the
MAP
from
HERE
to
THERE

Also by Emery Lord

Open Road Summer
The Start of Me and You
When We Collided
The Names They Gave Us

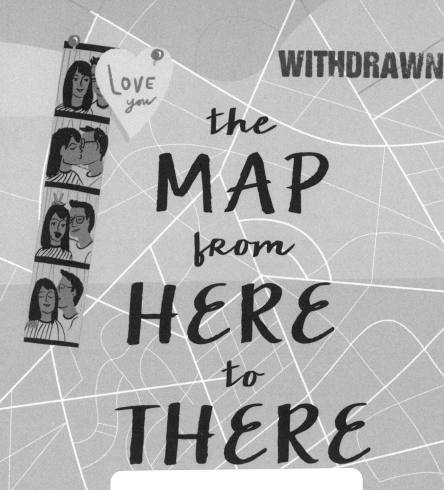

the

MAP

from

HERE

to

THERE

emery lord

BLOOMSBURY

NEW YORK LONDON OXFORD NEW DELHI SYDNEY

BLOOMSBURY YA
Bloomsbury Publishing Inc., part of Bloomsbury Publishing Plc
1385 Broadway, New York, NY 10018

BLOOMSBURY and the Diana logo are trademarks of Bloomsbury Publishing Plc

First published in the United States of America in January 2020 by Bloomsbury YA

Bloomsbury books may be purchased for business or promotional use. For information on bulk purchases please contact Macmillan Corporate and Premium Sales Department at specialmarkets@macmillan.com

Library of Congress Cataloging-in-Publication Data
Names: Lord, Emery, author.
Title: The map from here to there / by Emery Lord.
Description: New York : Bloomsbury, 2020. | Sequel to: The start of me and you.
Summary: High school senior Paige knows there is so much more to life after high school, but is it so terrible to want everything to stay the same forever?
Identifiers: LCCN 2019019170 (print) | LCCN 2019022114 (e-book)
ISBN 978-1-68119-938-2 (hardcover) • ISBN 978-1-68119-939-9 (e-book)
Subjects: CYAC: High schools—Fiction. | Schools—Fiction. | Friendship—Fiction. | Decision making—Fiction.
Classification: LCC PZ7.L87736 Map 2020 (print) | LCC PZ7.L87736 (e-book) | DDC [Fic]—dc23
LC record available at https://lccn.loc.gov/2019019170
LC e-book record available at https://lccn.loc.gov/2019022114

Book design by Jeanette Levy
Typeset by Westchester Publishing Services
Printed and bound in the U.S.A. by Berryville Graphics Inc., Berryville, Virginia
2 4 6 8 10 9 7 5 3 1

All papers used by Bloomsbury Publishing Plc are natural, recyclable products made from wood grown in well-managed forests. The manufacturing processes conform to the environmental regulations of the country of origin.

To find out more about our authors and books visit
www.bloomsbury.com and sign up for our newsletters.

For my spectacular girl

the
MAP
from
HERE
to
THERE

CHAPTER ONE

Of all the places to spend a hot August day in suburban Indiana, Cinema 12 had to be one of the best. Snacks, ice-cold air-conditioning, and endless opportunities for screen-writing analysis. At least, I thought so when I got the job in July.

Instead, Cin 12 gave me spilled nacho cheese, coagulating on the floor. Gray-haired men demanding student ticket prices but yelling at me when asked for a student ID. People complaining about strong perfume, about back-row make-outs, about the movie's ending, about the ice-cold air-conditioning itself.

Every time I tugged on my itchy, ill-fitting tuxedo uniform, I chanted: *College tuition. Room and board. Meal plan.* I got to wear my own white collared shirt, at least, but no shade flattered me in the low theater light. I'd gone through more blush in half a summer than I usually did in half a year, coaxing my skin from "vampire-adjacent" to "peachy."

"Okay, if you didn't know what happened in these last five

minutes," Hunter said, his voice low in the darkness, "how would you write the ending from here on out? Same way?"

"Hmm." I shifted my weight, leaning against the broom handle. Hunter's taste skewed toward big explosions or heart-warming football movies, but he'd taken to asking me about screen writing. "I'd end it more quietly. Instead of her running after his cab, I'd have him turn around, walk back to her front door, and knock. Roll credits."

"What?!" He glanced up at the smattering of viewers, all too enraptured to notice his outburst. "Hancock, you're kidding me."

My other coworkers called me Paige, but not Hunter. Hunter Chen spoke to all of us like we were his baseball teammates.

"You don't like the sprinting-after-him scene? Those are classic."

"No, I do," I said, damping down a smile. In fact, on the last day of school in June, I had sprinted after Max Watson, and I'd kissed him in the empty junior hallway. It was adrenaline and a lifetime of rom-coms, yes, but also something very true. "It shows the pivotal moment of dropping everything to chase what matters."

This summer, my screen-writing-program friends had teased me for preferring TV shows to film. When a movie closed with an inevitable, iconic kiss—atop a building, at the altar—I liked it fine. But I grew up with miserably married and then divorced parents, so I'd always known that wasn't really the end of the story. A TV relationship, though, could bear out for years, through the mundanity and will-they-make-it lows. It made small moments big.

On-screen, the beautiful lead reached the taxi, her russet hair tousled. She was breathless and lovely, no trace of sweat even after sprinting. The musical score held its note, violins in waiting.

"Oh my God." Hunter squeezed my arm in mock suspense. "Is he going to get out of the cab? He is!"

Of course he was. We'd seen the end a dozen times. They kissed as cars around them honked, and I shook my head. "See? A quiet realization would be more poetic—something as quotidian as showing back up. Choosing each other when there's no fanfare."

"Quo-what-ian? Okay, Honor Roll."

"Commonplace. So everyday."

He waved me off. "I like the running scene. Cheesy, sure. But packs a punch."

"Oh my God." I snorted. "It's, like, the closest you can get to an action movie sequence. That's why you like it."

"Or maybe," he said, hands on his chest, "underneath this stone-cold exterior, I'm a big softie."

I rolled my eyes, used to this after a month of coworkerdom. For a while, I'd wondered if Hunter's friends ribbed him about his good looks, about his training regimen. Maybe he made the jokes before anyone else could. Or, I wondered, was he possibly a little vain and drawing attention to himself? Finally, I realized: it's definitely both.

We rotated through three stations at Cin 12: box office,

concessions, and usher shifts. Our manager, Donna, had taken to pairing me with Hunter because he'd worked here long enough to help train me. And I, apparently, "kept him in line" better than Hunter's best friend, Lane, whom he'd sweet-talked Donna into hiring.

The credits rolled to the beat of "Say Yes," this summer's "Live in the moment!" anthem. People filed out of the theater, and I smiled thinly as they passed. "Have a good one."

"Take that chance with me," Hunter added, speaking the song lyrics. The girl he directed this toward glanced away, bashful and thrilled. He had one of those full, semicircle grins, with dimples and a square chin to frame it. "Make a running leap and see."

In June, "Say Yes" had pulsed out of bodega speakers and open windows as I walked to classes in New York. I'd bobbed my head happily. By mid-July, I was groaning at the intro's percussive handclaps as I swept up crushed M&M's. Now, though, Hunter and I had come back around to "Say Yes." Was it because the song was terrible and we'd succumbed? Was the song great and we'd embraced it? I had no idea; it was simply part of us now.

" 'Say yes, say yes,' " Hunter sang in an atrocious falsetto, shimmying up the steps. He'd apologized early on for his terrible voice and for the fact that it would not stop him. The universe, I'd supposed out loud, would only allow him greatness in one type of pitch. He was delighted by my willingness to both mock him *and* laud his baseball prowess, which I'd gotten a crash-course on these past few weeks. Hunter used to be singularly focused on playing Major League Baseball someday, but the rigor of year-round ball had twinged his elbow and his enjoyment. He'd scaled back, healed, and landed a full athletic scholarship to Indiana University, on his way to PT school or school counseling. But he still hoped to play pro ball—following in the footsteps of his hero, and fellow Chinese American pitcher, Vance Worley.

I knew at least a thousand percent more baseball trivia than I had at the start of summer. And Hunter, I suspected, knew a thousand percent more about screenwriting.

"So, what's the countdown on The Boyfriend? Cutting it pretty close to the start of school," Hunter said. My coworkers called Max "The Boyfriend" with implied air quotes, like they didn't fully believe he was real.

Perfectly real, in fact. Just in Italy for the second half of the summer, thriving in his preferred lifestyle of Latin, ancient relics, and gelato.

"He's home Friday morning." The closer Max's arrival, the joltier my pulse. I imagined the sharp lines on an EKG, its alarm beeping with increasing urgency. Even with good anticipation, my body didn't handle feelings well sometimes.

"Friday morning? Don't you mean thirty-six hours, twelve minutes, and forty-two seconds?" Hunter clutched his hands together like a Disney princess daydreaming of her true love. "Forty-one. Forty!"

I chucked an empty popcorn tub at him, which he dodged, laughing. I didn't even talk about Max that much! Or maybe I did. But who wouldn't? I'd spent the first half of summer in Manhattan. By the time I got home, Max had left for his Italian study abroad. And since I hadn't confessed my feelings for him till the last day of school, our relationship had been spent almost entirely apart.

I leaned down to an aisle seat, examining what appeared to be—yep, lovely—a small glob of white gum, newly stuck to the armrest. "Honestly. What compels a person to remove something from *inside their mouth* and press it somewhere another human being will sit?"

Hunter smiled, looking past me like a sailor gazing fondly at the horizon. "You've truly become one of us, Hancock."

He pretended to be jaded by this job after two years of part-timing it. As far as I'd witnessed, though, Cinema 12 was Hunter Chen's personal center stage. He flirted with elderly ladies, let his many buddies in with discounts, and wheedled every grumpy coworker until they smiled.

"Yeah, it's a real treat." I reached for a napkin, wrinkling my nose before I even neared the gum.

"So, hey," he said. "You tell your parents?"

Yesterday afternoon, I'd shocked myself by confessing to Hunter that my parents didn't know I planned to apply to film school in New York and LA. We were in the box office during a lull and venting about college anyway—Hunter may have been committed to IU for baseball, but he still worried about injury and balancing his coursework. And the words fell out, clumsy and unbidden. I hadn't even told my best friend yet. And I hadn't told Max.

"I did. Last night."

I was hoping the screen-writing thrill would dim as summer wore on. I expected to stay the course: an English degree in-state, with screen writing as a quirky side interest. But when

I helped my friend Maeve begin her writing portfolios for applications, I ended up starting my own, almost helplessly. Ideas that energized me, new pieces that challenged me.

"And it went well . . . ?" Hunter prodded.

"Okay, I think."

My dad went on about his pride in my go-get-'em aspirations, and my mom tempered the conversation with reason—ruminating about loans, job prospects, the fact that screen writing would likely keep me on either coast beyond college. It was like watching a bizarre table-tennis match: My dad on the left, rallying about my big dreams with the fervor of someone giving a commencement speech. Volley to my mom, reminding me that Indiana has great schools, that education is what I make of it.

Now I just had to tell Max. We'd talked about college abstractly, always assuming we'd both stay in the Midwest. Before this summer, I'd figured I'd land at IU like half my friends planned to. Then, even if Max went to Notre Dame or Purdue, we'd be a two- or three-hour drive apart—totally doable for weekend visits or meeting halfway.

Max would be supportive; I knew that. But as a helpless devotee to worst-case-scenario planning, I feared he'd also want to break up now, before we could get any more attached.

"Good thing this is our last showing," Hunter said. "That look on your face . . . man. You need a drink. And not just coffee at Alcott's."

I wrinkled my nose at him, and we bagged the remaining trash, working silently and fast. Once in the lobby, Hunter spun back.

"Hey, for real, what are you doing tonight? You should come out with us." He threw a glance at Lane, who was finishing up ice-bin clean-out behind the concession counter. Hunter described their best friendship as "siblinghood" after years of living in the same condo building. "Tell her to come out with us."

"You should!" Lane ran a hand through her red hair—a pixie cut with long layers that she wore pushed back. "Bella said the more, the merrier."

I had no idea who Bella was. Maybe someone from Linwood High—Oakhurst's neighboring town and rival, where Hunter and Lane were seniors. But they seemed to know everyone at my school, too, plus the local private school and a bunch of college campuses. Always a party, always open invitation.

"Maybe next time," I said, moving toward the door. "I have curfew. But thanks for the invite."

"She always says that," Hunter grumbled to Lane.

"Hey, I go out sometimes."

"Only when we're going to Waffle House." Hunter cupped both hands around his mouth. "It's senior year, Hancock. Say yes!"

"Have fun!" I called. "Be safe!"

The first time we met, Hunter rattled off the names of his friends at Oakhurst, hoping that I knew them. Aditi Basu? A little—I really liked her. Nate Song? I knew of him. Kara Cisse? *I'll save you some trouble*, I wanted to say. *At that enormous public high school, I socialize with between three and six other people.* I figured Hunter—star athlete with an endless stream of high-fiving friends stopping by the theater—would be glibly nice and not retain my name.

But during the second shift Hunter and I worked together, one of my mom's PTA friends walked up to the snack counter. I knew, with slow-motion certainty, what was about to happen. And sure enough, she very kindly mentioned that she thought of Aaron often, and of me, and hoped I was well. I said I was; I thanked her. I handed her a box of Sno-Caps.

Hunter didn't ask what happened because he didn't have to; everyone in the tristate area knew that an Oakhurst student named Aaron Rosenthal had drowned in a freak accident right before our sophomore year. And plenty of people knew he was my boyfriend at the time. He was sweet and smart and I liked him as much as you can like anyone you've known for two months when you're fifteen. Grieving him was slow, in jerky stops and starts, and it had never become easier to feel people's thoughts of him like a projector flickering images across my face.

"You wanna hide in the stockroom?" Hunter had asked. "Scarf some Reese's? I'll cover for you."

"I'm good," I'd assured him. "Although, good guess with Reese's. Peanut butter is at the nexus of all my emotional eating."

"The *nexus*?" Hunter repeated. "Okay, Hermione Granger."

I tipped my head. "Did you just mock my nerdiness by . . . citing Harry Potter?"

After that, Hunter invited me to every place he and Lane were cruising off to after work. But I'd always preferred being poolside at Tessa's, sneaking out to Kayleigh's rooftop with a laptop, watching a movie under the stars. I visualized myself at one of Hunter's parties: pressed into the corner of a sofa, praying for someone to talk to me and also fearing that someone would talk to me.

I walked outside into what felt like a screen door of August humidity—heat so heavy it seemed nearly visible. The feeble AC in my car tried its best, more an exhale than a gust. I was finally thinking of the sedan as my car—formerly my dad's and recently bequeathed to me for my seventeenth birthday. It was ancient, and not a cool car even when it was new. But I loved it—the console stocked with hand sanitizer, wipes for dashboard dust, a few old CDs for the player. Driving home from work was a small pleasure, me and the quiet, tree-lined roads.

When I pulled onto my street, I startled to see my dad's current car in the driveway so late. I used to consider my parents' marriage a tragedy, with bitterness that lingered even after they signed divorce papers. So when they started dating each other last year, I could only see a dark comedy. These days, though, even I could admit it had romantic dramedy potential. They were really happy, but obsessed with "maintaining boundaries," which included my dad staying at his own apartment.

I stepped around a hulking armoire in the garage, then a rolltop desk and a corner hutch, all furniture models posing in wait. After my grandmother died last spring, my mom refurbished her old desk for me, in the kicky red lacquer of a maraschino cherry. Since then, she'd been transforming flea market finds and free roadside furniture in her spare time—channeling grief, I suspected. Our garage looked like a re-creation of *Beauty and the Beast*'s penultimate scene, servants frozen in household form.

When I put my hand on the doorknob, I caught a raised voice from inside. My mom—not angry, but stricken. "It's not just the tuition and debt. We wouldn't be able to afford to see our daughter, Dan!"

I settled back on my heels, stunned. I knew my mom wasn't thrilled that Way-Out-of-State was my Plan A, but I genuinely hadn't expected this level of strife.

"We couldn't fly out there on a whim," my dad reasoned. "But in an emergency . . ."

I shook my head, sure that my mom's chin was quivering at the mention of an emergency. *Rookie move, Dad.*

"She's never even been to LA," my mom said. "*I've* never been to LA."

I needed to de-escalate, so I stamped my feet, as if just arriving home, noisily.

"Heyyy." I opened the door and pretended to look surprised that they were both right there at the kitchen table, papers spanning its surface. My dad was pointing at two different pages like a cartographer charting a course.

"Hey," my mom said, straightening. Her eyes flicked to the kitchen clock, not nearly as subtly as she probably intended. The cinema's last showing was a little earlier than usual tonight.

I stood there, tuxedo jacket held at my side. "Everything okay?"

"'Course." My dad's voice was clear. Confident. And he wasn't necessarily lying, in his own mind. My dad viewed most problems as challenges, obstacles on the way to greater good. But I knew the thin-pressed line of my mom's lips.

"Is this college stuff?"

My mom started stacking the nearest papers. "Yep. Boring parent to-do list. Forms due in October."

I examined her through squinted eyes. My mom was not a "yep" person. She said "yes"—maybe a "yeah" here or there if she was feeling tense.

Even if I hadn't overheard them, I'd have smelled the money stress like a trail of smoke. When you grow up with occasional income dips—a lag in freelance work, layoffs at the paper—you sense the tension long before you witness the fire. My parents' work had stabilized, as far as I could tell, in the past few years. My mom primarily wrote for and edited a parenting magazine, and my dad was at the city paper. But most of my life, their bickering had spiked highest around finances.

"So, honey," my mom said to me, all false cheer, "I was reading online today that there are some very good screenwriting master's programs. Lots of people go that route!"

"Right . . ." But I could also get my screen-writing degree in only four years of undergrad. Why would I tack on more time and debt?

"You *could* still get a more versatile English degree in-state, like you planned. And if you still want to pursue screen writing then, you can move on to grad school!"

If. I nodded slowly, not because I agreed but because I heard her loud and clear. I'd changed the plan on her last night, and she didn't like it one bit. Fine—I'd rather know where she stood.

"Katie," my dad said, quiet.

"Well, she could!"

"Or," my dad said, "she could pursue it now, full on. You read what her professors said."

I flushed, taken aback. I'd shared copies of two glowing recommendations to prove I might have a future in this. I hadn't necessarily expected them to be referenced.

"No, I know," my mom said. "Just a thought!"

For the first time since I was little, I walked upstairs feeling entirely sure my parents would have a whisper-fight in my wake. *Because* of me.

"Hey," I said, nudging my sister's half-open door. Cameron's room was eternally messy, more clothes on her floor than in her closet. She looked up at me from behind her laptop. "You happen to overhear anything downstairs?"

"Not really." Cam believed wholeheartedly in my parents' togetherness because she didn't remember the pre-divorce years as well as I did. Sometimes it felt like the three-year age gap between us made for two different childhoods under the same roof. "They were just discussing your college stuff from different points of view."

So, bickering. "Was dance good?"

"Mm-hmm," she said, eyes already back on her baking show, and I shut the door behind me.

I stripped off my work uniform, the smell of stale popcorn clinging to every fiber, and I keeled onto my bed, straight as a felled tree. Before this past spring, I would have called my grandmother for reassurance—waiting to hear her voice from a few miles away in her retirement community.

When I hauled myself up, it was only to read the sole finished piece in my writing portfolio. To remind myself why all this was worth it—why it had to be this way.

Why Screen Writing?

500-word maximum

My grandmother, for all her efficiency and no-nonsense worldview, loved watching television. Sometimes I think her recollection of *The Wizard of Oz* airing on TV in the 1950s was the first love story I ever heard. For most of my childhood, I hopscotched around my parents' disagreements and, eventually, between their houses when they split. Through it all, I loved TV; I loved Lucy. And I loved sitting beside my grandmother. She taught me about Madelyn Pugh, who had *GIRL WRITER* on the back of a director's chair on set. She was a girl and a writer. But she was also a writer of girls—Lucille Ball's character, specifically—and she had lived in Indianapolis, like me.

Shortly after I turned fifteen, the boy I'd been dating over the summer drowned in a freak accident. I spent days—weeks—in my room, curled around my laptop and desperate not to be alone in my mind. The television shows I watched in those days seeped in—fused with who I am. Eventually, I began to wonder, *Why do I like this particular show so much? What makes it good? Why am I invested?* Those questions became Google searches and script reading and every podcast that has ever featured a writers' room.

My grandmother died last spring, right after I found out I'd gotten into NYU's summer screen-writing program. I had the nerve to go, in part, because I was reeling again. Grief-stricken and desperate for distraction. Hoping to honor her.

I found more than that. I found my TV-writing spark could be easily fanned to fire—by professors, by classmates, by critique. By the sketch comedy class I hated but grew from, by the late-night debates with my bright, weird, interesting classmates.

Screen writing is my path because it's my passion, the creative space I come home to. But it's also a love story. The first act: my childhood with TV as a reprieve from hurt. In the second act, I learned to harness my pain to create. The story needs a third act, and in it, I plan to become one of the people who makes TV—for little girls whose parents are splitting up, for teenagers shocked by heartache, for anyone who needs to live in another world for a while.

I've been a grateful inhabitant. I'm ready to be a builder.

Things would be so much easier if the essay were an exaggeration. But I really felt this way—clear-eyed and certain.

I switched over to my e-mail, hoping for something from Max in Sicily, his last excursion before heading across the Atlantic. We'd texted and video-chatted all summer, but when the other person was asleep and we couldn't wait, we e-mailed. I was glad for the documentation, snippets of who we were, how we were. Thirty-five hours, two minutes, and counting.

CHAPTER TWO

The next day, I hustled into Alcott's for my lunch break—a daily practice that had been Max's idea. Why eat my paper bag lunch in the dingy cinema break room when my favorite place in Oakhurst was one intersection away? This bookstore had been my small salvation more times than I could count, the cove I steered toward in any storm. Now I ate my sandwiches by a sunny window, book in hand. This week, *Americanah* on recommendation from Tessa's girlfriend, Laurel. I nursed a small iced coffee—cheapest thing on the menu—and nestled in.

My break was almost over when something swooped into my line of vision. Blinking, I set my book down.

A tiny paper airplane hit the wall and dropped back onto the table beside me.

Max. The word rushed through me like a whisper, a quiet magic that could only ever be his. But he couldn't be here. Not till tomorrow morning—I'd taken the day off work, even. I swiveled my head a full one-eighty, searching, but no.

My heart punched at my rib cage as I reached for the airplane, its sharp nose bent from impact. *OPEN*, it said across the flat wing. In his handwriting. On what appeared to be a folded-up boarding pass. My fingers trembled, nearly ripping the neat angles of paper.

In the dead center, two words: *Miss me?*

I rocketed up, combing both hands through my hair. Why—WHY—had I clipped my bangs back this morning instead of doing something with them? In less than zero of my daydreams about our reunion was I wearing my work shirt and stupid baggy-legged tuxedo pants.

"Max?" I stepped into the nearest aisle, searching, but only glossy-magazine-cover faces looked back at me.

"Are you serious?" I said, louder. Because I couldn't get out the full sentiment: *You're home early? You have the patience to wait even one more second?*

He stepped into view, grinning and different and exactly the same. His denim button-up shirt and Converse and Maxness. I squealed something unintelligible—"Oh my God!" or "You're here!" or "It's you!"—and flew at him like a freed bird. It was nearly a tackle, sending him off balance.

"Hey, girl," he said, laughing. I kept my arms around his neck, stunned by the realness of him, solid and graspable.

This time last year, I didn't even know Max Watson. He'd started as the dorky cousin of my actual crush, Ryan Chase. Max had transferred to Oakhurst from private school, sat beside me in English class, and, somewhere along the way, became a true, trusted friend. He slid into my life like some part of my heart had always been saving a seat for him—this

boy who matched wits like fencing, who read me like a favorite book.

Max eased his hold, freeing me to drop down, but I stayed
pressed against him.

"Sorry," I said. "You have to live like this now."

It was some kind of ecstasy, to hear Max's laugh right next
to my ear. To feel his chest rise and fall against mine. No
ha-ha via text message, no laughter distorted through computer screens. Sometimes I imagined my feelings for him rivaled
any commercial airplane. They could soar out of Indiana, over
Ohio and Pennsylvania, cut through Connecticut. They'd propel themselves across the Atlantic and flamenco through Spain
and then swim the final sea-length to Italy.

When my feet hit the ground, I took him in, trying to
believe he wasn't a mirage. His darkest-brown hair, grown out
and thick. His usually pale skin, as tan as I'd ever seen it—a
souvenir from the Italian sun. New glasses I hadn't seen in
person until now, frames that looked nice with the green of
his eyes.

I could feel the goofiness of my smile, but Max's smile was
just content—the feeling of waking up late on a Saturday
morning.

"You're here," I said, only barely convinced. "How are you
here?"

"One of our excursions in Sicily was canceled, so I caught
an earlier flight. I got in at four a.m."

"You could have told me!" I said, stepping back to push his
shoulder. "I would have tried to switch shifts!"

I didn't add "I would have looked cute," even though

I thought it. On some level, he was still my friend Max, and I didn't want to admit how much I cared what he thought of me. How he thought of me.

"And miss seeing the tuxedo in person?" His eyes flicked up and down the work uniform he'd been joking about since I got the job. "I don't think so."

"Oh my God." I attempted to cover the awful pants with both arms.

"I didn't think I'd actually make my connection at JFK. Figured I'd rather surprise you if I did." He linked our hands together. So many times last year, I'd imagined reaching for his hand, and now it was simple—an invisible barrier dropped.

"How am I supposed to go back to work?" I demanded. "My break's almost over. I can't stay there knowing you're a few miles away!"

"Well, good. But I need a nap, and I want to catch up with my mom. But tonight, do you want to—"

"Yes."

He glanced down at his sneakers, smile tucked into his mouth.

"Oh," I said. "Wait. Laurel's bon voyage party is tonight."

Tessa had plans to send her girlfriend off to college in style, with favorite snacks and a nautical theme.

"Oh, right." Max's mind was working quickly, his eyes ticking around before they landed on mine. "How about a quick dinner, then we can head over there? I'll have to modify my excellent first-date plans, but . . . needs must."

I would have eaten dinner curbside in the smoldering

cinema parking lot, wearing my tuxedo, if he was the one sitting beside me. "Sounds great."

"Oh, and I'm, uh, not going to mention to anyone else that I'm home," he said, watching for a light of understanding in my eyes. No influx of text messages from our friends, no demands to see him right away. One dinner, just us.

I mimed zipping my lips.

"Good. I'll text you later?"

"You'll *see* me later," I said, and he squeezed both my hands.

I reentered the theater in a haze, a cartoon with hearts circling my head. Donna was standing with Hunter, glancing between her watch and me. "Cutting it a little close, aren't we?"

I did not care for Donna, overall.

"I'm here," I said, fingertips quick on the clock-in screen.

She turned toward her office, perhaps to note that I'd been flippant about my near lateness. It didn't matter. Even the hideous theater carpet—drab maroon with flecks of teal—suddenly looked celebratory, like confetti on a velvet backdrop. I turned back to Hunter, close to bursting. "Max got home early!"

"Yeah, he stopped by, looking for you. Told him you were at Alcott's." Hunter crossed his arms, appraising me. "Wow. I knew The Boyfriend was a big deal, but you are *beside* yourself."

"I am, yes."

"Go 'head," he said. "Do the little dance that you're clearly bottling up. Let's get it over with."

I did a little skip-around thing, with a twirl, then some hip movements.

"Wow," Hunter said, leaning his cheek against his hand. "Cute."

"Yeah, pretty good, right? I think it's only missing . . ." I turned to him, continuing the whole routine with my tongue stuck out at him.

"You could take this on the road! Stage show. The big time."

Lane walked past us, halfway out of her jacket for break. "Do I want to know?"

"It's a good day, Lane!" I said.

After work, I raced home for the quickest shower of my life, where I frantically scrubbed the smell of butter and salt from my skin. I tousled my hair as I blow-dried it, hoping to override Max's memory of my clipped-back greasiness. Scrutinizing the finished product in the mirror, I tried to believe I was a cute and together person, capable of minimal awkwardness in a date scenario.

Downstairs, my sister hunched over her latest batch of sugar cookies, a hobby she'd picked up around the time my mom started taking in stray furniture. I'd learned by now not to interrupt her while she was piping—a process that required a stern, almost glaring concentration.

When she stood back up, surveying her work, I cleared my throat and gestured to my outfit. "Yeah?"

Cameron looked over the rims of her trendy glasses, inscrutable. I'd chosen a striped T-shirt dress, a SoHo clearance-bin find. "Let me see the shoes."

I lifted one foot. She had no particular love for my Keds, but they were me and, in my opinion, immune to criticism.

"Good," she said simply.

I pointed at the cookies, glossy red apples in neat little rows. The pencil shapes were cooling, waiting for goldenrod icing—an homage to our school colors. "Back-to-school bake sale?"

"Mm-hmm. Practice run." She tapped one finger against her lip. While baking, she kept her hair piled like a haystack on top of her head, apron knotted at her waist. We'd always looked alike, but lately I saw more flashes of my mom's features on Cameron's face than on my own. "I added lemon zest to the base recipe this time, so we'll see. Max on his way?"

"Uh-huh."

"Are you, like . . . nervous?" Cameron peered at me. I hadn't realized I was rapping my fingers on the island until she nodded toward the sound.

"No." I pulled my hand back.

She gave me a look as if anxious behaviors were a new development for me. "Why? It's just you and Max."

Before I could reply, my mom came in from the backyard, blotting her face with a bandanna. "You look nice, sweetie!"

"Thanks." Why did I care so much? This boy had seen me in ratty, study-marathon clothes, on the school mornings when I'd hit snooze too many times.

"She's flipping out," Cameron said, twisting the icing bag for better control.

I glared at her. "No, I'm just rushed. We don't have a lot of time before we need to be at Tessa's."

Cameron gave my mom a knowing look. "Translation: Max and I don't have time to talk to you two."

"That's not—" I began, but what was the point? She wasn't wrong. I feared they would pull Max in, ask him about Italy, and fawn like this was senior prom instead of a casual first date.

"Oh, honey," my mom said. "We won't keep you! And we won't embarrass you."

"I know," I lied. At any point, Cameron could tell Max how long I'd taken to do my hair. She didn't need that kind of power.

My mom picked up a mixing bowl Cameron had left by the sink. "You do realize . . . we have met Max before? He's been in this home? Repeatedly?"

I did know. Still, I bolted up when Max knocked. I strode down the hallway, affecting the posture of a more confident girl. I had hated my required improv class at NYU, truly, but at least it had some real-life applicability.

I opened the door expecting the Max from earlier today, with tired eyes and thick hair rumpled. Instead, he looked bright-eyed, his hair neater on the sides.

"When did you get a haircut?" I asked.

"My mom cleaned it up," he said, sighing. "She said I wasn't presentable."

"It looks good!"

"Yeah?" His hand went to the back of his neck. "She was overenthusiastic, in my opinion."

"Well, I like it."

"Good." He'd stood in this same place at least a dozen

times before. Coming over to study. Picking me up for Quiz-Bowl practice. After my grandmother's funeral, wearing dress pants and a worried frown. And one windy afternoon last April, before the first time we'd ever really fought.

I motioned him in, but before we even made it to the kitchen, my mom and sister popped into view like two nosy little birds on a windowsill. *Please, God. Make them not be like this.*

"Hey, sweetie! Oh, look at you." My mom gave Max a quick hug. "Tell us about Italy. Was it a dream?"

"Absolutely. Like walking around in a movie." Max gestured at the countertop, full of Cameron's icing handiwork. "Gotta say, they're even better in person."

"Why, thank you." Cameron dipped her head, a little bow. So often, my snippy back-and-forth with my sister seemed inevitable. I assumed she bickered with everyone in her life. But I had noticed, all summer, Cameron commenting on Max's photos on social media: *OMG* and *so jealous!!!* and *bring some of that gelato back to Indiana.* The most I'd ever gotten from her, on one photo of me that Tessa had taken, was *cute.* Max, in turn, liked every one of her baking posts.

"I know you two have to get going," my mom said. "But come over for dinner soon, okay? You're welcome anytime."

"I'll be here," Max said. Then, to me, "You ready?"

He smiled over at me as we settled into his car, and I shoved away the guilt, the weight of my film school plans hidden in my back pocket. He'd asked once, when I first got home from the city, if I would apply to NYU. And I wasn't lying when

I said no. It was too expensive, too far, too improbable a career. *You're playing small!* Maeve had huffed on one of our last nights in the city.

"So," I said, straining. "Where are we off to, maestro?"

Why did I just call him that? I mean, he was orchestrating the date, sure. *But honestly, self, at least* try *to act normal.*

"Well, the original plan was Arpeggio's," Max said, "Then the drive-in, to see *Ghostbusters*. Only movie I could find that's set in New York. But you've seen it before anyway, right?"

Arpeggio's for Italy, *Ghostbusters* for Manhattan. Both our summers in one night—who thinks of that? I looked over at Max, at his profile while he watched the road. He glanced over, a lopsided smile—puzzled about why I hadn't responded to his simple question. *Because sometimes, Max, you are literally a bit breathtaking.*

"It's one of my dad's favorites," I managed. "He got *emotional* about the reboot, obviously."

"Really?"

"Oh yeah. Sitting with his two daughters, watching women bust ghosts? Dan Hancock Kryptonite. As soon as the theme song played, he was a goner."

"I guess that doesn't surprise me. His column's pretty sentimental sometimes." My dad was one of the few old-school newspaper writers hanging on to his weekly column. It made him what he called a "Z-list" local celebrity. Since his headshot was featured, he was occasionally stopped at brunch by readers with a kind word. Or a less than kind word, especially as his columns had become more blatantly political.

"Yeah, he's such a kidder usually, but when it comes to me and Cam . . ." I raised my eyebrows. "He'll openly cry at graduation."

Max considered this. "Come to think of it, I bet my mom will, too. She's normally good at compartmentalizing. But ceremony really gets her."

He pulled into the parking lot near the Little League fields and Riddle Park, the spot where a couple of food trucks often congregated, including Oakhurst favorite Pagano's Italian To-Go.

"Perfect," I decided, though Max looked a bit reluctant.

"Some first date, eh?" he joked. "Cheap food from an idling vehicle. You're welcome."

"Hey, food trucks serve some of the best cooking in the world—Tessa's always saying that. And I love cheap. I *prefer* cheap."

He grinned, quick and sly—a sight I'd missed terribly all summer. "I'm, uh, not sure how to take that, as the person you've chosen as your boyfriend."

We ate Italian subs messily at a picnic bench, napkins like drop cloths in front of us. Sharp red wine vinaigrette and salty salami. We split a sparkling water, and my heart fluttered each time I put my lips to the bottle where his had been.

"So," I said, during a brief lull. It was a weird spot, being old friends in a new context. What did most people reuniting in August discuss? "How was your summer?"

Max laughed, immediately in on the joke. "Um, not bad! Saw a bit of the world, learned a lot."

"Sounds lovely."

"Mm-hmm." He reached for the bottle. "It was. But I started going out with my dream girl, and I didn't get to see her at all."

I blanched, losing control of this comedy bit. Heat filled my cheeks, and I struggled to connect with my brain's language center. "Dream girl"—it should have been cheesy, but he said it with a lilt. Not a joke, exactly, but not serious.

"Well, hope you two can pick back up," I managed.

He nodded solemnly. "I'm working on it. Plying her with cheap food."

"Do you miss Italy yet?"

"I miss Liam and everyone," he said. Max's summer *coinquilino*—roommate—was a Welsh rugby player, burly and soft-spoken and excellent at Latin. They'd gone from trepidation to good mates in mere days. "And I really miss the antiquity."

He said it so earnestly, like he *yearned* for columned cathedrals and palazzi, for bricks cracked with age. I didn't say a word, but I also couldn't suppress my *oh, Max* face—a closed-mouth smile that betrayed my adoration for this total nerd. He must have noticed because he added, "I'm serious! Most of Oakhurst was built in the past fifty, seventy-five years. Rome was founded in 753 BC. *Before Christ!*"

"I *know* you're serious." And now I definitely couldn't quash the smile.

He laughed, too, fidgeting with his watch. I hadn't even realized how much I missed the full effect of him, the physicality. His laced fingers, his habit of jamming rolled shirtsleeves farther up his forearms. The way he leaned back in a chair when he knew he was right, arms crossed like an arrogant young professor.

"What about you?" Max asked. "You miss New York?"

There it was, the perfect segue to college plans, but I couldn't fathom launching into why I'd changed my mind about film school. It would ruin our dynamic before we'd even reestablished it. "I do. The energy of it, the food, the art."

My first week in Manhattan had been hard—so hard. The search for subway entrances, the beautiful but disorienting Village streets, the unmoving summer heat that made the city feel like a sewer grate. In my first workshop, my classmates— *especially* some know-it-all named Maeve Zaher—eviscerated my spec script, and I barely made it to the bathroom before crying. I missed my friends and Max like physical pain. At night, struggling to fall asleep, I chocked the week up to an expensive lesson: screen writing and big cities weren't for me.

But I couldn't go home—not when it cost so much money, not when my grandmother had been so proud. So I did a gut job on my script, editing it as mercilessly as it had been criticized. Because why not? It didn't matter. To my surprise, the instructor heralded my revision as the strongest in the room and, to my greater surprise, Maeve Zaher strode up to me after class and asked if I wanted to work together over coffee— the first of many. I met people I liked, friends who wanted to debate the merits of classic sitcoms, of laugh tracks, of voice-overs. And then, New York buzzed electric—late nights spilling into the streets, shared appetizers at the cheapest diners we could find. Working on scenes, trying to get lottery Broadway tickets. Walking the same streets as so many renowned writers. It felt like being part of something, this long history mapped out behind us. Waiting for us to add to the story.

"Janie . . . ?" Max said, calling me back to earth.

I laughed at myself. "Sorry! Yes. Hi."

His eyes narrowed, the briefest study of me. Wondering where I'd gone. *This week*, I promised myself. I'd tell him.

"So, does Ryan know you're home?" I asked.

"Yeah. He stopped over to say hey, but promised he wouldn't tell anyone. So I'd say there's a fifty-fifty chance that everyone already knows."

Maybe some people inch closer, but for the next hour, Max and I millimetered closer—true last year, emotionally, and true physically now. I adjusted my position, getting comfortable, but wound up grazing his leg with mine. He leaned in at one point, but he was reaching for a napkin.

Last time I kissed Max—the first and only time I'd ever kissed him—I flew on pure moxie, unstoppable. Now I'd had three months to sit with reality: I'd only ever really kissed one other boy, and that was two years ago. Could you forget how? Had I ever really known?

We stayed until Tessa texted, wondering if I was on my way. As Max and I gathered up our trash, my nerves sang with the particular anticipation of a pending surprise. "They're going to flip out when they see you."

And when they saw us, together. I bit a groove into my lower lip as Max drove and wished for a week of alone time with him, figuring out togetherness in the same zip code. Our friends had rooted for us all last year, and I loved them for it. But I dreaded the attention, the expectation—their eyes like spotlights on a relationship I didn't want to perform. Max parked on Tessa's street, the driveway already full of cars, and I wiped my palms on my dress.

"They're out back," I told him.

The McMahon house was the kind of fancy that included landscape lights on a stone path, which we followed toward the pool. Our friends' laughter floated above the tall wooden fence—Kayleigh telling a work story to guffaws and *Whats?!* Outside the gate, Max turned to me. "Ready?"

It was rhetorical, I knew. Was I ready to make our entrance as Max and Paige, Couple? I hadn't even kissed him yet, and this would be our last minute alone for the next few hours. He was watching my face closely enough to see my hesitation.

Of all the places I'd imagined kissing Max Watson again, "a dimly lit side-yard with our friends nearby" was not in the Top 100. I'd envisioned that cinematic passion, frantic mouths—the way we'd kissed the first time.

But instead, I looked up at a boy who was being so careful, reading me slowly. His hand on my cheek—the whir of my heart, almost pained by anticipation. He leaned down most of the way and paused. Giving me a beat—letting me choose, and I did.

I'd been worried about remembering how to do this. But

that wasn't relevant, as it turned out. I'd never kissed anyone like this, like Max right now—familiar but entirely surprising. I gripped his shirt to steady myself, relaxing once he got an arm around me.

When we pulled away, dazed, I bit both my lips, shy after such intensity. Sure, we'd flirted from afar all summer. But I had almost a year of friendship muscle memory, and being so obviously into Max felt a bit embarrassing, a side of me he didn't know.

"Okay," I said, smiling. "Ready."

Max blinked at me, then nodded back up to the car. "Well, now I think we should definitely ditch these guys."

I laughed and opened the gate.

Our friends were bunched around the patio table, hands reaching into snack bowls. Laurel with a white captain's hat over her waist-length box braids and Tessa on her lap, wearing yellow water wings. Morgan lounged in a purple halter suit and green capris, an homage to fellow lily-pale redhead Ariel. Kayleigh was luminous in a long seafoam-green wig. Malcolm and Josiah were pirates in tricorn hats, and Ryan made a shorter, broader Gilligan in a red polo. A few of Laurel's friends who hadn't left for college yet sat together, in everything from foam lobster pincers to some kind of anime costume.

"I'm guessing we missed a theme here," Max whispered.

Before I could apologize for blanking on that part, Morgan spotted us. "Hey, there you are! . . . Oh my God! Wait! What?"

"I brought a plus-one," I said. "Hope that's okay."

Every head snapped in our direction, where Max stood

with a hand in his pocket, casual as could be. Our friends became a flurry of arms and shrieks. Tessa got there first, nearly plowing Max over.

Considering that she was my best friend and he was my boyfriend, Tessa and Max's friendship didn't really have much to do with me. They had taken to each other right away during a shared lunch period, bonding over snobby music tastes and dry humor. While I spent my June scampering between purple-flagged buildings in New York, Max and Tessa carried on, at record shops and lunches they sent selfies of. I liked the idea of them together at home, even when I felt vaguely sick with missing them.

"Interesting," I said as Tessa pulled away from him. She had her blond curls in a low ponytail, a style she'd taken up this summer. "I recall no such greeting when I got home from New York."

"Well, that wasn't a surprise!" Tessa huffed. Morgan squeezed him with a side hug.

"Pasta did you good, Max-O," Kayleigh said, sizing him up. She'd highlighted her cheeks with a mermaid palette, reflecting like a prism on her golden brown skin.

Max pretended to doff his cap, but I could feel him go squirmy. Even with all that confidence, he sometimes faltered under the attention of my adoring friends.

"Excuse me," Laurel said, hands on her hips. The pose showcased the temporary tattoos Tessa had ordered: glittery boats on Laurel's dark brown arms, sailing toward an anchor and a pinup mermaid. "It's my party and I'm last in line?"

Max gave her a good solid hug. "Came home early to see you off."

"Yeah," she said, laughing. "Just me, I bet."

Max greeted Laurel's friends and Malcolm, a friend of his since elementary school. I knew Malcolm through QuizBowl, and was pleased that he'd started hanging out with our friends this summer, bringing his boyfriend, Josiah, into the mix, too.

Laurel's gaze slid from Max down to me, then back. "This is wild. Like that very satisfying moment in Concentration."

We must have looked confused, because she laughed. "You know, the card game? Trying to remember where all the cards are so you can match them? I finally got the pair together!"

"But no costumes?" Ryan chided. "Boo."

He swung an arm around Max's neck anyway, drawing him into the fray. After everyone was settled in back around the table, Tessa stood up. She cleared her throat and raised her glass—a girl Gatsby, presiding over the festivities.

"To Laurel King and her reign at Northwestern, which begins tomorrow. You will . . ." She paused, searching Laurel's face for the right word. "Dazzle them."

The apples of Laurel's cheeks went rounder because, well, Tessa was proclaiming this from firsthand experience. I'd never seen Tessa so grandiose, baring her heart. When she looked around, she seemed briefly surprised that the rest of us were still there. "To Laurel!"

I was close enough to hear Laurel whisper, "Thanks, baby," and I flushed at the grown-upness of it. Max had called me Janie almost as long as he'd known me, a reference to the shyer, eldest Bennet sister. I could never imagine him calling me "baby"—it was . . . sexy, or something, in a way I couldn't imagine Max seeing me.

Shortly after, Ryan cannonballed into the water, and Tessa, never to be outsplashed in her own pool, followed behind. Everyone else eased in, but Max and I sat near the shallow end, our bare feet pale in the water. Last year, he'd nudged me back toward swimming, an attempt to help with what had become a full-blown drowning phobia after Aaron's death, and it didn't go well. I'd needed to jump back in on my own. But when I did, I wore Max's belief in me like wings.

He leaned back, one arm stretched behind me, and I moved close, my right leg warm against his left.

"Hey." His eyelids looked heavy, jet lag catching up with him.

"Hi." I nodded to the other side of the pool. "Happy to be back with this bunch?"

"Happy." The way he looked at me when he said it—with a sigh and the slightest smile. Being together was like sharing a docking station, finally able to rest and refuel. "But feeling a little underdressed. I mean, Kayleigh ordered a *wig* for this?"

"Oh no. She's had that for years. Sixth-grade Halloween, I think?" Kayleigh had collected illustrations of Black mermaids since childhood—something her mom started and her aunts continued. They swam in their framed kingdom above her desk, near Kayleigh's rainbow of volleyball ribbons and a Polish-style paper chandelier her *babcia* made. "Mermaids are a thing with her."

Max smiled, unsurprised to hear it. "My life had so much less whimsy before I met you all."

"You were missing out."

He looked over and said, seriously, "I really, really was."

How to explain why I kissed Max Watson, for the third time ever, in full view of our closest friends? I don't know. I couldn't not.

Brake, I warned myself. *Slow it down.* Hadn't I seen how love could pulverize someone? Didn't I still have to tell him what next year might have in store? Instead, I rested my hand on his chest, electricity conducting up my arm.

My heart blew through the red like a girl in a convertible, already gone.

CHAPTER THREE

In the morning, I woke up to a text from Max, inviting me over for breakfast, and I pressed my smiling, ridiculous face into a pillow. We didn't need excuses to hang out anymore; no studying or QuizBowl or plans with our friends.

Outside Max's front door, I swept a hand over my shirt, dismayed at wrinkles from the drive over, and took a deep breath before I knocked. The fanciness of his house wasn't in size—it appeared, at street view, to be a cheery bungalow. But the inside felt grander, with dark wood floors and sharp lines of white molding on every edge.

Max swung the door open. "Morning."

"Morning." I stepped inside to coffee and cinnamon, savory spices and maple. "Wow, smells great in here."

"Ah, yes. The aroma of every food item available in central Indiana."

"Oh, stop," his mom called from the kitchen. "It's only three things."

"Fighting jet lag with burritos," Max said. He ushered me in, where Dr. Watson stood at the stove in slippers and sleek workout wear. She'd once told me to call her Julie, but it sounded too casual even in my mind. "Ms. Watson" sounded disrespectful to her MD, but "Dr. Watson" too formal.

"Ah, sweetie." She stepped away to give me a good squeeze, something she'd done even the first time we met. "So nice to have you here."

I liked Max's mom so much that I often went quiet around her. A funny, warm pediatrician who raised my favorite human being during her dozen years of school and residency? It was a lot. Sometimes, around her, my inner monologue spat out only: *Please like me, please like me.*

"I'm very glad to be here," I said, because that seemed polite and demure. And then my stomach chose to groan, miserably and loud. My hands shot to my waist. "Um, clearly. Sorry."

They both laughed, with eyes scrunched and wide, mirror-image smiles. Subtracting their shared features, I imagined Max's dad must be tall with that same dark-roast brown hair. Max stood a head above everyone in his Oakhurst family—his mom, Ryan, Ryan's sister and parents, all caramel blonds. I never asked about Max's dad, who wasn't much of a presence after Max's mom got pregnant in college. But I wondered sometimes.

"Sit, sit!" she told me. "I've got eggs, chorizo, and roasted veggies for the burritos, and there are a few types of cheese."

"Can you tell she missed me?" Max asked, nudging my elbow.

Dr. Watson looked my way, eyebrows raised. "My son tells me he missed big breakfasts while in Italy and this is what I get! After watching an entire slideshow of all the delicious food he ate this summer!"

Max grinned, and she shook a spatula at him, pure affection.

I figured he annoyed her in the usual teenager ways—*Is your homework done? Is there still carpet in your bedroom beneath this layer of unwashed clothes? Can you cool it with the video games?* But she genuinely liked him. My own mom always seemed more concerned with parenting me to even consider if she enjoyed my company. It simply wasn't relevant. More importantly: Was I getting good grades? Making safe choices? Being respectful and polite?

"Wait," I said, registering the entirety of what Dr. Watson had said. I slid my gaze to Max. "There's a whole slideshow?"

He shrugged. "She requested one."

"So I could live vicariously," his mom added. "Start planning my own trip."

"Do I get to see it?" I asked.

"You want to?" Max asked, surprised, and I gave him an extreme *duh* look that would have made my sister proud. "Well! I'm paranoid of being that guy who comes home from traveling and won't shut up about it."

"Excuse me." Dr. Watson arched a thin eyebrow. "I didn't fund your Italian summer for you to act like Mr. Cool Guy about it."

"Huh." Max sat back, like he was having a revelation. "The first time I've ever been called cool. It's a strange sensation. Powerful."

After breakfast, we went downstairs to the basement rec room, where a U-shaped couch faced the big-screen TV, complete with projector capability and all of Max's video game stuff. My nerves shrilled—half with the realization that this was the perfect time to tell Max about my college plans, and half with mortification that his mom might have thought "watch the slideshow" was unsubtle code for "be alone to make out."

But we really did watch the slideshow. He'd sent me some of the photos over the summer, but it was different on a giant screen, with his excited explanations. Lots of crumbling monuments. Alfresco tables with plants on the balconies above. The Cinque Terre, sherbet villages cut into the cliffs. Even the pasta plates were artful—fresh basil and dustings of Parmesan.

Around Milan, I started feeling sweaty, obsessing about how I'd break my news. What if he wanted to end things before we could get more attached, and this was the last time we were ever happy? Was I really going to risk that for a pipe dream? By the Roman basilicas, I was tracing my hands against the couch fabric, unable to be still.

When the last slide flashed "The End," followed by the Italian translation, "*Fine*," I made myself smile. "Incredible."

"Okay," Max said. "That was an obvious missed opportunity to make a pun about the slideshow being fine. Are you all right?"

All the saliva disappeared from my mouth. That content smile of his threw me—I didn't want to ruin it. But I couldn't keep carrying this around. Two crinkles appeared on Max's forehead, right above the bridge of his glasses.

"I need to tell you something," I said, and he angled toward me immediately. I forced a laugh and blew my bangs from my face. "Um, sorry, that sounded dire. It's not. It's that, um, I know I said, after I got home, that NYU wasn't a possibility, but . . . I was boxing myself in, I think."

All the blood from my face rushed to my chest, where my heartbeat tapped like frantic typewriter keys. I made myself stop talking so Max could react.

"You're going to apply?" he asked. "That's great! God, you scared me there."

"That's great?"

"Yeah! I mean, kinda figured you would, with the way you talked about NYU this summer." He cocked his head, with a smile like *C'mon*. "I think I know what your face looks like when you're falling for something."

I glanced down, lips pressed in a sheepish smile. Yes, I supposed he did. When I looked back up, Max wore an expression I recognized from QuizBowl—any time he gave an answer he was only ninety percent sure of and heard the moderator say: *Correct*.

"I'm applying to some places in LA, too."

He flinched in surprise, blinking quickly as he recovered. "Oh. Okay. California? Huh. Guess that makes sense—you didn't mention the West Coast, though, so I . . . huh."

"I didn't consider it till recently."

"Will you do school visits before then? Stay with Maeve?"

I imagined his brain circuitry, always so fast, zapping through the new information. "I will if I get in, which I probably won't. But if I don't go for it, I'll always wonder."

Would the next words out of his mouth be *But what does that mean for us?* I would certainly burst into tears, wailing that I had no idea. That I wanted to be with him but I understood if he thought we should return to friendship.

Mercifully, he gave me a slow, knowing smile—another expression I recognized. Since I'd met Max Watson, he'd looked at me, in turn, like I was the most perplexing, unexpected, delightful person on earth. Maybe my favorite, though, was this look right now—when he was thoroughly, blatantly impressed. "All right, then. Wow. Good for you, Janie."

For some reason, his reaction pained me in a way I hadn't anticipated. What fool would consider leaving this wonderful, supportive guy—my match in so many ways? My lower lip wobbled as I tried to speak. "But your 250-mile-radius rule. If I get in, we—"

"I know," he said, nodding. As the only child of a single mom, Max wanted to stay an easy weekend drive from home, which still left tons of options. I imagined Oakhurst as the center dot on the map, with a penciled-in circumference stretching from St. Louis to just beyond Columbus, Ohio. "We'll be apart."

"Far apart. But the odds of me getting in are so slim . . ."

"Janie," he replied, gentle. "We can't cross a bridge before we reach it. So let's wait till we're there, yeah?"

The confidence in his voice—his relaxed posture. He really

wasn't freaking out, and the energy calmed the whole room. I inhaled, like I could feel the oxygen reach all the way to my fingertips.

"Are you sure?" I asked him, lighter now. "Because I'd be happy to painstakingly diagram every possible way across the bridge and worry which one it will be. No? Torture myself, and you, with worst-case scenarios?"

Max smiled, pleased to have jostled me back toward humor. "How about just kiss me?"

I did, but quickly. If there was a relationship stage where you stopped caring about post-breakfast-burrito breath, we were nowhere near it.

"So," he said after I sat back. "You've really got a plan. I'm jealous!"

I rolled my eyes, smiling. "Please. I've, like, reluctantly accepted that this one expensive, fat-chance plan is something I'll regret if I don't try. You have a *bunch* of plans that you'd be happy with!"

"Ha. Fair enough." He paused, probably tallying up the many places he planned to apply to: IU! Purdue! Notre Dame! Northwestern! Wash U! OSU! UC! In premed! Or engineering! Or education! He had so many interests, and the willingness to be open to all of them. "So. What do you want to do today?"

"Well, I was wondering," I said. "Gondolas on the Canal in downtown Indy: depressing, compared to Venice? Or a fun way to relive it?"

"Fun," Max said.

"Maybe we do the boats and then meet up with everyone

somewhere?" I raked a finger across my lip, thinking. "If Tessa needs a distraction."

"Laurel will have hit the road by now?"

"Yeah," I said, reaching for my phone. Tessa had been upbeat last night, but I also imagined her last, clutching-on hug with Laurel before a three-hour drive and at least a month apart. "Let me check in with her real quick and see."

"Sounds perfect," Max said, glancing over my shoulder as I typed to Tessa.

Laurel take off?

Yep!

You okay?

Yeah. Sucks. But, ya know!

I narrowed my eyes at the exclamation points—like two fake smiles, which I didn't buy for a second.

I'm totally fine. Have the best time with Max!!

Then an actual smiley-face emoji, meant as reassurance. But by then, I knew: she was not even sort of fine.

"Double exclamation points?" Max grimaced. "Yikes."

"Right?" I studied her words again, my instincts clanging. If she wanted to be alone, no problem. But she could have said that. Instead, she was pretending. And not even pretending well. I frowned at the screen.

"Go," Max said, one finger brushing my bangs from my eyes. I didn't fully register the gesture for a few stunned seconds, but then felt overcome by the sweetness of it. Like I was his to fuss over. "Text me if you need the Cheer-Up Committee B-Squad. I'll bring Ry."

"But the gondolas . . ." *And you just got home, and I missed you so much, and school starts so soon, and and and* . . . And Tessa had stuck by me for years, through grief like fog that extended farther than either of us could see. Going to her wasn't even a question.

"Eh, I'm happy to wait when something is worth it." He lagged his head toward me, and my God—that pleased-with-himself smile. "Source: all of last year."

I tilted my head, mimicking his pose. "You're pretty great, you know that?"

"Oh yes," he said, solemn. "That's all I ever heard in middle school. Every kid was like: 'Man, that Max Watson. Pretty great.'"

I breathed out a laugh. Max getting bullied as a kid wasn't funny, but I figured he owned the experience and could joke if he wanted to. I rested a hand on his cheek as I kissed him, my fingertips against his jaw, and I only pulled away at the sound of the basement door opening, followed by footsteps on the stairs.

"Sorry to interrupt," his mom said cheerfully. "Just throwing in some laundry!"

"Very subtle, huh?" Max whispered to me.

"What was that?" Dr. Watson asked.

"Nothing, Mom!" Max called amiably. "Love you!"

———————————

Tessa's grandmother opened the front door, her expression relaxing at the sight of me. "Hi, sweetie pie. I'm so glad she called you."

Well, something like that. "Is she in her room?"

"She is." Then, a little sadly, "I suppose I should have known today would be hard on her. I loved the sound of her laugh all summer. Laurel's, too. Filled up the whole house."

I nodded. I should have seen it coming, too—the moment when love and leaving hit like a head-on collision.

"Well, Norah and Roger are home tomorrow." Gram McMahon gestured me toward the stairs. "I think that'll get her mind off it, at least."

Tessa's parents were sophisticated and full of bright energy, blowing into the house like a spring breeze. Her mom would rouse Tessa from bed, take her shopping; she'd overnight desserts from fancy bakeries in New York. But she wouldn't notice if Tessa needed to feel it, to be told it was okay to be sad. Enter me.

I stood outside Tessa's bedroom door for a moment. Music was playing, of course—strings and a soulful voice. And beneath it, a sniffle, then another. I tapped with one knuckle.

"I'm really okay, Gram." Tessa's tone was almost convincing—the vocal equivalent of a brave face. "I'll come down in a few minutes."

"It's me," I said, mouth close to the seam of the door.

A few beats of silence. "You're supposed to be with Max."

"And you're supposed to tell your best friend the truth about your well-being," I said cheerfully. "But here we are."

Rustling from inside, and—I could have sworn—a defeated sigh. "You can come in."

She'd never looked smaller to me than she did now—cuddled into a pile of pillows against the tufted headboard.

A little girl with a scraped-knee heart. I shut the door behind me and climbed onto the bed.

Up close, my best friend looked like an amateurish oil painting of herself. It was definitely Tessa, blond curls gone fuzzy in a topknot, but the details weren't quite right. Pale cheeks blotchy, eyelids puffed.

"Hey."

"Hi." A new song warbled from her phone on its nightstand perch, in easy reach. Before I could launch into my reassurances, she cleared her face. "I'm being a giant baby. I know it's not that big a deal—I really do."

This was something people had done with me since sophomore year—stopped when they caught themselves struggling with anything that wasn't full-on death. I appreciated the perspective, of course. I'd lost people permanently, to far worse things than distance. But sadness links at the joints, a gossamer web connecting loss, heartache, strife.

"Hey, don't do that," I said, frowning. "This is hard."

"It's a little hard," she admitted, voice squeaking. "I didn't want to waste time being sad while she was still here, so I bottled it all up, and now . . ."

She wiped at her face, still tear-streaked.

"I got home . . ." Tessa held her hands out to her room, where the summer light landed, golden. We needed the drum of April rain, the frozen lace of winter. "And my first thought was: 'Huh. What do I do now?' Isn't that so stupid?"

It wasn't. Even Tessa's bedroom reflected the way Laurel had changed things. A strip of photo-booth pictures taped to the mirror. Tickets from the concerts they'd attended together. A small ceramic rooster that was part of Tessa's birthday gift—an inside joke I wasn't privy to. A few spiky plants, alive thanks to Laurel's coaching.

"And it's so stupid," Tessa repeated. "But all of a sudden, I'm panicking that she'll dump me any second. Like, she'll meet all these cool people in Chicago, and they'll love her—of course they will. And I'm stuck here, some high school girl who—"

"Excuse me," I said, interrupting. "I'm 'some high school girl.' Morgan and Kayleigh, too. Does that make us any less smart or interesting or fun or loyal or—"

Tessa crossed her arms, grumbling. "I guess not."

"No." I gave her a knowing look. "And can I tell you something else?"

She nodded. Her lashes were still wet, stuck together.

"This playlist," I said, "is the most depressing succession of music to ever fall on human ears. Since the dawn of time. And we have to turn it off now."

She laughed, surprised, and then wagged a finger at me. "I'll have you know that Laura Marling—"

"Is not helping. I'm texting Morgan and Kayleigh to come over."

Her lips parted, like she was going to try to stop me, but instead, she sighed and laid her head down on the pillow. I finished typing and stretched out beside her so we were face-to-face. We hadn't huddled up like this since early this summer, in her parents' New York hotel. She'd met Laurel a few weeks before and still seemed stunned by her feelings. While Morgan had crushed her way through middle school and high school, and Kayleigh had flirted like it was a game of expert chess, Tessa had barely seemed to notice anyone. I chocked it up to introversion, to years of extensive travel as she tagged along with her hotelier parents, zigzagging across the world atlas. And when you've met people in over a dozen countries, what could Oakhurst, Indiana, hold for you?

Laurel, as it turned out. They met at the Carmichael, Tessa's go-to venue for music no one else had ever heard of. No one but Laurel, who was on the dance floor like it was redemption.

"Tell me about finally being with Max."

"Wonderful. Surreal." And then, without exactly giving my mouth permission, I blurted out, "I just told him I'm applying to film school."

She leaned back, startled. "I thought you said NYU was . . ."

"Out of the question. I know. But I want to see what happens, at least. There and a few places in LA."

"Huh." She squinted like I'd recently trimmed my hair or tried a new volumizing mascara—something was a little different, but what? "And your parents are okay with it?"

"Ish. They're okay with me applying, anyway."

"Well." She let her mouth spread into a real smile. "What if I wind up in New York or LA, too? Wouldn't that be incredible?"

Those cities, along with Nashville, had music-business

programs that Tessa was interested in, though she'd only spoken about them vaguely so far.

"Incredible," I agreed.

She searched my face. "But Max is staying close to home."

"Right." I tucked my arm beneath my head. "He was amazing about it, though."

"If you got into LA," she said, "you really think you'd go?"

Los Angeles seemed almost mythological, a place I couldn't simply move to. But my friend Maeve did a lot to demystify her hometown, promising to drive me around and take me home for dinner in the burbs with her family. "Maybe. The programs there are a huge deal. But it's daunting. And I don't know what Max and I would do."

"Well, it's you two," Tessa said. "You made it work all summer, no problem. You'll be fine farther away."

But for four years? I clamped my mouth shut because Tessa could afford flights to visit Laurel from anywhere. Her concept of long distance didn't work in my reality. If I moved to either coast, I wouldn't come home till the holidays.

Morgan arrived shortly after, and Tessa gestured around her room. "Welcome to our personal problems summit."

Bouncing onto the end of the bed, Morgan glanced at me. "You have personal problems, too?"

I filled her in, to supportive squeals and a brief speech about young women taking over Hollywood.

"Do you have anything to contribute to our problem collection?" Tessa asked Morgan.

"Uh, let's see. Yes. I have to get a transvaginal ultrasound to check my cyst situation tomorrow? The ultrasound wand goes *inside* you," she said, motioning upward with two fingers. "And also my work crush officially fizzled out."

"I'm sorry," I said. "What now?"

"Yeah, I thought he was quietly soulful, but it turns out he's just boring," Morgan said with a little pout. She'd been ready for love since the moment she saw Li Shang cast an admiring glance at Fa Mulan.

"No," Tessa said, "the wand thing."

"Oh, right." Morgan made a face. She'd finally gotten an appointment with a specialist after years of painful, unpredictable periods and being told she'd probably grow out of it. The doctor suspected an endocrine disorder, and Morgan was grateful for answers, but still processing—a cycle of relief, frustration, anger, and jokey updates that included hand gestures. "I'm glad the doctor will be able to see what's going on in there, but so awkward, right?"

We bemoaned her reproductive organs and her erstwhile work crush until we heard Kayleigh arrive downstairs. She appeared at the bedroom door with a hefty white box, nearly obscuring her work polo.

"Hello, children," she said, cheerful.

"What's that?" Tessa sat up, eyes big as a Pixar character. She loved restaurants of all kinds, anything inventive or new to her. In her spare time, however, she ate like an unsupervised child on Halloween. Kayleigh's bakery job was the second-best thing to happen to Tessa this summer.

"Well," Kayleigh said. "It's what happens when Jenna thinks she might be better at hand-lettering than I am."

We all scoffed in disbelief. Kayleigh excelled in anything that required precision and an eye for design. Sitting at the end of the bed, she opened the box to reveal a round cake with red-icing letters veering downward: *HAPPY BIRTH-DAY, MARFY!*

"It was supposed to say 'Marty,'" Kayleigh said, producing several plastic forks from her side-slung purse, "but the sloping was unfixable. So voilà! A long-distance-sucks cake."

"It's beautiful," Tessa said, already shoveling a fork into one side. She sampled a bite and sighed. "Ah. Exactly what I needed."

And then, in the next breath, she erupted into tears, hands flying to her face.

Morgan and Kayleigh snapped to attention, and I gasped, "Whoa! What is happening?"

"I don't want to be away from you all next year," Tessa cried. She'd buried her face from view. "Now I know how terrible it feels, like my whole world has been disrupted, and—"

"Hey," Kayleigh said, reaching a hand to her leg. "Come on—we have so much time. I've already started planning spring break, and that *alone* will be a hundred memories. Best is yet to be."

"She's right," I told Tessa. "And that's coming from me."

Max liked to joke that I saw the world as what was most likely to happen, instead of hoping for what I most wanted. Clearly, with my college choices, I'd taken the note.

"You know what?" Kayleigh said. "We need a list."

"Is that your Paige impression?" Morgan quipped. "It's good."

I made a face at her, and Kayleigh ignored us both. "We list every single thing we want to do together in the next year. Everything greater Indianapolis has to offer—places we haven't been in ages, places we've always wanted to try."

"Like a bucket list?" Tessa wiped her cheeks.

"Exactly. Then, any time we feel even a little sad: list."

"Come to think of it," I said, pulling out my phone, "I think I jotted a few things down . . ."

When I was in my tiny Manhattan dorm room that first week, looking at photos of my friends carrying on without me, I'd coped by listing things we could do once I returned. The list had been forgotten as I found my place in New York.

"Of course you did," Kayleigh said. "God, how far down are you scrolling? How many lists do you *have* on that app?"

"A few. Okay. The Fourth of July fest, Shakespeare in the Park, picnic at that one park we like downtown, mini-golf. Obviously, I was a little summer-focused here."

"Mm, I feel like Max can go to the Shakespeare thing with you," Tessa said, and I rolled my eyes.

"Holloway's Pumpkin Patch," Kayleigh said, dictating over my shoulder. "Senior trip over spring break."

"And Ditch Day," Tessa said. "Senior tag—"

"Homecoming and prom," Morgan finished, while I typed quickly, trying to organize their suggestions in roughly chronological order.

"And some of this needs to be Core Four only, okay?" Morgan said. "No boyfriends."

I was the only one with a boyfriend, so I gave Morgan a *What the heck?* look. As if these three hadn't steered me toward Max with the single-mindedness of Captain Ahab on the damn *Pequod*.

"No offense," Morgan said mildly.

"Some taken," I said, and I passed my phone around for any additions.

<u>The Senior Year List</u>

Sleepovers

Indy Zoo

Newfields

Roller rink

Karaoke place

Rave Lanes Bowling

Football game student section

Holloway's Pumpkin Patch

Homecoming

Fun new restaurants

Party

Ice-skating downtown

New Year's party

Senior trip

Prom

Senior Ditch Day

Senior tag

Senior prank?

Graduation parties

Summer road trip

Concert(s)

Picnic

Botanical gardens

Oakhurst Fourth of July fest

Shakespeare in the Park

Outlands mini golf

"Good. And we can always add to it," Kayleigh said.

Morgan waggled her eyebrows. "But which one should we do first?"

The List was how we wound up at the bowling alley, where Max, Ryan, Malcolm, and Josiah met us later. The List was how we planned for our last days of summer, mini golf and a trip downtown on a night I wasn't working late.

It was how Tessa wound up smiling the day Laurel left for college, when the final, wobbling bowling pin fell. Tessa spun, arms raised in her favorite Dolly Parton T-shirt, sleeves cut off. "Finally! Victory!"

She slapped Ryan's hand as she hopped off the lane, and I applauded from my spot on Max's lap. There weren't enough seats for all of us, but I'd still hesitated—*I can't initiate contact with Max; he'll know I like him as more than a friend!* He didn't miss a beat, though, curling one arm around me as he laughed at something Josiah was saying. As with nearly everything in his life, Max seemed sure of himself. It was hard-won, I knew—after years of the jerks in our grade taking him down every peg—but I still envied him.

Tessa sat down across from us, breathless from her celebration.

Kayleigh swung an arm around her shoulder. "Happy birthday, Marfy."

"Happy birthday, Marfy," Tessa agreed.

CHAPTER FOUR

"Please tell me that you're kidding," I said, staring at my dad's delighted face.

He thrust the backpack at me. "Nope! And I didn't save it for thirteen years to have you weasel out of this, so go on."

It wasn't enough that he still insisted on turning his night for dinner into "Back to School Bash." A banner always marked the event—some foil thing he'd found at the grocery store years ago. He made baked ziti, Cameron's favorite dinner, during the inaugural bash.

I trudged to the tiny balcony off his apartment and contorted my arms to fit the backpack—a purple number designed to look like a kitten's face, complete with plastic whiskers shooting off. I sighed and looked over my shoulder—re-creating the picture from my first day of kindergarten.

"Say 'twelfth grade!'" my dad prompted.

My sister smiled. "I'm so glad this is happening."

"I saved your backpack, too, Cammy. A few more years and this'll be you."

Her smile dropped as mine widened. I craned my neck back with a final pose. "Good?"

"Yeah, I've got a few to work with." He motioned me inside and shut the sliding door behind me. "Seems like just yesterday we were loading up that backpack for the first time. You were so nervous that you puked right before getting on the bus."

"Did I?" I'd always had a bad stomach, one that clenched like a fist when I got nervous. And I got nervous a lot.

"You did! With the kitty backpack on, no less. So sad. But cute."

"It's comforting to me," Cameron said, "that you have always been essentially the same person."

The oven timer went off, and I scowled at Cameron as my dad dashed to the kitchen. Stomach problems weren't even the defining complaint of my young life; insomnia was. For whole swaths of elementary school, I lay wide-eyed at night, staring up at my ceiling. I worried about my parents dying, about bad grades, about being yelled at by teachers; I worried about floods, about waking up in a different reality. Some nights, the only way I could fall asleep was to read, to get lost in someone else's world until I finally nodded off. Even then, nightmares often shook me awake with both hands.

Cameron placed the salad we'd prepped on the table and slid my phone closer to me.

"Max is texting you."

I gave a quick *don't look at my phone* glare, which I'd learned from her.

"How's my brother-in-law readjusting to American life?" Cam asked.

The glare became several shades darker.

My dad put a hand over his heart. "Oh, Cammy. Cameron, my youngest, my baby. We don't joke about that in front of dear old Dad. It's bad for my health."

I scooped out some ziti, and something—the smell of melted mozzarella and oregano, a constant in my dad's apartment for years—shifted in me, nostalgia taking root. For all my groaning about the kitty backpack, I knew this night was the last of its kind.

"So," my dad said. "I have some pretty big news to share with you both."

I held my chin still, barely resisting a glance at my sister. I could feel her doing the same. We'd expected this announcement for a few weeks now—that our dad would be moving back into the house.

"I accepted a new job!"

"Wait, what?" Cameron said, at the same time I managed, "You quit your job?"

"Well, I got an additional job, I should say. Wyatt State University asked me to teach a few journalism classes. So as of next week, I'm Professor Hancock on a part-time basis downtown. Cool, huh?"

"Oh." My sister spread her hands, as if laying the situation out before her. "Yeah. Cool."

I couldn't get words out, my mind flashing with the image of my parents across the kitchen table, reacting to the idea of film school. My mom's horror at the cost, at my future debt. Had my dad gone out and gotten a second job because of it?

"That's amazing, Dad." I slid a smile onto my face like sleight of hand. *Watch this ace of facial expressions, as I sneakily hide my panic up my sleeve!*

"Yeah, it's pretty neat. I'll also get tuition remission to take a class or two, which is major. Journalism is changing so fast! Gotta bone up if I want to hang around this field for another twenty years." He tugged his collar, joking about the pressure. "It's good news, girls."

My sister had picked her fork up and was digging in. "It's great! We just thought you were going to say you were moving back in with us and Mom."

"Moving back in?"

Cameron gave him a *duh* look. "Oh, c'mon, Dad. We're not children."

"You are, in fact, children. You're *my* children. And we have to maintain some boundaries." He looked to me, known relationship pessimist, for backup.

"At first, sure," I said. "But you guys have been dating for over a year. I think we've crossed the threshold where it's weirder that you're not there."

Cameron spoke around the cherry tomato in her mouth. "Agreed."

"We're trying not to mess with the balance."

"And we appreciate that," I said, an understatement. "But let the record show: both daughters are firmly on Team Stop-Making-It-Weirder."

"Your votes are duly noted."

"'But this family is not a democracy,'" Cameron and I said, in mocking unison. A favorite refrain of our mom's, over and over any time we tried to outnumber her in the divorce years.

"So, tomorrow," my dad said, clearly hoping for a topic change. "My girls back in the same school for the first time in years. You nervous for high school, Cammy?"

"No," she said reflexively. My sister was usually much better at acting cool. But even I could hear the too fast response for what it was: a cover-up. "I mean, middle school sucked, so bring on freshman year. Can't be worse. Plus, you know, I already have my Dance Team friends."

In that moment—in so many moments—I envied Cameron. What if I hadn't been born feeling everything so deeply? What if my parents had split sooner, before I was old enough to remember how bad it was for so long? What if I hadn't faced down unexpected loss at age fifteen? Sometimes, watching my sister's life felt like watching a strange parallel universe: a more carefree version of me, on a three-year delay.

This was my dramatic streak: introspection. Weighing experiences carefully. Helplessly examining. Cameron, meanwhile, did drama in the form of proclamations that she'd *die* if my mom wouldn't let her pierce her nose.

After dinner, I helped with dishes while my dad made brownies from a box, the smell of powdery cocoa filling the room. Cameron burrowed into the living room chair, phone in hand.

"The teaching job at Wyatt," I said quietly. "Is that because of my school? Because of the costs?"

He waved this off, like he'd anticipated my hang-ups. "I'm diversifying my résumé, Paiger."

So, not exactly a denial.

"We won't know about financial aid for a while," he said. "Your job is senior year and applications, okay?"

The cost-benefit ratio of film school was risky at best. Debt blinked like a giant minus sign, hovering over my future in red neon. But last year, my grandmother had admonished me to live my life. And for once, I trusted myself to do exactly that.

"Mom sold that china cabinet she refinished," I said, realizing. Last week, she'd listed the powder blue piece online, and it got snapped up for a modest profit.

"Of course she did," my dad said. "What was she gonna do—keep every piece of redone furniture in the house? She'd have to kick Cammy out to make space!"

"Funny," Cameron called from the other room.

I frowned. "Right. Yeah. I guess not."

"Relax, kid," he said. I gave him a look that I hoped would convey: *Oh, just* relax? *Is that all? All this time, my whole entire life, I just had to* decide *to* relax? "You're gonna get into your top schools; you'll work your butt off like you always do. And I'll be watching your shows on TV before we know it. You know, Shonda was only thirty-five when *Grey's* first aired!"

Over the summer, he'd listened to every podcast he could find about showrunners, and now quoted them like they were his personal friends. *Well, Shonda Rhimes says,* he'd begin, advising me on all matters related to TV writing. *You know, Mike Schur's philosophy is . . .*

"Okay, but she's an actual genius? I'll be lucky to get into one film school."

He rolled his eyes. "You get this attitude from your mother. Let me plan my watch parties."

"Dad," I said.

The timer beeped, and my dad raised his eyebrows pointedly, as if the oven was chiming in to agree with him.

"Cammy!" he called. "Come eat brownies before your sister implodes from worrying about things she can't control."

CHAPTER FIVE

Three times before, I'd entered this building for the first day of school. Freshman year, nervous and wide-eyed. Sophomore year, in a haze of blurry grief. Junior year, on coltish legs as I tried to move forward.

And today, finally, steady on my feet. I looked over at my friends, at the changing-leaf red of Morgan's hair, at Kayleigh's easy half smile as she waved to someone, at Tessa's gaze finding me, checking in. I gripped the feeling in my fists, the history between us, the comfort.

My sister scuttled off to her friends, and I almost called after her, wishing her a good day. But Cameron didn't need me.

I'd gotten so used to this building, the banged-up red of the lockers, the lingering fumes of fresh paint on cinderblock. The squeak of new shoes, bought at back-to-school sales. In a TV script, I'd write for the camera to pan around, capturing the blur of detail.

God, how many times had I fantasized about leaving Oakhurst? I'd wanted a new beginning, somewhere my face didn't make strangers think of a boy who died too soon. In the past year, though, I'd cut and pasted my life back together like a collage. Friends who knew me. Max. My quiet, happy room and Alcott's. My scripts. My job at Cin 12. And now, when it had all fallen into place: time to plan my departure.

"Stop that," Kayleigh said. When I glanced up to see who that comment was for, she seemed to be looking at me.

"Stop what?"

"You're about two seconds away from chewing the ends of your hair. Just *enjoy* this. We're finally seniors. No worrying."

Why did people keep telling me to stop worrying, like it was a light I chose to keep on, a bulb burning at all hours? By what instant magic, honestly, could I rewire my core self?

As we walked toward our lockers, I felt a pulse throughout the senior hallway—somewhere between a thumping heartbeat and a ticking clock. The last first.

Some loud guy in our grade whose name I could never remember—Bryan Ames? Bryce Ames?—came down the hallway with some buddies. Loudness seemed to be his dominant trait, along with his belief that volume alone made him charming. While passing us, he called, "Hey, girls. Have a good summer? Happy senior year!"

I thought that was it, but he turned back, pointing at Tess.

"Tessa McMahon! Heard you're gay now—congrats!" And before we could respond, he was hollering to someone else, "Whoop! Seniors."

Tessa looked back at me, with the flat expression of

someone sitting through an extended commercial break. "God, this town is predictable."

"Do you want me to correct people?" I asked. Last we'd talked about it, Tessa preferred "queer" and said she would let us know if that changed.

She snorted. "I'm fine with 'gay.' The 'now' can kiss my ass, though."

"Ignoramus," I muttered. "Wait. Ignor-*Ames*. Ha!"

"You are . . ." Tessa trailed off, smiling, and said, in her fondest tone of voice, "my favorite dork."

I took notes throughout my first classes, even though the syllabus information would be online. Writing out notes in longhand felt satisfying—peaceful, even—until AP English, which should have been my easy class.

"I imagine all of you consider language your forte," Mrs. Ramirez was saying. "If the reading list looks daunting, it's because I'm preparing you not just for the AP test but for collegiate coursework."

All my friends were in another period, so I had no one to share grimaces with until next-period lunch, where Kayleigh immediately asked, "English syllabus?"

"Yes!" I fell into the food line with her, hoping to grab a snack for after my senior appointment. "When am I going to read that much?"

Kayleigh clucked her tongue. "And if *you're* worried about that . . ."

"Big news on the personal front." Tessa joined us with a drink. She talked around the red straw. "The school has a milkshake machine now."

THE MAP FROM HERE TO THERE   67

"I'm sure you two will be very happy together," Kayleigh said.

I craned my neck, hoping to spot Max cutting past for his calc class.

"Well," I said, pocketing a protein bar. I handed a dollar to the cashier. "Senior appointment time."

"Who's yours with?" Tessa asked.

"I got a spot with Pepper." At this overcrowded school, there weren't enough counselors to meet with every senior before applications. Fortunately for me, my QuizBowl adviser and favorite teacher was an auxiliary graduation adviser.

"Lucky. I'm with Davis on Friday. I don't even know him."

"Good luck!" Kayleigh told me. "Hope you're graduating!"

Behind me, I heard Tessa smack her arm. "Don't joke about that. You know she has nightmares about missing credits."

I liked Ms. Pepper for a lot of reasons: she was smart and funny, one of those teachers who could read the room. But also because she seemed to like her students. When kids joked with her, she gave it right back. And though she had quite a poker face, she often seemed to be masking amusement, like she enjoyed our company.

She was seated at her desk, eyes so affixed to her laptop that I didn't knock right away. Even from here, I could see summer freckles, more pronounced than usual on her fair skin. I wondered what she did outside. Gardening? Swimming? I could only imagine her in a blazer on a lounge chair, reading a serious novel.

"Paige!" she said, spotting me. "Hey! Get in here! How's it going?"

On my way toward her, I trailed my palm over my former desk. This musty junior classroom had become an unexpected holy ground, the place where a seat next to Max Watson changed everything.

"How was New York?"

"Amazing." I settled into the chair nearest her desk. "Well, terrifying and overwhelming. But amazing."

"You liked your classes? How'd you fare in workshop?"

"Oh my gosh. Ha. Not great, at first."

"No one does," she said. "But you thrive on constructive feedback, so I bet your work improved quite a bit."

I smiled a little, flattered that Pepper knew me so well. "It did, yes."

Ms. Pepper looked genuinely happy for me, as she had last year when I told her about the program. "I'm so glad you had a good experience. And Max is well? I haven't seen him yet."

"Max is great. He loved Italy, of course."

"Of course. And you two are . . ." She pointed between me and a nearby empty seat, as if this somehow meant "in a relationship of some romantic nature."

"Yep," I said, trying to sound casual and not like my cheeks could explode into phoenix flames, ash out, and rise again.

She nodded, but I could tell she was resisting a smile. I had the sense that she'd been rooting for Max and me from the start. I imagined the two of us plotted like meteors, in different corners and hurtling through dark sky. Ms. Pepper saw our trajectories toward each other when we were still in different quadrants of the universe.

Before we were so together that I picked up his sci-fi lingo.

"So let's get into this, eh?" Pepper said. The screen reflected in her glasses, but I couldn't make out the details of what I presumed was my student file. Grades, state test scores. Anything about my first-ever boyfriend dying right before sophomore year? The guidance counselor checked in with me a lot back then, but left the heavy lifting to the therapist my parents found for me.

"Excellent grades, exemplary ACT." She clicked the mouse, scrolling. I resisted making a crack about having no life for most of high school being a huge help to my academics. "You've got some activities from freshman year. QuizBowl last year."

"And I work. At the movie theater."

"Right. That's good. The NYU program this summer is a great addition to your CV. Will you be asking any of your professors for college recommendations?"

"I did already." In her letter, my favorite professor called me a workhorse of a writer—eminently teachable without surrendering my point of view. *Green, of course*, another professor said, *but a whip-smart grinder with a great ear*. I reread those words a dozen times, trying to internalize: I was good at this. Or maybe, I *could* be good at this.

Pepper looked impressed. "Fantastic. Will NYU be your number one choice, then?"

"I think so? USC and UCLA are huge long-shots, but on the table." I almost added that my decision might rest on where my writing partner landed, but that was hard to explain without sounding codependent.

More than even workshop, Maeve brought out my best

writing. She charged into every element with a confident opinion—a natural consequence of being a Taurus with an Aries rising, she claimed. Normally, brashness like that would shut me down to huffy silences and deferred opinions. But Maeve prodded me to defend my ideas; she listened thoughtfully and considered. Alone in my dorm room, I could stare up at the ceiling for an hour trying to solve one problem. Across from Maeve at a coffee shop, ideas whizzed between us like sparks.

"What about Indiana schools? Any options with in-state tuition?"

"IU is a given." I'd visited with my parents and felt right at home, confident in the major offerings and how I'd fit in. It was my favorite locally, so I didn't see the point of paying application fees for other Indiana schools.

Pepper tapped a pen against her chin. "Are there any film-related activities here at Oakhurst?"

"Um, there's supposed to be an A/V component to my journalism elective?"

She toggled her head, unsatisfied. "What about the fall play or spring musical? Could you shadow the director, maybe? Or do stage crew?"

"Um, maybe. But I think they rehearse after school." I cleared my throat, trying to sound grown-up. "I have a work release to get some hours in at my job."

"Well, that's that, then. I think you're in fine shape. Let me know if I can glance over your application materials for you." She made eye contact, like she knew I needed the reassurance. "You'll be fine. And I'll see you at Warrior Night tonight, yes?"

"Yep." I'd been tasked with representing QuizBowl at the annual event for freshmen and slacker upperclassmen to peruse school activities. "See you. Thanks."

On my way out the door, I told myself she meant it like "fine china" or "fine wine."

Fine. I was fine.

That evening, I hesitated at the gym doors, indulging in a brief daydream about fleeing Warrior Night. Tables lined the high-gloss floors, already full of fellow seniors and their clubs. Kayleigh would be heading up the volleyball table somewhere around here. Morgan was manning the Empower booth, or, as she put it, *womanning* it.

Max, team captain of QuizBowl, had also been elected president of the robotics team. They worked on projects of their own, but also visited elementary and middle schools, trying to draw kids into the wild world of engineering. All good stuff, except that Max's robotics presidency left me speaking to strangers about academic and pop culture trivia. Luckily, our friend and third QuizBowl teammate, Malcolm, had positioned the student council table next to my station. Maybe he'd jump in if I blacked out from excess chitchat.

Max found me in the sea of people, sidestepping early-bird parents, students, and younger siblings dragged along. "There you are. It's been weird hardly seeing you all day."

"Yeah, I'm not into it."

"Wait for me after?" he asked, and I nodded. "Good luck—try to lure in some solid recruits."

"I'll try . . ." I gave a wary expression and swept my hair back, mock vanity. "But last year's rookie set a pretty high standard."

He grinned, eyebrows raised. "Oh, I don't expect *that* level of perfection."

For the rest of the evening, I chatted gamely with anyone who approached—emphasizing that QuizBowl was a very low-pressure commitment. And fun! Once, I called it "a brainy but whimsical addition to your résumé," which I hoped was true. During the lulls, I restacked our flyers and chatted with Malcolm.

The biggest surprise of the night was Aditi Basu. Junior class vice president, soccer goalie, and one of those rare people with genuine popularity, not status popularity. She ran the most-liked photo account at Oakhurst, colorful shots from her job at the ice cream shop and snaps of her family cooking together. But sometimes, makeup-free selfies with captions about beauty standards, posts about her migraines—and frustration with the pain, medication trials, missing days of school. She often liked my posts, rare as they were, so I felt as if I knew her, even though we'd only talked a few times.

"Hey, Paige." She smiled the way she always did—warmly, with a hint of shyness. Maybe a fellow introvert underneath the public vulnerability.

"Hey, Aditi. How's it going?"

"Good, good." She gestured at the poster board. "So, Quiz-Bowl. You guys did pretty well last year, right?"

"Yeah, we held our own."

"I had a class with Max," she admitted with a laugh. "He talked it up. Are there openings on the team this year?"

"Yeah! There are."

"Cool. Could I . . ." She reached for a flyer. "Thanks. See you at the info meeting."

I could almost feel people at other booths watching this exchange, QuizBowl's social capital rising with Aditi's mere presence.

So all in all, a good night. The last first day, over already. I walked out with Max's arm around me, Morgan teasing me about going home to color-coordinate my syllabi into binders. Ryan and Malcolm chatting with Kayleigh about weekend plans.

"That's a wrap, kids," Ryan said, peeling off for his Jeep. "First day down!"

"Oh, hey," I said, touching Malcolm's arm. "Are you and Josiah around on Saturday?"

"I think so," he said. "Senior Year List?"

"Yeah, we're thinking roller rink," I said. This was how I held on for now, how I readied myself to let it all go: enjoying every last first, savoring.

Kayleigh reached one arm up to the sunset, calling to everyone and no one, "Seniors!"

After being surprised by two sudden losses, I'd learned to be suspicious of the moments when everything felt right.

As soon as I caught myself relaxing toward contentment, I winced—eyes darting for the shoe that would inevitably drop. But for now, my worries had parted enough to let everything else rush in: fresh asphalt, the August sky with clouds in full bloom. The tiny buzz of freedom, my own car, my senior year waiting like a canvas I'd constructed and was finally getting to paint. The way that when my lips touched Max's, the parking lot fell out from around us like a flimsy wooden backdrop on a theater stage. I was fine.

CHAPTER SIX

On Saturday, a slow hour at the Cin 12 ticket counter converged with Donna's break, and I took the opportunity to rethink my schedule. Across the ticket counter, I laid the components of my life on index cards like a storyboard: *SCHOOL, HOMEWORK, WORK, COLLEGE APPLICATIONS, FRIENDS, MAX, QUIZBOWL, FAMILY, SLEEP.* Which needed priority right now? Could anything be combined? The only area that had obvious wiggle room was sleep, the glue that held my sanity together. Family and homework? Maybe I could work on my history paper at the kitchen table while Cameron baked and my mom shopped online for drawer handles.

"What do we have here?" Hunter's voice appeared nearby. His shift had started later, owing to a doctor's appointment. "Hmm! 'MAX' next to 'SLEEP.' Interesting."

"Oh, honestly." I pushed the cards apart.

Hunter slid into the booth beside me, mimicking my pose, elbows on the counter. "I take it your first week of school went well."

"Yeah, it was good."

"So this is just . . ." He trailed off, motioning at the spread before us. "The inner workings of an average, chill senior?"

"I have never claimed to be *chill*," I said with a sniff. "And not everyone has things figured out like you do."

His mouth quirked up on one side, dimple arcing from cheek to chin. "Do I?"

He looked pleased that I thought so, anyway. I searched through our previous conversations in my mind, flipping through pages of dialogue. He did seem to worry a lot about losing his scholarship to injury. About balancing college ball with coursework, since he might do graduate school eventually. He was a youngest child, a surprise to his parents later in life, and he seemed regretful to leave them for school.

I peered at him. "Wait. Are you as big a mess as I am?"

"Yes, Hancock!" He laughed. "Of course. I'm also just trying to have fun sometimes. Which I notice is not one of your cards."

"'FRIENDS' is. And I can have fun with any of these things!" I said, chin raised. "In fact, I made a *list* of things that my friends and I—"

Hunter cut me off, shaking both hands. "Please don't finish that sentence. It's very sad."

"Oh, really?" I spun, looking smug. "Is it sad that I'm going to the roller rink tonight?"

Hunter's eyebrows shot up. Not that I'd ever tell him so, but I'd maybe never seen such nice eyebrows on a guy—full and straight, as dark as his hair. "That place off Braemer Ave? Man, I haven't been there in years."

I pointed at myself with both hands. "Yeah, and it's fun."

"Well, Hancock," Hunter said. "That is very wholesome. Tell the gang from *Happy Days* I said hi."

"I know you're making fun of me," I said primly. "But I'm actually very pleased with you for that classic television reference."

He stared down at my cards as if it were a chessboard. After a moment, he moved *WORK* next to *HOMEWORK*. "I could help you study. Be your lookout, anyway."

I studied him in profile, the neat slope of his nose, the jut of his lips. "Are you being serious?"

"Sure. It combines something I like—sneaking things past Donna—and something you like: the full nerd lifestyle." Before I could retort, he flashed a card between two fingers. "Does this or does this not say 'QUIZBOWL'?"

———————

The roller rink had been forgotten since our elementary school birthday parties, but it hadn't changed—the Skee-Ball machine dings, the neon track lighting, the heavy clunk of wheels on sheened floors. Back then, I gawked at the high school couples, scandalized by the hand-holding and moony expressions. Now I was skating beside Max Watson, watching the tiny mirrored lights shimmy across his skin. Those couples might have felt butterflies, but I felt—I don't know. Loops of skywriting.

"Did you come here a lot as a kid?" I asked him.

"Um, only every weekend of sixth grade. How do you think I developed these sweet moves?" He skated in a slow figure-eight pattern, nearly losing his balance.

I caught his hand. "Easy, Tiger."

"I wasn't really falling," he said, grin flashing. "Just trying to get you to hold my hand."

"Uh-huh."

Kayleigh waved from across the rink, where she and Morgan had their arms linked. She gestured to the table where we'd set up camp an hour ago and where Tessa now sat alone. From the looks of it, she'd purchased the snack counter's entire menu. She looked as solemn as Jesus in *The Last Supper*, only with chicken tenders instead of disciples.

Max skated with me to the exit door, and I wagged a finger at him. "No fancy-skating attempts while I'm gone."

He gave a delighted grin. "I'll only fall for you."

I managed to spin around, so he'd have the full view of my grudging smile.

"Hey!" he said. "Look at those moves!"

"It's just how I roll," I said mildly. Then, over my shoulder, "Guess you punderestimated me."

I could *hear* his open-mouthed grin in the stunned silence. He called after me, "Dream girl!"

Josiah, reentering the rink, gave me an appraising look. "We're all pulling for a spring wedding."

We were still getting to know each other, so I liked that he'd ventured out with a joke. I swatted back. "You're one to talk."

As if on cue, Malcolm mimed something to him from the snack line.

"CHER-RY," Josiah said, slow and exaggerated. Malcolm

gave him a thumbs-up, and Josiah turned to me, pleased. "Double wedding, then."

I laughed and headed toward Tessa.

"Something tells me," I said, easing off my wheels, "that you are not having a skaterrific time."

Outside, a mural featuring this word and a giant, anthropomorphized roller skate spanned half the parking lot. We'd posed with it on our way in.

A bite of soft pretzel bulged out Tessa's cheek. "What gave me away?"

"We finished the first week of senior year!" I said weakly. "No? You missing Laurel?"

"No. Well, yes, obviously." Laurel had posted a few photos from her first week—a morning latte scene and a skyscraper shot. In the former, Tessa was tagged as the coffee mug, maybe an inside joke. Or maybe Laurel was tagging where her thoughts were as she sipped her drink.

Tessa stared at our friends, going round and round beneath the lights. "I had my senior appointment yesterday. Davis said he's alarmed by my lack of plans. *Alarmed*, Paige."

Normally, Tessa would scoff this off—the opinion of someone who didn't even know her. But Laurel's absence chiseled a line into Tessa's tectonics, a thin crack that was shifting every other plate.

"Lack of plans?" I repeated. "You're applying to a few universities, you know your intended major, and you have good grades. That's, like, exactly what I'm doing."

"Except you have a portfolio and experience with screen

writing. For music business, I have . . . what? A drawer full of ticket stubs? And I haven't clicked with any school the way you love NYU, like Morgan and Kayleigh love IU. But I should, right?" She reached for a French fry and nibbled at it. "What if I don't, no matter where I visit? Or what if I do, but I get rejected?"

It sounded like my own mind, worries tapped out like frantic ticker tape. Morgan skated past, Kayleigh holding on to her waist, and they both made goofy faces at us. Tessa smiled a little around the straw of her fountain soda.

"A drawer full of ticket stubs isn't nothing," I reasoned. "Not if you're pursuing a music business degree."

"Davis said my résumé needs at least one 'school-affiliated activity.'" Tessa made air quotes with her fingers, a gesture that I hadn't realized could be executed with such scorn.

"QuizBowl?" I sat up, hopeful. "We need a fourth member and some alternates."

She held out the basket of fries to me, and I took one. "Eh, that's more your thing."

"And Max's!" I said, indignant. "And Malcolm's."

"Yeah. Maybe," she said, but she scrunched up her nose. Rudely, in my opinion.

"You like photography," I ventured, thinking of her photos online. The yoga studio in the morning, a ficus casting shadows like webbed hands on the floor. The stage at the Carmichael, Laurel in silhouette. Kayleigh leaning back on her car's bumper, one lick into a soft-serve cone and looking like summer itself. "And you're great at it. You took Kayleigh's profile pic! And mine!"

When she'd visited New York, Tessa had caught me looking back on a crowded street, lips parted as I began to say, *Are you coming?* Behind me, a blur of yellow paint and red tail lights—a taxi whooshing past. It looked how Manhattan felt to me. A little too much, a little too fast, finding stillness within it. It reminded me of my favorite photo of my grandmother in Paris.

"True," Tessa said, frowning.

"Also," I continued, "music business isn't a traditional major. Why have a traditional application? Have the sound guy at the Carmichael write you a recommendation!"

"Steve?" she asked, skeptical. He was an older guy, shaved head and bushy, graying beard. Sometimes he let her sit in the booth with him during shows; she stayed out of his way and listened intently when he talked acoustics or soundboards.

"Why not?"

"Well, I don't know his last name, for starters. And every other word out of his mouth is censorable."

"He'd clean it up for a recommendation. Then you use your essay to talk about how music is this constant in your life, how you've heard it all over the world, how you've lived the hustle of business through your parents. You can even structure the essay with specific songs."

After a moment, she peered at me. "You'd help me with it?"

"Obviously. And you know what? I second-guess screen writing every day."

"Oh, please. I once witnessed you dissecting a *Mission District* scene, passionately, for an hour with Maeve."

"Yeah, but can I hack it? And will I hate it once it's work and not a hobby? Can I ever really make it my job?"

"Okay." Kayleigh slid to a stop beside us, swiping one hand across our presence before her. "What is this? Why are your faces like that?"

Morgan was right behind her, and plopped down. "Everyone okay?"

"Yeah," I said as Tessa demanded, "What's wrong with my face?"

Kayleigh gave her a pitying look. "Your stress expressions—stresspressions? exstressions?—are going to give you wrinkles by age twenty-one."

I relaxed my face from its grimace, but Tessa harrumphed. "Your face would look like this, too, if you weren't basically born a Hoosier."

All the Hutchins kids went to IU: TJ had graduated a few years ago, Brady was a senior, and Reid had just started sophomore year. Kayleigh knew the campus, owned the apparel, and had reeled Morgan in somewhere along the way, too.

"I'm applying other places, you know," Kayleigh said curtly. "It's good to keep some options open."

"Where else?" I asked, surprised. This was Max's philosophy, too. At last count, he planned to apply to eight schools across Indiana, Illinois, and Ohio. But I didn't know Kayleigh was bothering with application fees anywhere but IU.

"Oh, here and there," Kayleigh said, and Morgan chimed in, "Yeah, like, I'm applying to St. Mary's, just to see. Hey, did you tell them your other news?"

"Did you decide on a spring break locale?" Tessa asked, perking up. Kayleigh had promised us updates about a beach trip soon.

"I'm making progress," Kayleigh said. "But no. My dad's officially proposing to Lisa at her birthday dinner next week."

I lowered the French fry I'd been about to shove in my mouth. "Wow! That's soon."

Kayleigh's mom died in a car accident over a decade ago, an indelible loss that Kayleigh would always grieve. But a stepmother wasn't the stuff of fairy-tale villains anymore, and Lisa had been dating Mr. Hutchins for years now. The progression from occasional dates to Lisa being a part of family dinners had been so gradual that it never felt jarring to Kayleigh. Lisa had a son of her own, in middle school, and she kept pretty firm boundaries.

"You talked to your dad, then?" Tessa asked. At our most recent pool day, Kayleigh had mentioned her dad and Lisa hoped to get engaged in the next year, but they wanted the kids to weigh in about timeline and comfort level.

"I did," Kayleigh said. "Reid and I decided we'd actually rather live with Lisa and Jayden for a few months next summer, when Reid is home from school too. It's less awkward than coming home for winter break to a new, three-person family unit, none of whom are Black."

Lisa, whose parents were white and Puerto Rican, respectively, had long been able to connect with Kayleigh about being biracial. But she understood that their experiences differed, too. The dialogue had been pretty open from the beginning, if weighted a little heavily on the kids' initiative.

"Was your dad surprised you'd prefer sooner to later?" I asked.

"A little," she said. "But really excited. It's a ton of changes for him—becoming a granddad, getting married, his favorite daughter leaving for school."

From the speakers overhead, a familiar song clapped out its peppy beat. I thought I'd left it in summertime, but no. Say freaking yes.

"God, this song is annoying," Tessa said. "But . . . I kind of have to dance to it?"

"Come on," Morgan said. She held her hands out, to help Tessa up, and Kayleigh and I followed. The guys had moved to the arcade area, and were crowded around as Malcolm steered a virtual car. So the four of us glided, yell-singing the dumbest, greatest song of the year.

There at the roller rink—with its musty carpet and out-dated wall decals from the 1990s—I wondered how we looked to the rest of the world. Young and silly, probably. I often had the distinct feeling that strangers watched us with annoyance, teenage girls with cotton candy lives. They could think that—that we were frothy and carefree.

Would they ever guess how strong we were from carrying each other? Would they guess that the year Aaron Rosenthal died, these girls hefted my pain onto their own backs, shouldering as much as they could? That this summer, we stayed up half the night, scripting and practicing how Tessa would

come out to her parents? Would anyone know that Morgan
and Kayleigh's friendship was forged the year Mrs. Hutchins
died? That Kayleigh drew me into her orbit the year my parents fought enough to finally separate?

We were young and silly—sure, maybe. But we were also
each other's mothers, sisters, keepers.

"We're doing fine," Tessa called over to me, breathless.
Fine. That damn word again. "At least we can admit that we
don't know what we're doing, right?"

In improv class, I'd learned more than "say yes." I'd learned
to say *yes, and.* So I nodded to Tessa, faking certainty, and held
up one arm in triumph. "Seniors!"

CHAPTER SEVEN

The QuizBowl informational meeting, two weeks into school, brought out half a classroom's worth of prospective members—many more than I'd dared to hope for. And sure enough, Aditi Basu showed up, bright-eyed and interested. As Pepper started the meeting, Malcolm leaned over and whispered, "Did we . . . make QuizBowl cool?"

Last year, the team had practiced only very casually, so we had to throw together a more structured practice in less than a week. Max e-mailed a packet of topics and ran a practice match with total levity, making everyone feel at ease. Aditi excelled—cranking out answers about Nella Larsen, rococo painting, and time signatures. There were other standouts, too, including a sophomore named Sofia with quick confidence.

I needed to stay sharp to make sure my own seat was earned. So, true to his word, Hunter helped me sneak in some studying on a slow Sunday shift at the ticket counter. "As the fifth vice president of the United States, this Massachusetts-born—"

"Elbridge Gerry," I said dully.

"I have . . . literally never heard the name Elbridge," Hunter said. "Can we do something else? Anything else?"

"You can keep a lookout while I sneak in some reading?" I asked, hopeful.

Hunter slid my hidden book out from under the counter, a bright pink paperback with a tiara on the cover. "This clearly isn't even for school. Or almost-adults."

I snatched it back from him, protective. "Excuse me. This book is a perfect cup of tea."

"Oh, it's your cup of tea, is it?" Hunter affected a haughty British accent.

"No, I mean . . . some books, the reading experience is like a cup of tea." I patted the book, a cherished favorite since my middle school days. "Comforting and, like, healing. It may seem simple, but there's a real art, and important ingredients, too."

He gave me a look I couldn't quite place—mocking? pitying? "Are you explaining tea? To a Chinese guy?"

I laughed at myself, cheeks flushing. "Fine. What would *you* like to do?"

Make meaningless little bets on everything, as it turned out: Next ticket purchase? Would the next person comment on how hot it was outside? Next person through the door: hat or no hat?

I pulled a little piece of paper from beneath the counter, scribbled down *BET MOVIE?*, and shoved it into my tux pocket. I would have preferred to type this into my existing idea list, but Donna had a one-strike phone rule. According to Cin 12 legend, she once fired someone in the first hour of his first day for texting.

"What would a Bet Movie be?" Hunter was nosy in a child-like way, totally unselfconscious about being in my business.

"Probably nothing. But maybe two characters start making arbitrary little bets until it escalates into bigger stakes: betting houses, cars. Screwball comedy." I'd sift through the ideas later and decide if any had enough potential to share with Maeve.

"I like it. How are your writing portfolios coming?"

"Better than the other application materials, anyway." I worked on both in the late hours of school nights, when my mother thought I was asleep. "Do you still have to write an essay for your application? Even with the scholarship offer?"

"'Course, Hancock."

"What did you write about for the Biggest Challenge topic?"

He leaned over on the counter, arms crossed. "I, um, wrote about depression."

I hesitated, unsure if he was somehow messing with me. "Oh. Cool."

"Yeah, I mean, not just that. Like, as it relates to getting treatment—model minority bullshit and stuff. I didn't say 'bullshit' in my essay, obviously. But it is." He grinned, wolfish. "Oh my God, your face! You thought I was going to say I wrote about sports as a way to learn cooperation and discipline."

"Kind of," I admitted. The truth was, I was shocked that Hunter Chen dealt with depression in the first place. He came off as utterly lighthearted, unburdened. A big assumption, on my part, that felt foolish now, and unfair to him.

"I'll have you know," he said, pointing a finger, "that I wanted to. But my adviser said no."

I shook my head, smiling. "Well, I'm impressed."

"I contain multitudes." Before I could agree, he added, "That's Whitman. Oh my God, are you in *love* with me now? Quoting poetry?"

How could one person be so interesting and so annoying inside of thirty seconds? Honestly, it was a feat.

"What are *you* writing about for that essay?" he asked, eager.

"I still don't know," I said. "That's why I asked."

"Holding out on me after I ponied up? Cold." He nodded toward the parking lot. "Bet you. Next person: your exact type. Ten out of ten physical attraction."

We went a few minutes without a customer, but when someone finally strode up—well, I'd have known him anywhere, yards away. Sometimes I thought that even in a *Where's Waldo?* crowd, my eyes would always land on Max Watson.

"What are the chances?" Hunter crowed. I'd temporarily forgotten his little bet. "It's too good!"

My face burned. "Ha-ha."

Max, reaching us, smiled hesitantly. "Hey. Sorry to drop by unannounced."

"It's okay," Hunter said, tapping his temple. "We saw you coming."

I clenched my teeth, praying that he would not elaborate. "Max, this is Hunter. I welcome you to ignore him."

"Yeah, hey. We met a few weeks ago," Max said. . . . Oh God. That's right—he'd stopped here looking for me after his first day home. What had Hunter said to him?

"And I've heard sooo much about you," Hunter added.

"All good stuff," I insisted. Shielded by the counter, I knocked my knee with Hunter's, willing him to shut up. "Isn't it time for you to go on your break?"

"Might as well. Give you lovers some privacy." He slid off the stool, saluting Max. "Nice to see you."

"Anyway," I said, smiling up at Max. "Hi."

"Hi. I tried to text you, but—"

"The no-phone policy. Ugh, I know. Sorry."

"I think our date is getting crashed tonight," he said, and I cocked my head. "Ryan asked what I was doing, and I said staying in to watch a movie with you. Next thing I know, he's saying 'Sounds good' and Tessa's texting me about snacks."

"They fully knew you did not mean to include them."

"Oh, I know," he said. "When I said 'THIS IS DATE NIGHT,' Morgan said, and I quote, 'lol, okay, Dad.'"

I jerked back, face scrunched up. In what bizarre joke scenario had our friends become our children?

"Don't ask me," Max said, hands brushing away the thought.

"Well, that's what you get for telling the truth. Next time, secret date night. We go off the grid."

His eyes lit up, and I held up one finger, sensing the direction his mind had taken. "We're not dressing up like superheroes or spies."

"No fun." He grinned, leaning close to air-kiss me goodbye.

After work, I changed into jeans and trooped to Max's house. Everyone was talking over one another in the basement, laughing through the movie that was the excuse to hang out, and I climbed onto the big couch next to Max. I didn't even realize I was nodding off until Kayleigh said my name, asking if I was paying attention.

I made a grumpy noise, my cheek against Max's shoulder. "Let her be," Max said. I liked the rumble of his voice from this close. I liked that he was protecting my rest, the one thing I couldn't multitask.

"I'm doing my big reveal!" Kayleigh said, and I peeked one eye open. Sure enough, she'd plugged her laptop into the TV, and the first slide said SENIOR TRIP: SPRING BREAK. I hauled myself up.

"I have officially finished planning," Kayleigh said. "We need to finalize and send deposits before it gets snagged by someone else. Okay. It's affordable, it's drivable, it's beautiful. Drumroll, please . . ."

The first panel burst open, a beach scene that read: PANAMA BEACH, FLORIDA! in a vintage postcard font. Kayleigh clicked past it quickly, to a cheerful little beach house, blue with a yellow door. She'd captioned it HERE WE COME!

Her audience buzzed with questions. All but me. Even as Kayleigh toured us through her slides, I knew: my mom would go straight to mayhem, unsupervised teens on the beach, hours away. One of those teenagers being my boyfriend.

Tessa was watching my face. "*Any* chance your mom gives this the go-ahead?"

Before I could reply, Kayleigh scoffed, "Oh, please. I've already considered Kate Hancock in this. And I have good news. As you know, my dad is getting married in early April. He and Lisa are leaving for their honeymoon right after, since it's her spring break, too."

Lisa taught fourth grade at a nearby school district. That, I knew. I had . . . no idea what that had to do with our Florida trip.

"The good news is about your dad's . . . honeymoon?" Josiah asked unsteadily.

Kayleigh ignored him. "I chose Panama Beach because they're going to the Florida Panhandle, too, twenty minutes away. Meaning . . . they can drive down with us and be nearby in case of emergency."

"And they don't mind?" This from a horrified Tessa.

Kayleigh shrugged. "We won't even see them except during the drive, I'm sure."

My face relaxed as it dawned on me. "Wait. So, I can tell my mom there will be parental chaperones?"

Kayleigh smiled, smug as a cardsharp laying out the winning hand.

"It might work," I admitted. "If anything will."

From beside me, Max slow-clapped. "Bravo, Hutchins. A masterpiece."

Kayleigh took a few sweeping bows. "Thank you! Thank you. It was my pleasure to do this instead of homework."

CHAPTER EIGHT

Sunday nights at my dad's apartment were the only remaining relic of our strict-custody-block days, more habit now than legal agreement. With my mom chaperoning a dance competition for Cameron's squad, I was getting a one-on-one night for the first time in ages. And I'd saved a sushi coupon specifically for the occasion.

"Well, this was great," my dad said, setting his plate on the coffee table. He'd moved our order from cardboard takeout boxes to serving dishes so we could admire the scene as we ate. "Might be the first time we ever have leftovers."

"I know we tease Cameron about not liking seafood," I said, and paused to swallow. "But I genuinely pity her."

"Well, next time you and I have a coupon, we can go to the restaurant," he said, then gestured at the Emmys Red Carpet, muted on TV. "Tonight, priorities."

I'd spent many Sundays finishing homework here, in my dad's armchair with his beloved, truly hideous Colts blanket over my lap. He often worked up column notes, but tonight, he was grading journalism assignments. So far, he'd complained three times about having to grade on his laptop instead of marking up physical copies in red ink.

"Oh, I *like* that," my dad said, nodding at Llewelyn Price and her earrings, gold orbs the size of grapes.

While my dress opinions were filtered through what I would personally wear, my dad delighted in the most interesting sartorial choices. The comment never changed. Giant ball gown in a bold magnolia print? *Oh, I* like *that!* Any tux that wasn't plain black? Yep—he *liked* that.

His surprise at his own enjoyment really made the experience for me.

"You'd wear that one." He touched my arm to get my full attention. "Am I right?"

I glanced from my laptop to Rose Odegbami, giving an interview in a lavender gown, cap sleeves with a sweetheart neckline.

"Definitely," I said. "I think she'll win her category, too. She should."

Maeve and I had been texting back and forth about the nominees and prospective winners. We wrote to our strengths, not trends, but it helped to understand the industry as a whole, according to our professors.

"You going to the homecoming dance?" my dad asked. "Senior year, after all."

"That's the plan."

"Attagirl. Gotta make the most of this time."

The older I got, the more adults did this—made cryptic

references to "this time" with far-eyed looks toward their own high school days. And yet, during a particularly bad stretch of sophomore year, my mom referenced Robert Frost to me: my only way out of high school was through it. Adults insisted things got easier someday—as you figured out who you were, as you made your own decisions. Meanwhile, they also sighed about their jobs and bills; they mused about high school with longing. Maybe it was easy to romanticize something that had already happened.

"So, Tessie's in Chicago, eh?"

"Yep. Probably on her way back by now." I'd seen snippets of her weekend online—Laurel looking out over the city from a high-rise window (*Her | Chicago | Sept 5*); their faces reflected in The Bean (*Obligatory | Chicago | Sept 5*); a crowded venue, raised arms visible in the dark (*The Hideout | Chicago | Sept 6*).

"Is she applying to schools out there?"

"Um, maybe! She's mostly focused on Nashville, New York, and LA. You know her." Music scenes full of up-and-comers, hole-in-the-wall restaurant gems.

"So, uh, you and our guy Max." My dad cleared his throat. "That a . . . serious thing?"

I looked at him uneasily. Had he watched a tutorial on talking to your teenage daughter? "We don't have to do this."

"Oh, so you only talk to Mom about this stuff?"

"I certainly do *not* talk to Mom about this stuff," I said, laughing.

"You're *secretive* about your dating life? Great. Just what a parent wants to hear."

"My dating life?" I made a grossed-out face.

"You're not . . . uh . . . I mean, your dream schools are still on the table, right?"

At this, I turned. My dad, I'd always thought, understood me. My mom and I were so similar—made of the same tense fabric, held together with alone time and our many organizational tactics—that I vexed her any time I did things differently than she would. But my dad got me. "You think I'd ditch screen writing?"

For debt, anxiety, homesickness, and self-doubt—sure. But for a boy?

"Hey," my dad said, shrugging, "first love is powerful stuff."

Over the summer, I'd felt secretly embarrassed by how often Max occupied my thoughts. I prided myself on academic excellence—on my busy, interested mind. And there I was, staring out a library window, daydreaming of a boy? I used my mooniness as fuel for a rom-com outline that Maeve criticized as saccharine but not without potential. From her, high praise. "Well, they're not mutually exclusive."

My dad nodded, satisfied. The problem was, I had increasingly come to believe that Max and screen writing *were* mutually exclusive. Maybe not at first. But how long, realistically, could we go without seeing each other? I couldn't think about it too much or my stomach gurgled, acidic.

Part of me wanted to muse about all my worries. To open my mind like a stuffed-full cabinet, let everything fall onto the floor so my dad could help me sort through the mess. But I didn't want to undermine his confidence in me or his bursting pride.

"Oh, hey," he said, sitting up. "I grabbed something for you from campus. I know you're pretty booked up but . . ."

He dug around in his briefcase for a single sheet of paper. On it, an advertisement for yearly theater auditions. A few shows were listed, and my dad had circled one called *2BD, 1BA*, showing in late March. Beside it, he'd scratched the name *Cris Fuentes* and an e-mail address.

"Two beds, one bath?" I guessed. Surely he knew I'd never audition. "You want to see it together?"

"No. Well, sure. But I met the director on campus. She's an adjunct at the college, and her day job is at that theater your grandma used to take you to."

"Mythos?" An impossibly cool contemporary theater downtown, lots of fringe plays and experimental work. I sat up a little.

"Yeah. She takes an intern or two each season. Wouldn't that look good on a résumé? I said you'd shoot her an e-mail." He looked briefly guilty, perhaps realizing he'd committed me to something without asking. "The show's so cool, kid. A modern take on *The Odd Couple*, and it's their under-twenty-one show, so all people around your age. And a young playwright, too—a local."

He didn't have to sell me so hard; I was interested the second he said "Mythos." But I enjoyed watching him try. "You have a copy of the play in your bag, don't you?"

"No," he said, indignant. "It's in my e-mail."

"Forward it to me," I said. "Thanks, Dad. I don't know if I can make it work with Cin 12, but I'll send the e-mail."

I returned to my screenplay software, hovering over a

character description that Maeve had noted as generic. But I could feel my dad still looking at me. When I glanced over, he was smiling angelically. "Can I read one of your pieces? Just one?"

"No *way*," I said, turning my screen away even more. "Would you let me read an unfinished draft of your column?"

Touché. He didn't say it, but I could see him thinking it. "At least tell me what it's about?"

"Well . . . ," I said, pausing for effect, "it's about a girl . . . with a really annoying dad."

He reached over to swat at my feet.

CHAPTER NINE

"I think the problem is that I can't tell who has the ball," Kayleigh mused, leaning forward as if several inches would make the football field easier to read.

"Or the problem is that you're still wearing your sunglasses. It's been dark for a good fifteen minutes." Morgan flicked the side of Kayleigh's red frames.

"Stop!" Kayleigh said, dodging away. "They're cute. It's a *look*."

"They are cute," Morgan conceded.

"Are we cutting out after halftime?" Kayleigh asked.

"Be supportive," I whispered, though no one wanted to cut out more than I did. We'd decided on the Oakhurst vs. Linwood game since it was the rowdiest, the full senior experience. This was, I hoped, my last football game.

"Yeah. Support me," Tessa said from behind a giant black camera. She'd agreed to do "supplemental photography" for the yearbook as her school activity. The lens extended twice as far as the camera itself, and Tessa steadied it with one hand.

Tessa had come home from Chicago bubbling over, giddy. I hadn't expected her to charge home doubly in love—not just with Laurel but with Tate College, an arts school she toured while there. I'd heard of it because I'd heard of every school with a film program in the Midwest, but Tessa finally knew what it was like to see herself somewhere. Her parents immediately agreed to a Nashville trip to see if Belmont resonated as strongly with Tessa.

"Shouldn't Max and Ryan be here by now?" Morgan asked me.

"They're on their way."

"That reminds me," Kayleigh said, pulling out her phone. "Ryan owes me food."

We stood in the lowest corner of the bleachers, behind several rows of our unruly classmates. Every game I'd attended as a kid, the student section overflowed, pressed against the railings—seniors with capital letters painted across white tank tops, zany wigs sprouting from their heads. Others went for Warrior apparel—gold plastic chest plates or replica Roman helmets, topped by scrub brushes. I didn't recognize the girl wearing full battle leathers, but I liked her.

I could do crowds like this—there was anonymity in the sea of red and gold, too many faces to take in. And while I was willfully unclear on the rules of football, I did appreciate that our school colors suggested we were here to cheer on a Quidditch team.

So it was apt when my boyfriend showed up in a Gryffindor shirt, slightly too tight on his skinny frame. I blinked at the fading House crest. "What is this . . . lie?"

"Eh?" Max looked down at himself.

"You're, like . . . fundamentally a Ravenclaw. You're Raven-claw's undisputed Head Boy."

Ryan Chase, Hufflepuff unto his very soul, barked out a laugh beside us. He was holding a few foil-wrapped hot dogs from the snack line, per some deal with Kayleigh. I wasn't clear on the details of what happened in their chem class.

"Well, *yeah*," Max said patiently. "But you know, when you're a kid, you just assume you're a Gryffindor like Harry. It's all I had clean in the right colors. And hello to you, too."

"Hello," I said sweetly.

"Gryffindor pride," Kayleigh said, reaching over us to grab a hot dog. "Ry, did you remember my—"

"Coke? Yes. Hoodie pocket."

Tessa put down the camera long enough to scarf some food. Afterward, she flipped through the past few shots, frowning.

"She's taking this pretty seriously," Max said close to my ear, and I nodded.

"Okay," Tessa said, sighing as she changed out another camera lens. The sticker on the side said PROPERTY OF OAKHURST A/V, but she owned a similarly fancy one for travel photos. "I'm going to interact with human subjects. Someone come with me."

"I'll go," Kayleigh said. She turned to us, pointing at her-self. "*Supportive*."

"Grab me a hot chocolate on your way back, will you?" Morgan brushed a crumb off her blouse. For the past few months, she'd really leaned into a vintage style. It started with a high-waisted bikini and tortoiseshell cat's-eye sunglasses this summer. Tonight, she wore a marigold top with a Peter Pan collar, tucked into a maroon corduroy skirt. It was nice to see, in our senior year, Morgan evolving into her most confident, Morgan-y self.

"I'll try to get a good shot of Cameron," Tessa called back to me.

It was my sister's first big performance in front of a hometown crowd. Dance Team performed at some games, but also inter-dance-team competitions on weekends. I didn't totally understand, but it took up a lot of her time.

On the field, the marching band's straight lines became wide circles. The form undulated out to various other shapes, until they eventually spelled *Warriors* in script—the crowd favorite.

I tilted my chin up to Max, eyes still on the field. "I kind of have a soft spot for the band."

"Oh yeah?"

The blare of the brass, the shine of the tubas in stadium lights. "Yeah. I only ever hear horns and brass like that at parades and games. It's so specifically hometown and . . ."

"Celebratory," Max finished.

I smiled up at him. Yes. Exactly that. He shifted a little closer, maybe resisting the urge to kiss me. My parents were in the bleachers somewhere, too. Instead, he brushed my bangs out of my eyes, which somehow made me feel kissed all the same. I'd let my hair grow out a little after seeing a Brigitte Bardot film this summer. I wasn't sure if I'd ever achieve the tousled look, but I was sure I liked Max fixing my hair.

"You guys are revolting." This was from Ryan. But he said it happily, like our revoltingness was a personal joy for him.

Next came the dance team, and I let out an uncharacteristic *Woo!* Ryan wolf-whistled, nodding at me to signal it was done on my behalf.

"She borrow that outfit from you?" Ryan joked. The team uniform included high-waisted leggings and a top that showed a slice of skin.

"Ha," I said humorlessly, through a bite of hot dog. "Team Cardigans forever."

Max laughed, like this was both an understatement and an endearing sensibility. I started to say *You're one to talk, Fandom T-Shirt Boy*, but I was distracted by a familiar Warriors windbreaker and hat, red worn near-pink after years of use. My dad, hurrying down the bleacher steps. He stopped at the railing, as close as he could get to the field, and held his phone up. "Go, Cammy!"

"Oh my God." I looked back at the higher-up seats until I spotted my mom, who gave me an *I couldn't stop him* shrug. She had the fondest smile on her face.

As Dan Hancock filmed or took pictures or whatever he was doing, he swayed his hips in time with the music. Dear Lord.

"Well, this is adorable," Max said, and I scolded myself for my reaction. Having a dad so present in my life that it was occasionally embarrassing? Not something to complain about, especially in front of Max.

When the routine ended, we all cheered. Cameron's bright

smile, which had been pasted over her nervousness, now seemed relieved. Proud.

On his way back up, my dad stopped by, clapping Max on the arm. "Hey, bud! Or should I say *buongiorno?*"

"*Buongiorno!* Good to see you, Mr. H."

"We've gotta have you over for an Italiano dinner some night!"

"Sounds great," Max said.

He looked to our other friends. "Hey, kids. Happy senior year! Better see you over for game night at some point."

Morgan watched him jog up the steps to where my mom was waiting. "Still going well?"

"I guess. I try not to think about it."

My phone went off, then again, a buzz from the purse resting on my hip. It was just Hunter, texting from somewhere in the stands across from us—our navy-clad rivals. I scrolled through several lines of all caps and emojis.

"Everything okay?" Max asked.

"Yeah. Just Hunter with a lot of big talk about Linwood. Why would he think I care who's winning?" I showed Max my text as I sent the words: *AREN'T THEY ALL FIELD GOALS? THEY ALL HAPPEN ON THE FIELD.*

"Hunter from work?" Morgan asked, nosing in.

Ryan scratched the back of his head, thinking. "You know, I saw him pitch against Lachlan last year. Unstoppable."

"Hey." I tagged Ryan's arm. "I've been meaning to tell you. He's committed to IU next year, same as you."

"For real?" Ryan said. "Is he cool? Give him my number— maybe we could carpool home and stuff."

"Kayleigh and I will join that carpool," Morgan said, beaming and obvious. "What? He's so cute!"

When she looked to me for confirmation, my eyes darted away. Of course Hunter was cute—his impish, high-watt grin and all that. But why would I ever say that in front of Max?

"He certainly thinks so," I managed, trying to sound bored and put-upon.

"Is he single?" Morgan asked.

I snorted. "And always mingling."

The crowd surged around us, people jumping to their feet to better see something on the field. I stood, too, if only out of instinct.

"Go!" Ryan hollered, fists clenched. "Gooooo!"

"Run the ball!" I yelled, and Max looked down at me, perplexed. "What? I'm ninety-five-percent sure that's relevant to the situation."

———

After the game, we walked out with the school-spirited droves, angling toward the parking lot.

"Remind me why this has to be No Boys Allowed?" Max asked, fingers laced through mine.

"So we can talk about you!" Morgan yelled from up ahead, climbing into her car with Tessa and Kayleigh.

"Because it's a sleepover." I lifted to my tiptoes. Even in a graceless parking lot full of amped-up football fans, kissing Max felt like a two-person oasis. I often visualized life like a day planner—my next day, next week, next year. But standing still with Max was like planting a *You are here* pin in my life.

At least, until the honking started. When we looked over, Kayleigh was leaning across Morgan, pressing on the horn.

Max's hand left my waist, and I pulled away to see him giving them the finger, smiling. I laughed on my way to the car.

"Thanks for joining us," Morgan said primly. "Another minute, and I was going to start reciting my junior research paper."

"Oh my God." I rolled my eyes, even though she couldn't see me. Her paper was titled "Sexual and Reproductive Health Teaching Practices and Outcomes in American Public Schools," and I knew this because she quoted passages from it regularly.

"Leave her alone." Tessa gave me a look of solidarity.

In the rearview mirror, Morgan waggled her eyebrows at me. "*Are* you and Max . . . ya know?"

"Morgan!" Kayleigh said, smacking her leg. But then she turned to me. "Are you? You'd tell us, wouldn't you?"

My mouth fell open. None of my friends ever discussed details like that—no dishing about which bases and when. It just wasn't our style.

"I certainly would not. My personal relationship is none of your business," I said, all daintiness and manners. I wasn't committedly abstinent like Morgan, but it felt like a huge deal, and still far away. "And we've only been together and in Oakhurst since August."

"Yeah, but it's you and Max," Morgan said.

What did that even mean? "Next topic, please. I don't see Tessa getting interrogated."

"Oh, they've tried," Tessa noted.

Kayleigh twisted all the way around in her seat, so she could see Tessa. "You and Laurel are going to stay together next year, right? Even if you go somewhere farther away?"

"I hope so," Tessa said.

I waited to be asked about long distance, but no—all three of them talked about my relationship in the future tense, Max and me always together in next-year scenarios. They thought we might be sleeping together because it was us, Paige and Max. Not for the first time, I thought that my own idea of my relationship—going out with a boy I knew well but was still learning about—might not match what people saw of us.

My thoughts circled like a whirligig, round and round and round. Did Max think we were seriously committed? Sure, he'd joked about me being his "dream girl," but that was a sweet compliment, in appreciation for my bad puns. Right? I felt woozy all of a sudden, and I cracked the window to breathe in fresh air.

"Paige!" Morgan was saying. "Hello? Dairy Queen or Kemper's?"

"Kemper's," Tessa insisted, in a tone that suggested I'd blocked out a heated debate.

I glanced over at her. "Didn't I see you with an ice-cream cone at the football game?"

She lifted her button nose into the air. "My personal relationship with ice cream is none of your business."

That did it, at least. I laughed, pushing at her leg as we reached the front of the exit line, on our way.

CHAPTER TEN

I came home from work one Thursday evening to my mom examining the kitchen cabinets, arms akimbo—the Wonder Woman of home design. She turned over her shoulder. "Hey, honey. I was just about to put your plate in the fridge."

She removed the aluminum foil cover over some chicken casserole and green beans, and set the microwave. It felt strange and grown-up to arrive home late, tired from a day on my feet.

"What's with the paint samples?" I asked, pointing to a gradient row of whites taped to an upper cabinet, where we kept the cereal. "You're redoing the cabinets?"

"I think so. Refinishing them. White would be brighter, don't you think? More modern?" She tapped a finger to her lips. "What do you think?"

"Definitely."

She moved to the side, considering the tones at a different angle. "But I don't want it to be *too* bright."

"Right. Like when new sneakers are so white, they're almost blue."

"That's precisely why I disqualified Powdered Sugar. Although anything off-white will look dingy." She looked back at me, a quick smile. "Oh, well. I'll figure it out. Anyway. How was work?"

"The usual," I said, gesturing at an oil stain on my vellum-thin shirt. "Glamour. Prestige."

"I'm worried," she announced. This was not exactly a big proclamation. Like me, my mom worried as a baseline of her existence. She removed her glasses and massaged the bridge of her nose. The frames were new, a dramatic burgundy color that had surprised me. And dramatic they were—she used them for a lot of exasperated gesturing. "I'm worried that you don't have time for classwork and studying and applications. Maybe it's best if—"

"Mom." I gave her a trying-to-be-patient smile. "We've talked about this."

"I know, but—"

"Cam has school and then dance practice, right? My schedule is like that, only I have a job instead of a club."

"Dance is not a *club*!" Cameron called from her Netflix nest in the living room. "It's a team."

"Okay!" I yelled back. My mom put her glasses back on, which I took as a signal that she was done with this topic. I pointed at the paint swatches, squinting. "I think the one on the far right."

"That's what your dad thinks, too. Swan Flight has a warmer undertone, but I'm not sure if that's a good thing. I might try one of each to see how they look in the light."

My mom factoring in my dad's opinions about the house: this, essentially, was why I thought he should just move back in. Once, after they split, he dropped Cameron and me off on a rainy Sunday night. With genuine concern, he asked that I remind my mom the gutters needed to be cleaned out. I conveyed that information as if it were my idea—my realization. *Water is dripping off the house pretty hard*, I told her as casually as I could. In hindsight, sixth grade wasn't exactly the peak of my still paltry acting skills. My mom huffed. *Tell your father I'm perfectly capable of caring for this house without his input.*

Now, they discussed paint colors together.

She looked back, her expression shifting back to Mom Mode. "You have a lot of homework?"

"Catching up on some reading. Then stuff with Maeve."

"I don't like how late you two talk."

"Well, she's on Pacific Time. We don't have a ton of options."

"You could e-mail."

"We do. And text." I chewed a bite of green beans hard, forcing myself not to get snippy. This conversation occurred every Thursday, and I couldn't tell if my mom forgot or if she just wanted to alert me of her continued displeasure. "But talking stuff out is a lot faster. That's why we only do it once a week."

She said nothing and began pulling plates from the dishwasher. You wouldn't think it was possible to passive-aggressively unload dishes, but Kate Hancock had a gift.

"You know, some seventeen-year-olds do actual bad things," I said, unable to resist. "I'm staying up to perfect college application material."

"I'm aware of that. But I'm your mother," she said simply. It was the high card in every argument. Turning toward the living room, she called, "Cameron Rose! Why am I unloading the dishwasher when you agreed to do it earlier?"

I saw my exit, and I hurried upstairs before I could once again become the subject of parenting. When I emptied my tux pocket, I found I only had four scraps of paper since my last chat with Maeve. And one of them read, in unfamiliar handwriting: *ACTION MOVIE FT. VERY ATTRACTIVE GUY. ASIAN, YOUNG, ATHLETE, CHARMING. POSSIBLE CHARACTER NAME: HUNTER.*

I texted him a picture of his little joke with a laughing emoji.

Wow, what a great idea on your part! he typed back. *Cinema gold!!!*

Maeve and I worked through the plot on my comedy piece—underdeveloped, according to her, though she thought the dry humor was reading well. I highlighted the too-on-the-nose dialogue in her family drama scene. We were just getting into potential shared projects when my mom ducked in, tapping an imaginary watch.

"Okay," I said.

"You need sleep."

"I know." When I heard my mom's bedroom door close, I looked back at Maeve's heart-shaped face—her soft cheeks sloping into a sharper, dignified chin. "Does she think I'll be in bed at ten p.m. next year? Truly, what is the point of this nagging?"

"My mom's doing it, too, even though I might be really

close to home," Maeve said. She rolled her eyes, lashes pumped up by mascara. "It's, like, their last moment to parent us, so they overshoot."

Simultaneously, we pointed at each other. "Mother-daughter movie."

"Flip-the-script humor?" Maeve's thick, black-as-ink eyebrows rose. "How do we reverse it? The daughter over-parenting the mom?"

"Maybe Mom goes to college?"

"Mmm. Romance subplot: Mom wants to date her pro-fessor?"

"Or she discovers one of her professors is an ex-boyfriend from her early twenties?"

"Ugh," she said good-naturedly. "Someday, I will be bet-ter than you at the love story hook. Someday!"

"Um, *Aoife and Ahmed*?" I said, citing both her parents' names and the working title of her most cherished project—a romantic drama beginning with their chance meeting at a grad school lecture, through twenty years of marriage. The draft had clobbered me; I could hardly read the last scene through the tears in my eyes.

"But I didn't craft the plot!" Maeve said. "It really hap-pened. Well, mostly."

My phone lit up beside me, Max saying that he was going to bed and hello to Maeve.

"Max says hi," I told her.

Maeve cracked a smile. "Did I summon him when I men-tioned dating a professor?"

"Ha!" I said. Because, well, Max and his rolled-up shirt-sleeves and his excited gesturing when someone got his obscure references. But also because Maeve felt comfortable enough with me to joke about my boyfriend. She'd insisted on "meeting" him on video chat over the summer. I'd known then that we would stay friends beyond our weeks at NYU. "I'm telling him you said that!"

"I'm jotting down the mother-daughter idea on the shared doc," she said, eyes fixed on the screen. "And, in parentheses, listing the professor's name as Max."

I realized, sitting across the desk from Cristina Fuentes, that I was not getting this job. Mythos Contemporary Theater was too cool for me, and the assistant producing director currently holding my paltry CV was definitely too cool for me. The only information my dad had offered was "she's awesome," which I now found to be a fair assessment. Her hair was short and blunt, revealing studs in tiny interior places on her ear. We were in her second-floor office, and the hopelessness of the situation relaxed me. If you're certainly not getting the job, you have nothing to lose. I'd chock the interview up to good experience and be glad for it.

She'd already asked me a few preliminary questions, tapping a pen on a large desk calendar.

"You took playwriting at NYU." Her eyes scanned the résumé page. "And an improv class. Contributed to a short film. But you're not interested in acting?"

"Correct." Extremely correct. But I'd learned at NYU that many aspiring writers and directors were also aspiring actors. Maeve wanted to be, in her words, the Irish Egyptian Mindy Kaling.

"And your traditional theater experience is fairly limited."

"Limited to . . . audience member, yes."

"Here at Mythos?"

"Yeah! In fact, walking through the lobby just now, I was thinking about the last play my grandma brought me to. About the earliest known version of Monopoly and the woman who created it."

"Sure. *Do Not Collect Two Hundred Dollars.*"

"Yes!" I pointed at her, a gesture that struck me—too late—as embarrassingly informal. I lowered my hand.

"I enjoyed that one," she said. "And this play, *2BD, 1BA.* You've read it?"

"Yep! Yes. Twice."

"What do you think?"

"It's great," I said. "I have more experience with film and TV scripts, but this play really pops for me."

"Pops," she repeated. "What about it?"

"Well, I think when you're vamping on a well-known piece like *The Odd Couple*, it's easy to dress it up with modern slang and issues but not really *say* anything new. But this play challenges some of the norms in the original and digs into what friendship means in adulthood more meaningfully. No offense to Neil Simon."

"That is . . . ," she said, leaning back in her chair, "what I think as well. What norms do you think it challenges?"

I nodded, giving myself a moment to layer what I'd learned in classes with my instincts about the script. "Well, in the original, there are a lot of throwaway jokes about Felix being suicidal. I noticed this play takes ideation more seriously. But it doesn't careen the tone into a maudlin place! It's an impressive balance."

We sat there for a few pleasant beats, long enough for me to register: *Oh, I think this is maybe going very well.*

"How'd you get into all this?" she asked, waving a hand. "Scripts, writing?"

"My grandmother. I was really into *I Love Lucy* as a kid, and she wanted me to know that a woman helped write the show. Madelyn Pugh was from Indianapolis, so that made her feel real to me." As relaxed as I was, I added, out of genuine curiosity, "What about you?"

"Um, that would be María Irene Fornés. Such an innovator as a playwright. And Cuban, like me. And Desi Arnaz, actually!"

I reached deep into my memory and said, hesitantly, "*Fefu and Her Friends.* That was Fornés, right?"

Cris sat up a little. "Right! You know it?"

"I've only read an excerpt for a class."

"You should read the whole thing." She glanced back down at my single sheet of accomplishments. "Well, Paige Hancock. Anything else you want to tell me?"

What did I have to lose, really? Might as well swing for the fences.

I was spending too much time with Hunter.

"I guess that . . ." I paused, searching, but I couldn't think of a better way of phrasing it. "I know it's a support role. So, I'll happily do coffee runs or pitch in with stage crew or whatever needs to be done. I'd be really grateful to observe and learn."

"Yeah," she said, "Rachel said you're good at putting your head down and getting to work."

It took me a second to realize she meant Ms. Pepper, who had offered to be a reference. I knew her name was Rachel; I could have told someone if they'd asked me. But I only ever thought of her as Pepper. "Rachel" seemed like the name for her outside-of-work identity, a person who had a beer with friends and wore sweatshirts.

"Oh, you talked to her. Great. Yeah."

"Can I be honest with you?"

I braced myself. I was too young, too inexperienced. At least, after getting used to my workshop classes this summer, I could take criticism without crying on the spot.

"I thought I was interviewing you as a professional courtesy to Dan. But I'm impressed." She leaned back in her chair again. "Your schedule is fairly limited, yes?"

She was . . . she was talking about this like it might happen. I cleared my throat. *Composure, Hancock. C'mon.* "Yes. I work Tuesday and Thursday after school and Saturday and Sunday, usually. I could be here three days a week."

Cris Fuentes nodded. "If you can get tech week and show week off in late March, I think that'll work. I have a college intern who's here daily, so you'll be her backup."

She continued to explain the schedule, but I lifted off my

seat, levitating a good foot above the chair. Cris Fuentes was using the future continuous tense to speak about my role here. Was she saying I had an internship?

"That sounds great," I said. Someone said. Probably me. I felt like a ventriloquist of my own self, puppeteering my mouth while I had an out-of-body experience.

"You're welcome to sit in on auditions in a few weeks, to observe the process. If you like."

"Yes," I said. "Yes, please."

CHAPTER ELEVEN

I didn't realize the problem until after a celebratory dinner with my family and the elated texts I'd sent to my friends. I opened my planner to add my internship, officially, but in late March, where I needed to add *TECH WEEK* and *OPENING NIGHT,* my handwriting already spelled out *QUIZBOWL QUARTERFINALS.* But no—certainly I could make both work. I could use a sub for QuizBowl that one night; we had so many new members, after all . . . But so much of tournament success was about knowing your teammates, their rhythms, their weak spots. It would be unfair to compete all year, knowing I'd miss a linchpin qualifier.

The choice was obvious: I wanted to be at Mythos, learning from Cris and her team. Standing in the theater that reminded me of my grandma, so present in my memories that I could almost smell her perfume. But QuizBowl had been so special to me last year, a strange and vital source of confidence, of camaraderie. It showed me that being wrong, even publicly, wouldn't kill me. It showed me that you have to keep trying if you ever want to get it right. But this was the right move.

At least, I was fairly sure, until I had to tell Max. Until I had to watch his face across the table at Alcott's on Sunday afternoon.

"You'd consider quitting QuizBowl?" He looked so hurt, like I was quitting my relationship with *him*.

I swallowed back a lump in my throat. "I don't want to, Max. At all."

"No, I know. It's just . . . QuizBowl's our thing," he said. His eyes were flickering around, like he was tallying a math error. "Would you still come to practices?"

"If I wasn't going to compete on the team?" I asked feebly.

"Yeah. That'd be weird, I guess."

"I'm sorry." My voice cracked, and Max jerked up like he'd been in a trance.

"Oh no, Paige! Hey." He grabbed my hand. "Don't apologize. It caught me off guard, that's all. The internship is amazing, and you've gotta do it."

"Yeah?"

"Yeah. Of course. It's just, when I imagined our year, I thought we'd have all this time together carpooling to matches. Like last year."

"I know." That was a big part of how we'd gotten to know each other, driving home from neighboring schools on quiet highways. "But last year, we needed an excuse to have that time together. Now I'll drive to Anderson with you any time you want."

His smile sloped, the effort there but still a little down. "Oh yeah?"

"Right now," I offered, moving my free hand toward my purse. "We can sit in my driveway talking after we get home."

"Talking," he repeated, the slack side of his mouth rising. "Or . . . ?"

I smiled at him, and we stayed at that table for an hour, joking, flirting, discussing. Being us. But I couldn't shake a feeling like the first plunking raindrop had hit, when the storm clouds still seemed far away. Was that . . . ? Did I just feel it? My career aspirations already coming between Max and me. In my mind, I wiped the water from my shoulder and stared across the table at blue sky.

———

I got to school early Monday morning, hoping to catch Ms. Pepper first thing and break the news about the internship. She all-out beamed about my Mythos news, and she took the schedule conflict in stride. I walked away confident in my choice and grateful for her guidance. Finally, I let myself feel relieved—happy, even. Paige Hancock: Student Intern. I'd add it to my résumé the minute I got home.

"Why did you let me choose photography for the year-book?" When I shut my locker door, Tessa's face was right there, grim as a museum portrait.

"I didn't *let* you. You didn't even *tell* me till after you signed up." I tilted my head, the closest I ever got to sass with her. "What's wrong with it?"

"Since I'm the rookie, and I can drive, they keep sending me to these awful away meets. Do you have *any* idea how boring cross-country is?" She gave me her most solemn expression. "It is literally just running outside for a long time."

"You talkin' about me?" Ryan had sidled up beside us, Morgan and Max with him. They'd taken to pooling around my locker at this time, my cool drink of water during these marathon days.

"I actually like your track meets," Tessa said. "The speed, the variety of events."

"The short shorts," Ryan continued in a dreamy voice. Morgan laughed, which Ryan was transparently thrilled by.

"How'd Pepper take it?" Max took my hand, turning to face me.

"Great. Totally supportive."

He looked briefly crestfallen but recovered the landing into a smile. I suspected he thought Pepper would find a way to make it work—that she'd never let me drop QuizBowl.

"So, better than I did?" he said, only sort of joking. "I'm gonna miss you, that's all."

"I know," I said, pained.

"Hey, this doesn't mess with your weekends, right?" Ryan interjected. "You better not miss the hayride place. Kayleigh will end your entire life."

"I won't miss any List stuff," I swore, as I peeled off with Max for our next classes. "Rehearsals don't even start for a while."

"You hear that, Miss Dance Ditcher?" Ryan was telling Tessa. She'd planned a visit to Laurel two weekends from now, so she'd miss Homecoming—something she didn't even pretend to regret. "Priorities."

Normally in this two-minute walk to our next classes, Max bubbled over with things to tell me since the morning. I glanced at him, suspicious of his silence. "What's going on up there?"

Max slid a hand to his shoulder, under the collar of his shirt, and rubbed at a muscle there. "Um, with Homecoming. You know I don't really, like . . . dance, right?"

I stopped walking. "*What?* This relationship is built on a lie."

"All right, all right."

"Yeah, I know." I put my hand through his arm. "I'm not exactly a dancer either."

"Okay." He still looked a little off, some of the bounce gone from his gait.

I would have continued to soothe his worries, but Kayleigh was running toward us, a blur with raised arms.

"She's here! The baby's here!" She brandished her phone at us, showing a squishy little face in a striped hospital hat, and promptly dissolved into tears. Her oldest brother's little girl.

"Aunt Kayleigh!" I hugged my friend close as she shook a little, face buried in my shoulder. "Congratulations!"

Get Morgan, I mouthed to Max, and he shot back down the hallway.

"This is a little early, right? But she's good?" I asked.

"She's good," Kayleigh said, pulling away to look at me. Her eyes were filled to the brim with water, dark irises swimming behind the tears. "They named her Sawyer, Paige. Sawyer Bloom."

Kayleigh's mom's maiden name. By the time Tessa and Morgan rounded the corner, the bell was ringing, and I was crying, too. We clutched Kayleigh in a group hug until she had to examine the photo again.

"Look at her," she whispered, zooming in. Her mother's granddaughter. A family first, a new chapter. "Would you just look at this spectacular girl?"

CHAPTER TWELVE

The next weekend, Morgan pulled into my driveway before noon. Kayleigh was off to visit Baby Sawyer in Chicago and Tessa was on assignment for yearbook photos. Max's mom was taking him to Wash U for a tour, and Ryan tagged along. And Morgan—well, she was doing Morgan stuff. Namely, driving to Indiana University to attend a workshop on sexual education. She'd invited me so I could look around at the campus again.

"So, remind me how Reid and Brady became a part of this?" I asked. Kayleigh's brothers were both at IU, of course, and their a cappella group had hired a presenter to do this workshop.

"At the end of the summer, Reid suggested I write a proposal for the Oakhurst school board, for more responsible and realistic sex ed. I was really upset about all my stuff," she said, gesturing at her lower body to summarize her reproductive organs. "And he thought channeling it might help. He was saying how colleges should step it up, too, so he got their group to bring Sexplanation to campus."

"Does Kayleigh know?"

"Don't make it sound weird. Yes, Kayleigh knows."

I knew Reid, Kayleigh's youngest brother, best of the three Hutchins boys. He was studious and passionate and really sweet to all of us, if always bickering with Kayleigh. Brady, now a senior here, shared Kayleigh's gale-force charisma and the natural leadership skills that landed him as president of two student orgs here at IU. Impressive guys—and cute, though Kayleigh would retch at the thought. I tried to imagine sitting in this seminar with them, while a presenter said the words "spermicide" and "cunnilingus." I would have blushed the entire time. "But aren't you a *little* relieved that they're in Chicago meeting Sawyer?"

"When," Morgan said thinly, "have I ever been relieved for people to miss a sex education opportunity?"

In a floral sundress and denim jacket, Morgan strode into the building like a sleek-haired, preppy Miss Frizzle of sex. She settled in to take notes, and I shifted in my seat, glancing out the window.

"You don't have to stay," she said. "You should explore."

"You sure?"

"I mean, I just invited you to sell you on IU instead of NYU," she said, only partly joking, I thought. "I'll text when they're wrapping it up."

"Wrapping it up," I said. "An important takeaway."

Morgan struggled not to laugh. "Go on."

I wandered the building, inside the perfume of old books and floor polish, and stared at students like they were animals

in a zoo. *Where are you from? Are you happy here?* I wondered at
them as they sprinted, late to class.

Outside, Bloomington's grid of streets felt like a Monopoly board—a little daunting at the start of the game, but I could
imagine chipping away at experience real estate. I could imagine studying in the local coffee shop, fellow students working
all around me on silver stickered laptops. Max visiting every
few weekends, holing up in my dorm to watch movies, then
nights out with Ryan, Morgan, and Kayleigh.

I walked past a kids' museum and smiled at the displays
inside—primary-colored play zones and large-scale science
projects come to life. Max would love it.

IU didn't scare me, but maybe that was good. Maybe college should feel like coming home. These burnished trees,
these quiet streets, these groups of girls walking three-wide
down the commons—it was easy to envision my place in it.

"I like it here," I told Morgan, on our way out of town.
She'd already given me the rundown of her seminar, a rush of
ideas for how she could pitch them to the Oakhurst School
Board.

"Why do you sound surprised?" she asked. "You toured it
with your parents this summer!"

"Yeah, I know." We'd come shortly after I got home from
Manhattan, and Bloomington—anywhere—seemed quiet and
small. Joltingly so. But now, after months at home in Oakhurst,
it seemed kind of perfect. "It's growing on me, apparently. And
I can really see you and Kayleigh here."

"Well, I can see you here, too," Morgan said. "Not even
because of me. I think you'd be happy."

It should have been great news—feeling like I'd fit in at a great school with my friends nearby and in-state tuition. But now it would be harder to justify a big-ticket school in a big city with my big, ridiculous plans. I had so much goodness close to home; why on earth did I feel pulled away? Proving something to myself? To my grandmother, to Maeve? Or was it just that nearly every big change in my life had happened *to* me? Maybe I wanted to be the driving force for once.

I watched out the window as Morgan merged, steering us back up the map and toward home.

The lobby of Mythos Contemporary Theater was full of people, pacing with folded-over scripts and moving their mouths in diction exercises. *2BD, 1BA* was the yearly young talent show, every actor under twenty-one, but I still felt conspicuously teenaged in the crowd.

"Do you have your audition confirmation?" a woman asked, over the top of her clipboard.

"Oh, um, no. I'm a student intern? With Cris Fuentes?"

She signaled me toward the door like an air traffic controller. "Through there."

I'd brought a notebook and a pen, an attempt to look official. But walking through the dark rows of seats, to where the creative team was huddled near the stage, I was sure Cris Fuentes would be shocked to see me. *Oh dear,* she would say, *you must have misunderstood. Why would we offer an internship to a hapless high school senior?* I'd crawl back to QuizBowl, mortified and traitorous.

Instead, Cris said, "Hey, Paige! Come meet everyone!"

After introductions, they scattered through the front rows to watch auditions at different angles. Cris propped her knees on the backrest in front of her like she was in the passenger seat on a road trip. This theater was her home, every nook a known place. I felt like an interloper, but—instantly and badly—I wanted to belong here, too.

It was hours of the same two monologues—one for party girl Olivia, one for uptight Flora, coming unhinged in light of her broken engagement. I'd read the script, but seeing it performed, I laughed more than once, from the humor and the familiarity of my odd-couple friendship with Hunter Chen.

The front-runners, it turned out, were obvious—the electricity in their bodies, the command. When an actress named Marisol recited one particular line, her voice caught on the last word, and suddenly it was the confession of a vulnerable girl instead of the wry commentary it had been in the past twenty auditions. It didn't surprise me when Cris and her team shortlisted her for a lead. I scribbled notes of the words and phrases they used to describe various performances—"sensitive," "flat," "playful," "self-conscious."

Callbacks would be in two weeks, on a Saturday I couldn't get out of at Cin 12, and rehearsals wouldn't start until after the first of the year. By the time I left, I could feel the theater's hum, like the space was a living thing—an old, friendly beast, ready to lead me through a fantastical realm. Mythos indeed. How could I already miss a world I'd only just glimpsed?

For the rest of the week, I found myself procrastinating on

writing portfolio work by reading *Fefu* and a few other plays, hoping to amass enough vocabulary to keep up at Mythos. *The Glass Menagerie*, at least, could be used as an elective read for my English class. Tennessee Williams called it a "memory play"—the events perhaps skewed by a narrator's recollection, by sentiment. I drummed my fingers and stared at the tacked-up ephemera above my desk: a photo of my friends, a note from Max, a map of New York, and an *I LOVE LUCY* sticker that my grandma found years ago. Was this, too, a memory play—how I retold my story to myself, omitting the tokens of anxiety, divorce, grief, phobia? I stewed in that question, uncomfortable, and outlined the idea as a paper for class. My existential crises made for material, at least. *Screenwriters' motto,* Maeve would joke.

I stared back up at my corkboard. For my entire life until last June, I'd thought I'd done it—compiled everything I needed. I was *happy.* What more could I want? But Manhattan taught me that other important friends might be waiting in the wings, their entrances written for my college days. I learned I could be good at things I didn't even expect, and I wanted to learn what else I could do when I pushed my boundaries. But I was beginning to wonder, with a growing sense of sadness, if the only way to find out was to be brave enough to start a new collage.

CHAPTER THIRTEEN

I'd seen enough movies to expect the awkward posing as our parents snapped pictures. I could have guessed that my dad would angle us toward better light, that my mom and Max's mom would keep saying, "Okay, just one more. Look here!" But I still wanted to experience it firsthand, to collect the details in my beaded bag.

"Regretting this yet?" Max joked, through a teeth-gritted smile.

I wasn't. The summer before sophomore year, I'd day-dreamed about Homecoming, hoping Aaron and I would still be together. I imagined a tutu-pink gown and his arms around my waist as the music played.

By the night of the dance, he'd been gone for months, and I hunkered down at Tessa's house with my friends, who art-fully sidestepped any dance-related topics. Later, I scrolled through photos of my classmates in satin, with heavy fake lashes and good posture. I expected to feel bitter—they were here and he wasn't. But mostly, I felt sad. And old. I couldn't fathom caring about Homecoming. Every high school tradition felt pointless.

Now I stood pressed against Max in a galaxy-blue dress, making those same stiff-backed poses I'd once sighed at. And I could feel it again: the excitement about every cliché slow dance heading my way. It felt like finding a childhood teddy bear I'd thought was lost forever.

We met our friends at Arpeggio's, the would-be site of our first date two months ago now. At a long banquet table near the back, we switched between intent conversation—Morgan's take on a young congresswoman! Ryan opining on his still undecided major—and obnoxious-to-other-diners laughter. Kayleigh caught a ride with Tessa to Chicago, off to visit her niece again, which left Morgan and Ryan as happily platonic dates.

By the time we paid the bill, the sky had gone fully dark. My heels clacked against the parking lot, a quick pace that betrayed my eagerness.

"Well," Malcolm said, "seems we'll be fashionably late."

"We could ditch the actual dance at this point." Max glanced at his watch. "Go over to my place."

Morgan snorted, motioning to her gold dress. "You think I look this good and I *don't* want the whole school to see?"

"She wants the whole school to see, Max," Ryan said flatly.

The homecoming dance took place in the gym, on the high-sheen wood floors of the basketball court. A DJ table sat under one of the hoops; black and white tiles of the dance floor barely visible beneath the pulsing crowd.

I stood at the mouth of the beast with Max, staring. It still looked and smelled like the gym—the place I once tripped running laps, with a splat that echoed into every corner of the room. Now the space was dimly lit and my classmates were milling around, dancing, or strewn across bleachers. Some teetering in high heels, unpracticed; some tugging at ties. Muggy air and sweat, piney cologne from every direction.

Leading Max into the fray, I turned. "Woo! High school!"

"High school," Max echoed.

We settled into the second row of the bleachers. The very definition of wallflowers, maybe, but I didn't mind. I liked being the one he leaned over to, speaking close to my ear. At one point, I looked up to find Clark Driscoll—Aaron's longtime best friend—walking past.

"Clark!" I said. "Hey!"

The greeting flew out of my mouth as soon as I registered Clark's presence. My brain had temporarily blacked out that when Max was bullied as a kid, Clark was one of the perpetrators. I rested a hand on Max's leg.

"Hey," Clark said, brightening. His date, a smiley junior, waved to us. "You look awesome."

Then, smiling between Max and me, he added, "And you look nice, too, Paige."

It was a bad dad joke—right up Max's alley, and he smiled easily.

"Thanks," I said. "Good to see you. Have fun!"

Clark held eye contact for just a second longer than I expected. In that gaze, an acknowledgment of the grief gone by and the loss that lingered, the solidarity in both of us being here tonight. "Yeah. You too."

"Sorry," I whispered, once Clark and his date were gone.

"Don't be." Max leaned over to kiss my cheek. Then, his eyes catching somewhere beyond us, he laughed. "God, they're goofs."

I followed his line of sight to Morgan and Ryan, hamming it up on the dance floor with zero inhibition. "I truly love them."

Before I could ask if he wanted to join them, he said, "Photo-booth line's dying down. Wanna do it?"

I absolutely did, and we made our way to that corner of the gym. "Should we plan our poses? Or keep it spontaneous?"

"Are you offering," he asked slowly, "to *not* plan? For me?"

I batted his chest. "I can be extemporaneous!"

After our photos were snapped, Max chatted with some friends from the robotics team. I was nodding along to phrases like "sensory feedback" and "end effector" when a pop song pumped out of the speakers, the recognizable handclap percussion getting a cheer from the crowd. "Say Yes."

"Oh my God, this freakin' song," I said, looking up at Max.

I knew, for the rest of my life, this song would take me back to the specific feeling of this past July. It already did—I could practically feel the heat, smell the garlic salt and sticky diet soda. Finally home from New York, my heart tripping at the sight of Max's name in my inbox, driving my own car with the windows down.

Morgan appeared at the edge of the dance floor, motioning severely at me. "Get out here!"

I glanced at Max, hopeful that he'd join me, caught up in the spirit of the song. His body looked planted, roots extending into the core of the earth. But he smiled, shrugging. "Go for it."

"You sure?"

Max held up a hand—a dignified pass, like declining hors d'oeuvres. *All right, then.* When I got near enough, Josiah grabbed my arm and pulled me toward my friends.

"Um, *finally!*" Morgan yelled at me. At this stage of the night, Ryan had sunglasses on and was bopping hard with an invisible microphone. Josiah and Malcolm were nearby, lip-synching to each other.

So, fine. Can't beat 'em, join 'em. I put my arms up.

"There she is," Morgan said, laughing.

Oh yeah, what are you waiting for? I mouthed with the song lyrics. I liked dancing to a song I knew so well, every pulse, every background vocal *ooh* and *oh*.

The last beat of the song dropped off, replaced with a slower piano ballad. It was an awkward transition—a big, breathy laugh to a heartfelt confession. We all stood there for a moment, the energy we'd been exuding with no place to go. Tessa would have commandeered the DJ's station and excused him.

The dance floor shifted from clusters to couples, single cells snapping into pairs. I glanced through the crowd, hoping Max would appear, dodging pressed-together bodies to get to me. After only a few seconds, I scurried from the dance floor, the embarrassment of it more than I could handle. How had I come with a date—my boyfriend—and still wound up feeling like a rejected Austen heroine?

In the same spot I'd left him, Max was still holding court with the engineers, but he slid out to greet me. "Have fun out there?"

"Mm-hmm. You're missing out . . ." I tried to say it temptingly, but he laughed happily, like it was a joke. I couldn't be upset, really. He'd told me, point-blank, that dancing wasn't his thing. Still. It reignited a simmering little worry, that I was his pal Paige and not, like, a cute girlfriend to be romantic with.

On our way out, we passed Aditi in a classic black gown and red lip.

"You guys have fun?" she asked. As junior class vice president, she was on the dance committee, which may have accounted for why the whole event was considerably less tacky than I'd expected.

"Definitely," I said.

"We miss you at QuizBowl," she said, which was generous. "But the theater stuff sounds so cool—good for you."

"Oh, thanks! Max says you're killing it on the team."

She shrugged. "Just trying to keep up with Columbia here."

I opened my mouth to say I didn't know the reference, but Max scoffed. "Oh, please."

"What?" She flashed a mischievous smile. "I'm sorry, but you can't tell me you're applying to big-name schools and expect to *not* get teased a little."

My gaze swung up to Max as he gave a tense laugh. He

hadn't mentioned Columbia College to me yet, but it made sense—he'd always liked Chicago, and he was already applying to Northwestern.

"All right, I better find my date. Nice to see you, Paige!" She nudged Max as she walked past. "See you Monday, Ivy League."

Ivy League? Columbia College wasn't Ivy. But Columbia University was. In Manhattan. My thoughts spun like a centrifuge, dizzying, and I gave a strained smile to no one. "I'm just gonna use the restroom real quick before we go."

"Okay . . . ," Max started to say, but I was already en route, heels snapping against the cafeteria floor to the bathroom nearest the parking lot, mercifully empty.

My chest rose and fell, and I placed one hand over my breastbone, wishing I could unzip my dress. Columbia? I shut myself in a bathroom stall as a clammy sweat whooshed over me, that pre-vomit stomach drop. Max would do that—go to New York with me? Did I want him to? I waved both hands, fanning myself and trying to shake the jittery energy from my fingers. But my stomach still clenched, and I winced, surrounded by the sound of water on water as I hurled, crouched in my pretty clearance dress.

I flushed the toilet, my breathing slowed. Okay. Better. Maybe it wasn't even panic, but something off I'd eaten at Arpeggio's. Food poisoning can come on fast.

The possibility of having both NYU and Max—that was a good thing, one I hadn't even considered before. My brain just worked like a faulty telephone switchboard sometimes, routing me to the wrong feeling. That's all this was.

I blotted my face with cold water, rinsed my mouth out. I'd brought a tiny travel toothpaste, prepared for our Italian dinner, and I swished some around. The humid air in the gym had flattened my bangs, and I looked, at once, too pale and too flushed, with eyeliner bleeding black. What a dream girl. I folded toilet paper and cleaned myself up.

This is good news, I informed my reflection. *Get it together.*

Max pushed off the wall where'd he been leaning, waiting for me. "You okay?"

"Fine!" I looped my arm through his, mostly so we'd be walking in step, obstructing his view of my face.

When Max started the car, I stared into my lap, into the ocean of my dress's fabric. "So, hey," he said. "I'm sorry Columbia came up like that. Aditi mentioned it as a possibility for herself next year, so I told her I've been considering it, too. Pepper said I should pick a reach school or two—figured it might as well be Columbia and Caltech."

"Oh!" My voice came out an octave too high. I pressed a hand to my chest like I could compress my heartbeat into normalcy. "Caltech, too! Okay!"

"I was going to tell you," he said. "Obviously. And it was just an idea. I won't apply if it bugs you."

Bugs me, like it was a gnatty little annoyance. As opposed to a gesture of willingness to fundamentally reroute his life choices based on mine.

"No, it's totally fine!" I said, lying through my freshly toothpasted teeth. "I just thought you felt pretty strongly about the 250-mile-radius thing."

"I do. Well, I don't know. When I mentioned that radius

to my mom, she kind of laughed it off. Here I thought she'd be lost without me. But . . . I think she might be looking forward to being an empty nester? Having some freedom. Kind of offensive, if you ask me." He looked over—I could see the movement in my peripheral vision. "I'm yammering. Sorry. I feel like I freaked you out with this."

"I was just surprised. It's fine. Great!"

"Yeah?"

"Sure. I mean, they're great schools, right?" That's how I'd feel if my brain were capable of processing emotions into their proper channels. If my brain hadn't taken "Boyfriend near Dream School" and funneled it into "Bad, Yikes, AHHHhhh" as it cliff-dove into the panic below.

"I'm also applying to U of M," he added, offering proof that there were other recent additions. "But, um, as long as it's come up . . . I know I'd like to stay together. Regardless of where we end up."

Right there, on the table. No dancing around it. A theme with Max tonight, apparently. I wasn't sure why I was surprised; it was Max. He knew who he was and what he wanted—Ryan had told me that once.

The light flicked to green, and Max put his hands on the wheel.

"I hope that, too," I said, my voice measured. "Obviously."

He gave a small laugh, hand rising to adjust his glasses.

"What?" I demanded, annoyed.

"Nothing. It's just very us. I'd like to; you hope."

"Well, I don't know what schools we'll get into! Or how we'll feel! I'm trying to be—"

"Realistic. Yeah, I know. You're planning for the most likely scenario. But I'm thinking in terms of what I most *want* to happen. Figured I'd put it out there."

Maybe on its own, this comment would have simply flattered me. But layered on top of the little "old married couple" comments from friends and near strangers, Max's casual admission felt like weight. Weight that was becoming heavy. "Well, we don't have to decide now. Right?"

"Of course we don't, Janie." He said it lightly, like he'd expected my reaction on some level. "Wow, are we growing up? Look at us, not spinning out about an impossible-to-know future?"

Okay, that got me. I laughed, shaking my head. It was just us, me and this person who clicked into place with me. This was really fine. Totally fine.

In the driveway, Max slid the car into park, and I leaned in to kiss him. That, at least, grounded me right here. It was just getting good when the porch flashed a bunch of times, a strobe effect inside the car. My mom at the light switch inside, very over me sitting out here in the darkness with my boyfriend.

I pulled back, sighing. "God, Mom. So uncool."

"Moment killer," Max agreed, his hand still in my hair. "I can't believe we wasted time talking about our futures!"

I gathered up my purse, trying to convince myself I felt as secure about our conversation as Max did. I'd probably wake up tomorrow elated that he might be at Columbia or Caltech.

"Love you," I said as I climbed out.

"I know," he said coolly.

I rolled my eyes, smiling. "'Night, Han Solo."

I'd made it a few steps away from the car when he called, through the rolled-down window, "Hey. Come here a sec. I need to tell you something."

Gamely, I walked back, and laid my arms flat on the ledge of his window. "You love me, too?"

"Well, yeah." He leaned in to kiss me once more. "But I really wanted to watch you walk away in your dress twice."

I backed away from the car, flattered and scandalized. "Inappropriate!"

"I do love you, though," he called.

CHAPTER FOURTEEN

"Mom!" Cameron hollered. "Were two of our cabinet doors . . . stolen?"

"That would be a very weird burglary, wouldn't it?" my mom replied.

She'd removed the two lower cabinets at the hinges, exposing Cameron's hand mixer, bags of flour, and plastic piping bags.

"Those are my test doors," my mom explained. "So I can make sure the color is right."

"Why my baking supply cabinets?" Cameron asked.

"Those doors are the least visible to anyone walking into the kitchen." My mom—diplomatically, I thought—withheld that all the cabinets belonged to her, even the baking supply ones.

"If anything, it's just easier to take your stuff out and put it away," I said, trying to be helpful.

Cameron's eyes shot to me. "I don't want my supplies to get *dusty*."

"Well," my mom said, terse now, "I'll be working on them today, so you won't have to bear it for long."

I joined my mom in the backyard, and watched over my laptop screen as she flicked on the electric sander. I stretched my legs out, yoga pants warming in the sun. On today's docket, my Biggest Challenge essay. I'd long known I wouldn't write about Aaron or about my grandmother—they were losses to be mourned, not lessons to be learned.

Since Homecoming, I'd settled into the idea of Max applying to schools near mine. But my body's absolute freak-out proved what I had to do: write, as best I could, about the anxiety that had trailed me for seventeen years—occasionally leaping out but always lurking.

When I considered scrapping the meager words I'd gotten down, I watched my mom with her surgical mask and determined brow, scouring off the layer that didn't work. I forced attention back to the page, to sand it down.

After dinner, Cameron went upstairs, but I stayed in the kitchen to help with dishes.

"I wanted to talk about the possibility of taking a senior trip." I pulled my shoulders back, readying myself to speak fast but steady. "Kayleigh planned a senior trip to Florida over spring break. Her dad and Lisa are staying in the next town over for their honeymoon, so it would be chaperoned. It's very affordable, and I'd pay for it myself."

My mom stayed quiet for a long time. Organizing, I knew, the many objections she'd level against the idea. "Next town over isn't exactly a chaperone, is it?"

"Well," I said, "we'd have parents very nearby."

I couldn't read my mom's expression—receptive? Annoyed? "It'd be you, Tessa, Morgan, and Kayleigh?"

"Yep. And Ryan, Max, Malcolm, and Josiah." I tried to sandwich Max's name in there, like she wouldn't notice. Rookie move—I saw that now. It sounded guilty.

"*Max* would be going?" She looked at me as if I'd asked her to sponsor a couples retreat to Cancún, complete with tequila discretionary fund. "You're asking to vacation with your boyfriend?"

"No, no! It's a whole friend-group thing. Max is part of the group—that's all."

She frowned, briefly picturing this, but shook her head. "I'm sorry; I have to say no. It's not appropriate, you cohabitating with your boyfriend for a week."

"It's not—" I huffed, cutting myself off when I heard my tone. "That's really not what it is."

"It's *not* you and Max living together for a week?"

Was she serious? "Are you intentionally trying to make this sound nefarious?"

"I am *intentionally*," she said, "making judgment calls as a mother."

I'd known she wouldn't love the spring break idea—the long drive, the distance, the possibility of drinking. I didn't expect her to get most caught up on Max's presence or how it would look to other parents.

Walk away, Paige. I felt the call in my chest, intuition singing. Instead, I doubled down like a reckless moron. "You're going to have to trust me to make good decisions on my own next year, you know . . ."

"Yes, I will. And until then, this is my jurisdiction," she said, gesturing to the entirety of our household. "And this isn't an appropriate scenario for two seventeen-year-olds."

Angry tears filled my eyes. Did I even need her permission if I was paying for everything? "So, should my friends all go without me? Or should Kayleigh uninvite just Max?"

My mom threw her hands up, right as the side door opened.

"Hey! I brought you that . . . ," my dad said. He stopped in his tracks, staring at our postures. "Drill bit . . . What am I walking into?"

"Parental distrust," I snapped. "Based on zero evidence."

"Your *daughter*," my mom said, "is asking to vacation with her boyfriend."

"I am *not*. Dad. My friends are planning a spring break trip. Kayleigh's dad and Lisa would be there. It's safe and cheap and—"

"And that doesn't change the inappropriateness of—"

"Whoa." My dad held his arms out, separating us and silencing us at once. He swiped his hands a few times, eyes squinted closed as he thought. When he opened them, he motioned to me. "You, upstairs. No, don't give me that look; I'll be up in a minute."

I went, feeling childish and frustrated at myself. What was the point of being well behaved if my mom didn't trust me anyway? I fired off a few ranty texts to Tessa before my dad knocked. He kept one hand on the doorframe as he leaned into my room. "What would the sleeping arrangements be?"

"I'd be upstairs in bunk beds with Tess."

"And our good friend Max?" he asked dryly.

"On a pullout couch with Ryan downstairs." I held my hands out, earnest and desperate to be seen as such. "Or whatever Mom feels comfortable with. I swear, it's—"

"Ah, ah," he said, cutting me off. "And you can cool it a little, okay? Your mom is only trying to keep you safe, which she does a pretty great job of, by the way."

Before I could huff that he owed my safety to *my own decision making*, he popped back out of the room.

I stewed in the silence, mentally enumerating my valid points. Did she have any idea about her incredible good luck? I followed rules to an almost pathological degree! She'd written articles about bullying, shoplifting, teens running gambling rings. But I wanted to go on a trip with my equally well-behaved friends and suddenly I'm a risk?

By the time my mom knocked, I was seething. "Can I come in?"

"Yeah." I said it in my "no" tone of voice, though.

She sat on the corner of my bed, leveling her field of vision with mine.

"I'm giving the trip a tentative yes." When my face lit up, she held up one finger, stopping me. "*Tentative*. And I have stipulations. I'll be talking with Mr. Hutchins at *length*. I might task him with surprise check-ins."

"That's fine," I said quickly. I mean, embarrassing as hell, but better than nothing.

Her lips pursed as she let out a long sigh. "If there's alcohol there, Paige—and I'm not naïve about that—it can lower your inhibitions."

"I know."

"And if you're with a boyfriend, unsupervised in a house for a week, you could feel caught up in the moment or even pressured. That's not a statement about Max; it's just the reality that making an informed decision when—"

"Mom," I said. "I've been friends with Morgan Sullivan for half my life. I understand consent."

Morgan didn't dial down her beliefs—not about sex and agency, not about her faith and personal abstinence—for anyone, even parents. So my mom knew full well that I'd heard my options.

"I know you do. But it can feel less straightforward in the moment, and I don't want you to ever regret something that . . ." She trailed off, sighing, and I startled at the realization that she might be speaking from experience.

"I hear you," I said. "Thanks, Mom."

She watched me for a moment, resigned. "Well, you can thank your father."

"Is he still here?"

"No, he went home. Had more grading to do." She stood up, turning to go.

My dad had swept in, helped my mom and me communicate, and then ducked back out. As much as I loved my own alone time, I imagined him returning to his empty apartment with sadness.

"Mom?" I asked, voice softer now. "Am I the reason he hasn't moved back in?"

She tilted her head, just a degree or two, like the question surprised her.

"No, honey," she said. "*I'm* the reason he hasn't."

I fiddled with the ends of my hair, longer now than it had ever been. "So, it's not because I took a while to get on board?"

My mom brushed back the wide-barrel waves I wished I'd inherited. "No. I have to think about boundaries—yours and Cameron's, of course. But mine, too."

"Well, I'd understand if you wanted him here more often, you know? Now that he's teaching." I wanted him here more. I wanted to see them both as much as I could before college. But I couldn't be a factor in their cohabitation. If it blew up, I'd blame myself.

She twisted my Grammy's wedding ring, a simple gold band she'd taken to wearing on her right hand. "I'm trying to do the right thing for everyone."

"I know," I said. Then, nodding to the ring, I added, "I miss her."

"Me too." She glanced up, a half smile lifting one cheek. "She'd have told me to let you go on the trip."

"Yeah. The whole 'live your life' thing."

"No!" She laughed, incredulous. "Because she knew from experience that if you say no too often, your teen daughter will lash out in rebellion."

My mom didn't have a sister, but surely she didn't mean . . . "You?"

"I have to save *some* stories for when you're older." She turned away, leaving me with that cliff-hanger.

"Hey, Mom?" I said, before she'd left the room. "Thanks for saying yes."

Once out the door, she called back, "I said *tentative* yes."

I stood from my bed and danced around in a circle, arms raised.

CHAPTER FIFTEEN

I worked the Saturday late shift, my mom's least favorite of my work obligations. Movies started until eleven p.m., so I wasn't walking out to the parking lot with Hunter until well after midnight.

"Good luck at your fall baseball game on Monday!" I called to him.

He laughed. "You can just call it fall ball! But thanks, Hancock."

Oakhurst was quiet this time of night, only a few bars open now. By day, the intersection outside the theater swarmed—clogged with cars, backed up from the next light near the highway. Now, though, no one. I cruised to a stop at the red light. Put on my indicator and used that moment to click on the radio. When the light changed, blazing green against the black sky, I eased onto the gas and made my turn . . . only to be pushed from somewhere, so hard that I wrenched back with a gasping *oof.*

A crunching noise echoed in my ears and, oh God, it was

my car. Skidding, skidding. Had I braked on instinct? Had I run into something?

The base of my skull sang against the headrest. I was grasping the steering wheel, then my own chest, my throat, my thighs. *I'm here, I'm here.* Was I dead? Would I know if I was?

I stared out the windshield, where a signpost of some sort bent over the hood of my car. But I wouldn't have just randomly hit it. My rearview showed a black truck I didn't recognize, sideways across the lanes behind me.

"Paige!" A voice roared it. Familiar. Once, again.

I blinked up at the window. Hunter's face appeared, ashen in watery streetlight.

"Oh God. Okay. You okay?" He pulled the door open and crouched down to me.

Hunter. Oh, good. Hunter. Nice. Safe. And talking to me, so probably I was alive.

"I . . . think so?" My voice sounded strange, as if I were hearing it underwater. "Did that truck hit me?"

"Yeah. Piece of shit ran the red—I saw it. Does anything hurt?"

My limbs felt cold, but okay. I wiggled my toes.

"No," I said. My thighs ached, for some reason, and my chest hurt from how hard my heart was beating. I glanced around. Someone was hurrying toward us—a middle-aged lady who had pulled her car over. Cell phone to her ear.

"Let me help you get out, okay?" Hunter said. "We should get to the sidewalk."

Suddenly, nothing in the world seemed more important than exiting the car. My mind played action movie sequences of cars blowing up, glorious and terrible. I tried to unbuckle myself, struggling with my visibly shaking hands. Hunter undid the seat belt, and I let him help me out.

"I've gotcha. Good. Nothing hurting still?"

I shook my head, though my legs felt gelatinous. He braced his arm around my waist, guiding me.

The woman reached us and asked if I was okay. I heard my voice say yes. She'd already called the cops. Cops. Huh.

I could hear a voice nearby repeating, "Oh my God, I'm so sorry, I'm so sorry." The voice kept cracking, obviously crying. *Was* I hurt?

"Could you please be sorry by shutting the fuck up?" Hunter called. I peered at Hunter's wrathful face. *He's yelling at the person who hit me.* Someone hit me.

Hunter eased me down to the curb, and only then did I have a full view of the car.

My car. My dad's car. The one he used to pick me up from school in. Before I was old enough to sit in the front seat, let alone drive it. The steering wheel I gripped as I got my learner's permit.

Crumpled, the back smashed.

I had been *in* there.

I lurched forward a bit, thinking I'd vomit, but all that came out was a choked gasp, then another. Tears dribbled out as I tried to slow my breathing. I could so easily be dead—until right now, I'd thought I might be.

"I've got ya," Hunter said. "I've got ya."

His arm, wrapped around me tightly, kept me earthbound. Two minutes ago, I lived in a different world. Now, I was someone who had been in an accident, I did not have a functional car anymore, and the fact that I was alive did not feel like a given. My mind couldn't grip those facts, so it tried to float away, above the scene like a loose balloon. When the cop crouched down to ask some questions, Hunter fielded the logistical ones, his voice calm while my ears rang like a bell's chime, sustained on and on and on. I longed to touch the metal, to make the reverberation stop.

"Miss?" the cop was saying. Her hair was parted down the center, combed back neatly. "Have you texted a parent or guardian?"

I blinked up at her. "Not yet."

"The other party has insurance. He's admitted fault. Those are good things."

Choppy film reel: pulling my phone from my tux pocket, staring down at the screen. Hunter gently suggesting I start by saying, "I'm fine." Dialing my dad, whose apartment was closer than home. I spoke to him calmly, downplayed it as a fender bender, and, all the while, felt separated from my trembling body. While we waited, I shivered against the cold—smooth-talking autumn passing the nights on to winter. Hunter got a blanket from the back of his car, thick cotton with his baseball number stitched in the corner.

I studied the asphalt of the road, the cracks and gravel bits unnoticeable except up close.

"Are you okay?" Hunter asked. "Honestly, Hancock. You can say no."

"I'm shaken up," I said. "But I think that's all."

The ambulance pulled up, its siren *woop-wooping*, and all I wanted was my bed and my parents. I wanted to go to sleep. I wanted this to be a bad dream. My dad arrived in flannel pajama pants and his navy gym sneakers, frazzled and hurrying. What a surrealist scene. Regular objects—and time—gone slippery, half melted like in a Dalí painting. Hunter Chen beside me. The EMT, who cleared me but insisted my dad watch for concussion symptoms. Near a stoplight we'd driven through a thousand times. I could have died right here. In my goddamn tux. How ridiculous. How incredibly stupid and ridiculous.

"Dad," I said, touching his arm. He looked ready to cry. The cop had said something to him about a tow truck, and I wanted to go home more than I had ever wanted anything. "I'm really fine."

"Oh, I know, kid." He smoothed my hair, staring at me like I'd disappear if he blinked.

"Did you tell Mom?"

"I did, yes." It was a testament to him, really, that she hadn't already showed up, frantic. "I'm gonna take you home to her now. We've gotta keep you awake for a bit, watch for vomiting, confusion. That kind of thing."

He thanked Hunter, who looked stricken, reluctant to part ways.

"Text me tomorrow, Hancock. Swear?"

"I will."

My dad wrapped an arm around me, like a bodyguard hurrying a celebrity through paparazzi swarms. I buckled myself into the passenger's seat, hands shaking. I'd seen it now, the way the metal could scrunch in like a wad of paper. I closed my eyes, pretending I was anywhere else, and my dad said, "Eyes open, kid. I've gotta know that you're awake."

At home, my mom kept stroking my cheek and murmuring that it would be okay. After being her daughter for seventeen years, I knew she was repeating this mantra to soothe herself as much as me. When they finally let me fall asleep, I drifted off to her voice: *I'm just gonna grab another blanket from the hallway closet. I'll get you a glass of water in case you feel thirsty. Is it warm enough? Let's check the thermostat. Everything's going to be fine.*

CHAPTER SIXTEEN

For the next week, I felt achy and detached. An accident that happened in four seconds was taking days to sink in. I stayed quiet, mostly, as my dad handled the car fiasco—unsalvageable, with meager insurance money for its supposed worth. My mom handled the hovering, offering me food constantly and inexplicably taking my temperature. Her fretful energy was matched only by Max, who all but searched me for dents. When his eyes met mine, I suspected him of checking my pupils for dilation—a doctor's son to his core.

"You still feel okay? No headaches?" Max asked the next weekend, stretched out on the couch. He brushed my bangs aside.

"No headaches," I promised. "I'm fine."

Physically, anyway.

After Aaron died, I spent months—and a year of therapy—trying to tend my scars. Not until last year did I finally internalize that not every good thing gets ripped away. But somewhere in that healing, I'd forgotten what it felt like when you've seen the truth: everything can be over in an instant.

In my waking hours, I helplessly played out imaginings of my loved ones gone, the phone calls to tell me, the sink-to-my-knees aftermath. But at night, for the first time in months, I dreamed of drowning. It began with my feet planted on the bottom of a pool. I looked up at sunlight breaking through at the water's surface—all I had to do was push off the concrete floor and propel myself upward. But when I tried to flex my feet, they didn't move, two hinges rusted shut. I was stuck, and then thrashing, and awake. Clammy and panting from terror, from relief.

My body protected me by resisting sleep. I imagined slumber like a black sky, polka-dotted with stars. On a rare good night, I could tip my mind backward into that space and float. But more and more often, I chased slumber, pounding on every door in the corridor. I stopped drinking caffeine in the afternoon, I counted backward, I downloaded a meditation app.

I used my post-midnight time to work. I decided two of my portfolio pieces were done, and I finally banged out a draft of my Biggest Challenge essay. *My brain is a little house, humble but beloved. The dwelling of my memories (flashes of my grandmother before her hair went gray), my knowledge (the quadratic formula and every Greek god from Achelous to Zeus), and my language function (perspicacious, in my opinion). But my brain has a panic button, and I don't seem to be in charge of when it is triggered. That has been—since my earliest memories, to the best of my knowledge, and in the simplest terms I know—my biggest challenge.*

"Look at you, all decisive," Maeve said, bottom lip out in an impressed pout. "I like it. But how will you end it?"

"Hmm. I guess by saying that it's not all bad? When I can harness the anxiety, I'm exceptionally efficient? And constant worry helps me anticipate problems. Makes me empathetic, I think?"

"No, not a pro column," she said. "A conclusion. What's the end of the narrative arc?"

Ha. Well. Backsliding into nightmares and even daymares, horrible sights flashing before my eyes out of nowhere, in class, at work. "I'll think about that."

"Good." She spun around, lying on her stomach with socked feet swaying. "I'm almost done with USC's writing supplement. But to actually press send . . . it's feeling real."

I nodded. God, I was so ready to have this all over with. To enjoy my senior year the way it was meant to be—late nights, small mistakes. Leaving it all on the field, as Hunter would say. It felt like I'd been old for half my life, and I was running out of time to try being young.

"Max's applications going okay?" she asked.

"Yeah, but it's a lot. Like, ten schools."

"Anywhere near us?" Maeve was applying to a few other Cali schools, but she didn't really acknowledge options beyond our top three.

"Uh, yeah. Reach schools. But yeah." I fought the embarrassment, the worry that I sounded like a lovestruck ballad on lite radio.

"He better not distract you from writing," she said, intending to joke, I knew. "You're going to be very busy taking over the cinematic world with me."

Before that stupid driver decided to text his way through a red light, I'd experienced my application deadline like a large countdown clock pointed directly at me. I could *feel* the seconds ticking down. Now, I wanted the weightlessness of sending it, gone, done. If that driver had hit me at a slightly different angle or a little faster, would I have died thinking *Oh no, my last pass on that character sketch?* No way. I wanted to rip up the *HOMEWORK* card, and *SCHOOL* and *COLLEGE APPLICATIONS* and *WORK*, too, while I was at it. I wanted sleep and Max and my friends.

During the week, Tessa drove me to school and dropped me off at Cin 12 after; Hunter drove me home, with my parents or Max occasionally picking me up. I felt like a child and also happy to be ferried around, safe. Safer, anyway. But on Sunday, my dad offered his car for my afternoon shift.

"Are you sure?" I'd already changed into my tux, already grabbed my purse.

"Yeah," he said. "Your mom and I are taking her car to the antique mall. As long as you feel okay being behind the wheel?"

"Yeah," I said, with no idea if that was true.

But driving again felt surprisingly comfortable. I'd somehow pushed past the anxiety and into a type of *who cares anyway* confidence. If I could be plowed over at any point, might as well enjoy my life—enjoy driving, even.

At work, Donna let me leave early, which I would have otherwise declined. But some spare time, during which parents would not expect me home . . . that, I couldn't turn down.

The most direct path to Max's house was, of course, through the theater's big intersection. I idled, waiting for the light to turn as it had that night, and the accident played out like celluloid film. Heat slithered up my spine, panic giving me tunnel vision. But with no cars behind me, I could back up, away from the intersection. I licked my lips, which had gone dry, and I took the back way, heart galumphing.

Max answered the door in a washed-to-gray fandom T-shirt, his preferred weekend wear. "Aw, where's the tux?"

I made a face at him, grateful to my last-week self for stuffing a change of clothes in my work locker. "What are you up to?"

"I was . . . doing something productive. Definitely not playing video games."

"Can I play, too?"

He waited for the punch line. After months of demurring to almost every activity that wasn't on the List or part of schoolwork, I couldn't blame him for his surprise. "Oh my God, yes. Definitely yes."

"Are there any games where I can have a sword?" I asked, and he laughed. We holed up in the basement, where it became clear I had no hidden talent for virtual-weapon-wielding. But it felt good to try, to swing and jab and not really hurt anything.

"Yes!" Max said as I successfully hit a combo of buttons he'd coached me on. "You got him."

The screen danced with some kind of digital victory, then transitioned to stats for the next level.

"Hey," I said. I was sitting on the floor beside him, our backs leaned against the couch. Late last night, when I'd been imagining my untimely death, I thought back over the past months with Max. I'd held my hands at my sides to keep myself from texting him at two a.m. "I love you, you know that?"

Max peered at me, puzzled by my drop into seriousness. "Yeah, I love you, too."

I turned back to the screen, but Max tugged my sleeve. "How're you feeling about college stuff?"

"Um, pretty good, actually! For once." My college choice wasn't life or death—not even close. And with that anxiety static quieted, I could finally feel excitement again, and the privilege of having a choice at all. "I've gone from IU as a safe choice to one I'd be really happy about, I think. I'm glad I went back with Morgan, because something connected. How 'bout you?"

"You know. Fine." He rubbed a spot over his eyebrow.

"Oh no," I said, sitting up a little. Was my worry contagious, passed to Max right as I got a reprieve from it? "I thought your Northwestern visit went well."

Maybe this was it: the moment we revisited the whole Columbia and Caltech thing. In light of the car accident, it just didn't seem to matter. Max could apply wherever he wanted, and we'd see what happened.

"It did," he said. "But my mom and I got to talking about my dad, obviously."

His dad? I shook my head, as that did not seem obvious to me at all. I knew nothing about Max's dad, and certainly hadn't expected him to come up right now. He and Max's mom were college sweethearts when she got pregnant with Max; that was the only information I had.

"He lives in Chicago," Max said.

"Oh. Okay. Did you . . . see him?"

"No, no. He was out of town when we were there anyway. But my mom thinks I need to be more open to it."

That surprised me. The way Max had briefly spoken about his dad last year, I hadn't imagined Dr. Watson wanted him around. "They're on good terms, then?"

"Yeah. Have been since I was pretty small." With one finger, he mashed at the game controller, making his player swing a sword around idly on the TV. "The more my mom and I talked, it was like . . . Have you ever been really sure about something from when you were little? And then an adult tells you more of the story?"

I smiled at him, like that was an understatement. "*Have* I? Perhaps you recall Dan and Kate Hancock reuniting after I was positive—like, stake-my-life-on-it sure—that there was nothing between them worth saving. Yeah. Blew my mind."

"Exactly," he said. "I'd kinda cast my dad as the clear villain. I knew little bits, and I filled in the rest. Now I'm wondering if I've been unfair about the whole thing."

"Hey." I looked at him severely. I had this mental image of gawky, middle-school Max, before he transferred to private school for a few years. "You were a kid. You *are* a kid. How could you have been the unfair one? You were protecting yourself."

"Maybe." He smiled sadly. "I prefer that over me being a self-centered jerk."

I turned to him and held unblinking eye contact. "You are many things, but never that. If you were, I'd tell you."

"Oh yeah?"

"Mm-hmm." I leaned over to kiss him, and I meant for it to be quick. But the press of his lips was more comforting than I'd expected, the warmth and presence and nowness. The controller thudded to the carpet, freeing up his hands. My thoughts could slow, right here with Max, here, *here*, and not in a smashed-up car and not states apart next year. I crawled onto his lap, some vague impulse to prove all that to myself. To keep all this, his hands warm on my waist. Here.

In the past, my instincts had thrown a wall up pretty quickly, shyness and inexperience kicking up inside me. It had so much potential for embarrassment—someone else's hands on skin that only I ever saw, ever touched. But it wasn't someone else, was it? It was Max. And if one distracted driver could exeunt me and anyone else from the planet, what was so nerve-racking about anything else?

Max pulled back, and our noses still nearly touched. "What's going on, Janie?"

"Nothing." I tilted my head to look at him curiously. "Why?"

His eyes flicked back and forth, looking for something in mine. I was breathing hard, mouth warm from his, and the embarrassment started to creep up my neck.

"I'm extremely not complaining," he added, maybe sensing my self-consciousness. Which, of course, made me want to melt in a hot, mortified heat.

He brushed my bangs to the side, and I closed my eyes. It

always felt like a shocking thing for him to do in front of others—so blatant, a smoke trail that hinted toward fire. He kissed me again, gentler this time.

We sprang apart only when we heard the garage door open, to which Max muttered a swear word and hurriedly reached to unpause the video game. We collected ourselves before his mom made it to the top of the basement stairs and called hello in a pointedly loud voice.

"Hi!" we called back, too eager. Oh God, Max's hair, even by its usual standard, was rumpled. My mouth felt warm and, I suspected with horror, pink from friction. I pressed my lips together.

She appeared on the stairs. "Hey, Paige, sweetie. I saw your car in the driveway."

Her tone was friendly enough, but her smile wasn't really a smile—she was prying up both sides of her mouth by sheer force of will. I wanted to sink through the rug and into the earth below the Watson home. I'd tunnel my way out so I'd never have to face his mom again. "Max told me about your accident. I'm glad to see you're driving again—you must have been so shaken up."

"I was. Still kind of am. Max is helping me get out my feelings by attacking zombies." I glanced at the video game screen.

"They're hellbeasts," Max said. "But."

"Great," she said, tentative. "Well. Are you done with homework, Max Oliver?"

"Yes, Mother." How was he remaining so casual?

"Well, I'll be right upstairs." It was a clear warning, as she smiled thinly. "If you need anything. Nice to see you, Paige."

"You too!" I squeaked out.

Oh God, I needed to leave. This house and also my corporeal form. I would poof into a mist of awkwardness, become one with the atmosphere.

Once she was gone, Max said, "Sorry about that! I thought she wouldn't be home for at *least* another hour."

I pressed my hands to my face, which I also planned to do on my way out of this home, now and forevermore. "She hates me. This is a nightmare."

"What? No way! I mean, *I'm* about to get a painfully uncomfortable talking-to," Max said cheerfully. "But that's it."

I crushed myself into the couch, peeking at him through my fingers. "How are you not mortified?"

"Rest assured that I will be later," he said, "when she launches into the 'correct condom use' part of the doctor-mom lecture."

I rocketed up. "Wait. Do you think she thinks that we're—I mean—" I stopped talking only because I ran out of air and briefly forgot how to inhale. A merciful God would strike me down now, just end it here.

"Janie, she really isn't judging you." He slid beside me, one hand on my knee. "But I'll tell her that point-blank, if it would make you feel better."

"No," I decided. "Well, maybe. I don't know. If she asks, I guess."

I pressed my face into my palms again, but this time I

THE MAP FROM HERE TO THERE   165

laughed helplessly. This situation—though I'd gone light-headed from embarrassment—strangely made Max feel more like my boyfriend than ever. It wasn't something I'd ever experienced with anyone else, and certainly not with Max when we were just friends. In this, he was a co-conspirator and, now, the only other person who shared the secret of us being awkwardly busted by his mom. Other than, well, his mom.

I let my hands fall and smiled at him, shaking my head.

Max leaned over to kiss me again, which I expected to be a quick *See? We're fine* smooch. But instead, it felt like a kick drum and a deep sigh, even after the panic of getting caught by Max's mom. When I put my hand on his jaw, pushing him away, he laughed. "What? I'm already busted!"

"Kill your zombies." I pointed at the screen.

He pressed a kiss on the back of my hand. "Hellbeasts."

Two weeks after the accident, my parents announced that my dad would be moving back in. They'd clearly rehearsed the speech, given jointly at the dinner table. Cameron clapped her hands, not in applause, exactly, but in childlike delight.

I made a show of supportive daughterhood, but it was mediocre improv. Sure, I'd wanted this for them, but was this reactionary? They'd both been reminded that everything can end in the flash of a stoplight, one bad decision later.

When I tiptoed downstairs after hours, I gasped at the sight of someone in the dark kitchen. My mom, leaning against the counter and holding one of Cameron's cookie containers.

"What are you doing up?" she asked.

"Hungry." Not true, exactly. The nighttime anxiety screeched like static, so I couldn't hear my body asking for food or water. But sometimes I made myself get up and eat, hoping to feel sated and calmer.

She frowned at me. "Are you feeling bad again?"

"No," I lied. She already hated my far-flung college plans; she didn't need more tally marks in the "Con" column.

My mom looked like she was considering sending me back up to bed, parenting a five-year-old instead of an almost adult. Instead, she held out the cookies to me, and I took one.

"Are *you* okay?" I asked.

"Oh, sure. I'm afraid you get your occasional insomnia from me."

In the daylight hours, the kitchen functioned as our hub—where my mom issued reminders, where we hurried through meals, where we exchanged practical queries: *Who ate the last yogurt? Where are my black flats? Did someone move my phone charger?* The whir of the dishwasher, the ding of the microwave, running water from the faucet. At night, the kitchen itself seemed to be slumbering, a workhorse asleep in her stall.

My mom, too, seemed different late at night, in her robe and headband—off-duty in a way she never was during the day.

The darkness made me bolder, like this extra pocket of time made room for straightforwardness. "Is Dad moving back in because of the accident?"

"No, honey." My mom studied me, perhaps realizing that her response was too quick, too simple. It sounded like a mother's instinct to soothe. "These things are clarifying, though."

"Clarifying," I repeated. That word was written in pretty script on one of Cameron's shampoo bottles, purporting to rid hair of product buildup. Could an accident do that with your life choices—strip away the gunk? Make things clearer, cleaner?

Is that what it was doing for me?

I looked at my mother, now sweeping her hand over the counter in case of stray crumbs.

"Okay," I said, trying to believe that it was.

CHAPTER SEVENTEEN

Since the car accident, I'd been eating my turkey sandwich in the Cin 12 break room. Fall was over like a good kiss, and the walk to Alcott's would be shivery. Even if it weren't, I'd have to go through that damn intersection and relive the lurch and ambulance lights, my dad showing up bewildered in pajamas. The musty break room offered no respite, but no flashbacks either.

When I returned from my half, a pretty girl lingered at the snack counter where I'd been stationed with Hunter all evening. He flipped a rag onto his shoulder like a sitcom barkeep.

"So, text me about this weekend?" she was saying.

I looked away, eyebrows raised, and went about my business restocking display-case Skittles. Hunter would be driving me home later, which was very generous and also wouldn't stop me from teasing him about this.

"Oh, I will," he called. In the silence that followed, I could almost hear Hunter watching her walk away—the shift of her hips and the bounce of her hair. After a moment, his voice was clearly directed at me. "I know her outside of work, Hancock. I'm not hitting on random customers."

I held my hands up, an innocent woman. "I said nothing! I have no opinion!"

"You have judginess, is what you have." He swatted the rag at me, and I dodged it. "Not everyone gets as lucky as you and The Boyfriend, you know."

"Oh, I think you're getting luckier than I am . . . ," I said, joking.

"Is it lucky to be embarrassingly hung up on an ex?" he asked. "Because that's where I'm at."

I startled at the admission, the earnestness of his face. "Anyone I know?"

The dimples emerged, bracketing his mouth. He'd meant to pitch me a curveball, and he sank it—perfect. "Nah. Her name's Julia. She graduated last spring and didn't want to be 'tied down' at college. So. Yeah."

"I'm sorry," I said truthfully. "I had no idea."

"Eh." He waved a hand.

A couple strolled up, an older gentleman in a striped scarf. His wife had her arm looped through his, a hat over coiffed white hair.

Hunter's extrovert charm sprang up without a beat. "What can we get for ya?"

When I took the man's credit card, I noticed he wasn't wearing a ring—nor was the woman. Maybe they were married and didn't like jewelry, but maybe not. Why did I always assume that older couples were married? The strangeness of my parents' relationship disproved that expectation in a very personal way, but I still seemed to forget that most love stories are more complicated than meets the eye.

They headed off to their theater, and Hunter surprised me by bouncing right back to our heart-to-heart. "So, yeah. She's at school, and I'm here, and it is what it is."

"You were ready to do long distance?"

"Ha. Well. She's at Ball State, so, really close. It was less about distance and more about her wanting freedom." Hunter shook his head regretfully. "The thing is—I get it. She's meeting new people at school, having fun. That's the time you should be trying things out. Sucks for me, though."

I finished lining up the Mike & Ikes, and checked expiration dates before shutting the case, satisfied. "So these cute girls who come by to flirt with you . . ."

"Are great. Fun to hang with, smart. That's it." He stood up straighter, eyeing me. "And they know the deal. I'm not a dick."

No, he certainly wasn't. A bit of a player, sure, but a more complicated one than I ever would have guessed months ago. I shook my head, marveling a little.

"What?" he asked, self-conscious.

Hunter Chen thrived on chatting up strangers. He never needed an excuse to dance around or to sing. He liked telling stories from the "dumb shit my friends did last weekend" genre and had very little patience for angst. I didn't relate to a single bit of it, and yet. "I like you more than I thought I would."

"Is it my effervescence? The fact that I just used an ACT word? Or is it . . . the bod?"

"I'm not dignifying that, obviously."

He tossed a piece of popcorn at me. "Yeah, I like you, too, Hancock. You gonna come see me play ball in the spring?"

After Christmas break, baseball would start up for real, and Hunter would scale back his hours at Cin 12 almost completely till summer. I could barely stand to think about working shifts in silence. "You gonna come to my play?"

"Depends. Can I bring a foam finger?" He held up his pointer, demonstrating. "Front row? Here we go, Hancock, here we go!"

I rolled my eyes, but only for show. His revelation about Julia and what would have been a short-distance relationship? It kicked up my worries about next year like dead November leaves, scuttling and scraping. "Hey, can I ask you something?"

A fresh crop of customers swarmed in, and we snapped to attention. But when cards had been swiped and butter-flavored oil pumped, Hunter turned and said, "Okay. Shoot."

"When you committed to IU for baseball last year . . ." I let my words fall off, hoping he'd see where I was going. But he cocked his head. "Did you decide on a place in-state because you knew Julia would be here?"

"Ah," he said, nodding. "Not . . . really? I tried not to. But it's kinda tough to separate out all the way."

"Yes! Exactly. Okay," I said, vindicated. My accident had happened so soon after Homecoming that Max and I never went back to the Columbia topic. Still, I wrestled with it. If he got in, he could decide to go based on the prestige, the quality.

But could he ever really separate me from the decision? And wouldn't I feel responsible if he hated Manhattan? He made this life-altering choice for me—wouldn't I feel beholden to spend four years together, come what may?

When I turned these questions over in my mind each night, sleepless, I could hear Max's voice countering me: *Or, Janie, what if it's really great?* And truly, meeting Max in Central Park after a brutal critique in workshop? A coffee somewhere in Midtown to recalibrate? Spotting his familiar face in the oncoming crowd? What if it *was* really great?

"What's goin' on, Hancock?" Hunter's expression went stern. "Because I know you're not thinking about following The Boyfriend to school."

"No. No, no."

"Good. Because I need to be cast in one of your shows someday. It's my long-term plan, after my MLB years."

"But . . . Max is applying to a school in New York. And one in LA."

"And you are . . ." He watched my face, ever the pitcher waiting for the sign. "Not into this idea."

"That's weird, right?" I blurted out. "Why am I not thrilled?"

"Uh, because you're seventeen? That's a lot of pressure." Hunter wiped the counters, probably in case Donna emerged to see me leaning a hip against the register. *If you have time to lean, you have time to clean.* "But who cares about the reason? I mean, you feel how you feel, right?"

"You would think." I sighed, knowing my next sentence would step over a line I couldn't return from. "But, um, my feelings aren't always reliable? Sometimes my brain devolves into, like, obsessive worry?"

"Ah. Hard to know if your concerns are legit or if that's the anxiety talking?" Hunter asked, as casually as when he'd brought up his depression. "Gotcha. What do your friends say?"

I picked at an old sticker on the register base. "Haven't told them."

"Because . . ."

"Because they treat Max and me like we're a sure thing. Because they're already in our business. Because they love me, but they're not impartial when it comes to him. Take your pick."

"Fair enough. Whew. This is kind of a doozy, huh?"

Everyone expected one thing or another—my friends expected Max and me together, Maeve expected I would get into film school, my mom expected that I'd stay in-state. "Yep."

"Here's a question. If you got into all your schools, and Max was going to school in Indy . . . would you be tempted to go with IU? Try not to factor in that I'd be there, too."

I snorted. Would it be tempting to stay an hour from my parents, my sister, my bedroom? Tempting to be on campus with Morgan, Kayleigh, and Ryan? And probably near Max? To take out significantly fewer loans for a more broadly applicable degree? "Yes. But not just because of him."

"Well, hey. An application isn't a decision. It's not even an acceptance. Right?"

"Right." I'd told myself that a hundred times the past week, but hearing it from Hunter, who had no stake in the situation, made it feel truer.

"The anxiety stuff," he said quietly. "You see a doc?"

"I did. All of sophomore year."

"Okay." He said it mildly, like that was that. Like it wasn't an extremely loaded question. I glared at him, annoyed at his reticence. "You wanna come out with us tonight?"

And oddly, I did, a little. The montage played in my mind: walking into a big, anonymous party, disappearing into Hunter's friend group, where no one knew me. I could be a Chill Girl, someone with a trilling, head-thrown-back laugh. Sit on the arm of a couch with a drink in one hand. I could set aside writing portfolios and worries about money. Do something a little wrong, even, just to prove I could. "My mom's expecting me home."

Hunter nodded, used to this by now. "All right. But next time."

"Next time," I said, and for once, I meant it. I certainly meant it when I bumped his hip with mine and said, "Thanks, Chen."

CHAPTER EIGHTEEN

My dad moved back in during Thanksgiving break, and I told myself it felt like a natural progression, no big deal—until our final Sunday dinner at his apartment. The last bastion of the divorce arrangements, the last glimpse at this part of my life.

We ordered Chinese since his cooking supplies were mostly boxed up, labeled HOUSE or DONATION. The cynical part of me—the girl who spent every third-grade library trip searching for books about parents who fought—worried that there wasn't a box labeled STORAGE.

"You okay, kid?" my dad asked.

"Yeah," I said, fast and guilty. "End of an era."

My sister whistled like a North Pole elf, closing up box after fully packed box. I'd never seen her do manual labor with any measure of cheerfulness. But then, Cameron had wanted this to happen for years now. To me, it was never a broken home, now repaired. Each three-person unit had been whole, and I belonged in both.

Max was always calling me a realist, but how could I not be? I'd seen love go both ways with the same two people. My parents loved each other so much they married in the first place—so much that they found their way back to each other. And that love still wasn't enough to keep them from years of discord and separation.

I was beginning to think that half of growing up was figuring out when to let go and when to hold on. The radio implored me to say yes; one of my favorite TV show creators wrote a whole book about the practice of saying yes; improv class at NYU taught me *yes, and*. But saying yes meant saying no to other things, didn't it? A yes to Mythos had meant a no to QuizBowl. A yes to one college would mean a no to all the others. A yes to film school felt like a no to Max, my family, my friends nearby.

"Hey," my dad said. "You wanna tell me what's going on in the old thinkbox?"

"Thinking about Shonda's book." He'd read it, too, of course, in his tireless pursuit of supporting my dreams.

"As you do." He seemed appeased by this, enough that he didn't notice me rubbing at my chest, annoyed by the tightness. All the lost sleep was adding up, and I felt dizzy, wishing the food would get here. Maybe low blood sugar. Or maybe I was coming down with something—the movie theater was a hotbed for germs, after all. I couldn't think about that too much or I'd walk out on my break and never come back.

Stepping into the near-empty bedroom I'd shared with Cameron all these years, I stretched my neck, rolled my shoulders, breathed. The hallway light illuminated a strip of carpet, up to a nightstand where a picture of my dad, Cam, and me had always been. She'd wrapped it up already, packed in next to my books and the lamp. How many nights had I stretched out in the bottom bunk that first post-divorce year, breathing easy? The knots between my parents finally detangled. I missed my mom here; I missed my dad there. But it was good.

My hands cramped, heat flooding down my arms. *Stop*, I told my body. I knew from experience: This was not a cardiac event. It was a panic attack. But that was almost impossible to believe as my heartbeat hiccuped, both arms gone tingly. I eased to the ground, stabilizing myself. If I'd had the air for it, I might have called for my dad. Instead, the wave crested, and I managed to inhale. Again. Again.

"Paiger!" my dad called. "Food's here!"

I wiped my lower lids, my mascara surely gray watercolor by now. The last thing I needed was for my dad to worry, so I cleared my throat and called, steadily as I could, "Coming!"

That Saturday, I allowed myself to truly lounge with my friends. We were marathoning reality TV before Tessa left to meet Laurel for a concert downtown—tickets they'd had for months now.

"I can't believe you let us watch this in your presence," Kayleigh told me, gesturing to a talking-head shot of someone explaining her side of the story.

"Well," I said, "it may not be scripted, but the narrative is certainly sculpted by producers, you know? And the nature of that is so dynamic, because—"

Kayleigh held up a hand to stop me, or so I thought. But she nodded toward Morgan, who was scrolling her phone with a darkened expression.

"Morgan?" I asked. "Is it a college e-mail?"

She held up one finger, silencing us as she finished reading. I truly feared she might launch her phone into the McMahon family fireplace.

"Well," she said, sitting up. "The school board e-mailed me back, just *completely* dismissive. Do you know how long Gabby and I spent laying out the argument for more effective health education? There's not even a mention of us being a topic at a future meeting. This is *egregious*."

"Those a-holes," Kayleigh said.

"Listen to this." Morgan's eyes scanned the screen, filling with fire as she reread. "'It was very sweet of you to compile resources relevant to Indiana's policy, but . . .' I'm sorry, very *sweet* of me?"

Tessa retracted her chin, offended. "What a condescending dick."

"Right?" Morgan said. "Sweet? Like I'm some sugary little cake?"

Kayleigh considered this. "I could make that happen. A simple round buttercream with some petal-tip florals. And, in bright pink letters, REVOLUTION."

"I couldn't even eat it! I'm supposed to 'watch my blood

sugar' now," Morgan said in a mimicky, nasal voice. Her doctor appointments continued to be a frustration, to say the least.

Tessa pointed to the kitchen. "Wanna get into my dark chocolate supply?"

Morgan didn't seem to hear her, irises wild. "They're elected officials; they have a responsibility to the district. This e-mail is insulting. I sing in freakin' church choir with one of them!"

Tessa looked startled by the fervor, but I understood. If Morgan could pry community change out of her diagnosis, it would be okay. It would have meaning—a story with a good ending.

"Ugh," Morgan said. "What do I do now?"

"Be mad," I said. "Vent to us. Take a breather. You'll come up with something."

"I guess. Because this is just . . ." She looked around, like Jesus himself would materialize in her room with soap for her mouth. "Horseshit. This is horseshit. Right?"

"This is a giant pile of horseshit," Kayleigh said. I nodded, as high and low as my neck would allow.

"Do you want to punch this pillow?" I asked, offering one.

"No, thanks." She sighed, though, prolonged and heavy. "I need to, like . . . go out or something. Burn off some energy."

Truthfully, my own instinct, after that night at my dad's apartment, was to let loose a little. All year, I'd been trying to manage my schedule, to multitask, to out-effort my problems. It wasn't working, so why not try Hunter's method? "Do you want to stop by a party, maybe?"

My friends turned to me, seemingly in slow motion.

"Who are you?" Kayleigh deadpanned. "If you're truly Paige Hancock, say your identifying phrase."

I rolled my eyes. "What would my identifying phrase even be? Probably 'I'm uncomfortable'?"

"Ha!" Tessa clapped, a little too delighted, in my opinion. "Is someone we know having a party?"

"Hunter will probably know someone."

"I'm going to drink," Morgan announced to no one in particular.

"I'll drink with you," Kayleigh said. "Paige, you okay to drive?"

"Oh, um—" Technically yes, but I'd just have to go through that damn intersection outside the movie theater. Which. Well. I could probably do, if I had to.

"I'll drop you off," Tessa said. "Linwood's on the way to the venue. And I can swing by and pick you up after the show."

Good enough for me. I pulled out my phone.

———————

"Well, well, well," Hunter said, standing on the porch with his arms crossed. A couple of guys were on the porch swing, smoking cigarettes and laughing at a phone video. "You showed."

I'd only ever seen him in the cinema tux, so the red half-zipped hoodie made him look bright cheeked, his hair more jet. It was like seeing a cartoon character—almost always in the same outfit—dressed up for a special-event episode.

"I said I would!" I gestured back to Morgan and Kayleigh. "You remember my friends?"

I braced for a line, something flirtatious. But he simply held up one hand. "Hey, ladies. Thanks for nudging Hancock out of the ol' Alcott's social scene."

"Can you believe we didn't even drag her?" Morgan asked him. "It was her idea!"

"Well," he said, pressing the door open, "she loves me. Come meet people."

The scene was quieter than I had imagined, not the pulsing, pressed-to-the-walls crowd I'd feared. Hunter guided us into the living room, where I spotted Lane on the arm of the couch.

"Whose house is this?" I asked.

"My buddy Gabe's. You've met him—tall guy? Super skinny?"

Lane leaped up from her seat, blue cup dangling from one hand. "Paige! You came!"

Hunter gestured to the group Lane had been sitting with. "Morgan, Kayleigh, and Paige, from the Cin House."

"The *cinema*," I said, smacking Hunter's arm. "Don't make it sound like I work somewhere seedy!"

"Well, I'm sorry to say that you sort of do. Drinks?"

"Sure." I slipped on the casualness like a velvet dress—how did I know it wasn't my style if I never tried it on?

"Chen!" a voice called from nearby. "Next game?"

"Yeah, man," Hunter called back. Then to us, "You in? Beer pong?"

Morgan and Kayleigh glanced at each other and nodded—their duo cemented.

"Cool. Hancock, you're with me?" Hunter asked.

"Oh, I don't know."

"I can drink the beer, if you want. Have you ever played before?" He said it without a trace of mocking. Some guys, I thought, would crow with delight over someone else's inexperience. Hunter seemed genuinely interested.

Still, a part of me wanted to scoff—*of course*. "Nope! Never."

"Well, that just means you'll have beginner's luck."

"Do I strike you as an athlete?"

He gave me a once-over. "The National Spelling Bee airs on ESPN."

"Jerk." I laughed, despite myself, and punched his arm. I'd never been the type of person to play-hit someone before, but Hunter acted like an annoying brother sometimes, and he deserved to be treated as such.

"See? Slugger!"

I did like the idea that next year, if someone asked whether I'd played beer pong before, I could honestly say: *Of course*.

Beer pong, as it turned out, had its merits. Sure, the spectators were intimidating, but they didn't seem to pick sides. They cheered for anyone drinking, in any scenario. After a few embarrassing whiffs, I got the hang of the Ping-Pong ball's hollow, plasticky weight. The first time I sank one, I stood stunned for a moment. Hunter high-fived me, and the group of strangers clapped, appeased.

Beer, however, remained disgusting, somehow both bitter and watery.

"Shots?" Hunter offered, when we'd finished. He cast himself as the host even at someone else's house. "We do have supplies for Lane's signature drink, the Redheaded Feminist. Her twist on another recipe."

"Redheaded Woman with Sexual Agency was too long," Lane said.

"Well," Morgan said. "That, I've gotta do."

"I like you," Kayleigh announced to Lane. "Your friends should be friends with my friends."

"Done," Lane said, laughing. "Consider yourself invited to my birthday party, which is going to be major."

Shots eventually devolved to a kitchen dance party, someone's phone hooked up to a wireless speaker. Hunter danced with goofy confidence, offering a hand to spin me. My friends bounced, hands raised, and we probably looked like total fools to any sober person. At that moment, though, I didn't care a bit.

"Paige!" Morgan said, mid-hop. "Guess what! My stomach feels *sloshy*. Ha-ha! Like a dishwasher inside of me. *Swish-swoosh*."

My feet pressed into the ground, and I took her by both arms. "Hey, let's maybe stop jumping."

"Okay!"

I guided her to the hallway, as she stared around, looking woozy. Executive decision: time to go. Morgan needed water and quiet and to sleep this off. And hopefully to not puke at my friend's friend's house.

"Hey," Kayleigh called, "I'm gonna text Tessa and get her here, okay?"

I gave a thumbs-up as I steered Morgan toward Gabe's mother's powder room, with its embroidered hand towels.

"Stupid school board," Morgan muttered, sinking to the tile. "Stupid Morgan. Stupid alcohol."

And with this litany, she laid her head down on the toilet seat. I found a stack of mouthwash cups and got her to sip some water slowly.

"Better?" I asked, after a few minutes.

"I maybe can't have kids bio-log-ickly," Morgan said, slurring. She licked her lips. "Biologic-all-ee."

"What?" My voice came out a whisper.

"Or it might be hard for me. Is what the doctor said. Don't tell anyone, okay?" She patted my knee.

I gripped her hands, trying to get her to look at me. "Of course I won't. Does anyone else know, though?"

"My mom. She had a hard time getting pregnant with me, so she gets that I am sad and mad and confused. I'm seventeen! I shouldn't have to think about fertilly. Fertality. FERTILITY."

There were a lot of other things I could say—that she could become a parent any number of ways, that medicine and treatment would likely make strides. That maybe the doctor shouldn't have introduced such an unknown hypothetical to a seventeen-year-old. But as someone who confronted all negative possibilities as a coping mechanism, I knew better than to downplay the complicated feelings here. "That really, really sucks."

"It does." Morgan nodded. She stretched her neck, then rolled her shoulders. "Okay. I'm fine. Can you please forget I blathered?"

"No," I said. "But I can promise not to bring it up again until you're ready."

"Okay. Thank you for sitting on the bathroom floor with me."

"You're welcome. Let's go home, okay?"

Kayleigh couldn't get through to Tessa or Laurel, who were surely on the dance floor near thumping speakers. So she did what I would have done: texted Max.

When I'd imagined the moment of him picking us up, Max strode from his car in his jaunty way, smiling at me like *Oh, you*. Pretending to be inconvenienced, but not-so-secretly amused by my tipsiness.

I stood up, waving as I saw Max's car pull onto the street. He rolled down the window. "You okay?"

"Fine," I said, surprised. I stood up straighter. His worry was sobering, if not literally. "Thanks for coming to get us."

"Sure." The muscle in his jaw worked so hard that I watched closer, wondering if he was chewing gum. He was not.

On the ride home, Morgan sang loudly, the nausea left behind now. Almost loud enough to cover the annoyance pulsating from Max Watson's entire being.

We pulled into Tessa's driveway, and Morgan jumped out of the car. "We are home, and I am so happy!"

"Thanks, Max-O," Kayleigh said. She kissed her palm and reached up to the front seat, pressing it against his cheek. He smiled a bit, to my relief, as she climbed out. I put my hand on the door.

"Stay for a sec?" Max said quietly.

Kayleigh made an *eek* face and scurried toward the house.

"Hope he doesn't ground you!" Morgan called back to me, and laughed at her own joke.

Drunk Morgan was kind of a turd, actually.

"I'm sorry," I said, before Max could get a word in. "We shouldn't have called."

"I'm not mad that you guys called me."

I crossed my arms, bracing for impact. "No?"

He thought for a while, his eyes looking straight up the driveway. "I'm just trying to understand. You were staying in for girls' night. Then I'm picking you up, drunk, from a Linwood party?"

"Morgan was having a bad night. She needed to get out of the house."

"I take it Hunter was there?"

"Yeah," I said. Oh. This . . . looked bad, didn't it? Like I told my boyfriend I was staying in and then went to some guy's party. "I snapped into crisis mode with Morgan—total tunnel vision. I should have texted you."

Max nodded slowly, but he didn't turn to face me. "What's goin' on with you, Janie?"

Part of me wanted to let every spiraling thought spring out of my head like Medusa's snakes. The unknowns of my own future, the doubled panic that Max might make his choices around mine, that my dad moving back in could be a complete disaster, that my damn nightmares were back, and that even the daily, lower-level anxiety gave me a too-fast heartbeat, my mind always scrabbling for somewhere safe to rest.

But he'd recoil—who wouldn't? It'd be like removing the mask of smiling, summer Paige to reveal the hideous drama below. Some dream girl.

"I'm really freaked out about hearing from colleges," I admitted. That seemed like the safest one, a tiptoe.

"I am, too," Max said. "I guess I'm just surprised your reaction was to go out and get drunk. That's not like you."

At this, I huffed. The past few years were decided for me, my life swerved into grief. Who would I have been without it? I had no idea.

Max must have heard the indignation because he added, "You've always said drinking isn't worth it to you. That all you'd do is worry about getting in trouble."

True enough. But look where my abundance of caution got me: sick with worry around the clock, exhausted from living in my own skin. Hit by a distracted driver when I'd done nothing wrong. "It was a few beers, with friends I trust. I don't think it's that big a deal."

"It wouldn't be for some people." He turned, his brows scrunched down like I was a particularly vexing algorithm. Which piece was he missing? There was an edge in his voice—a tell that he was losing patience. "But it is for you. That's what I'm saying."

My stupid eyes flooded, beer loosening my hold on composure. "*I* don't know what is me and what isn't, Max. I was really sad and messed up when we met, okay? I emotionally unenrolled in high school. But I'm back now, and I don't think I should feel bad about doing normal stuff like going to a party or Homecoming or whatever else!"

Oh, okay, so the Homecoming part just snuck out. I sank back in my seat, desperate for a way to walk it back.

"I made you feel bad about Homecoming?" Max stared, genuinely surprised. "I thought you were going mostly because Morgan wanted to. Because it was on the List."

"Well, partially. But it would have been nice to be danced with."

Max blinked, absorbing this. "Well, it also would have been nice if you had, I dunno, told me that it mattered to you?"

At his tone, I returned to glowering. That night ended in a panic attack for me, the memory marred anyway. "And it would have been nice if you had, I dunno, told me about Columbia and Caltech."

He shook his head, smiling in his forced, gritted-teeth way. "I *knew* you were upset about that. Why did you tell me it was fine if it wasn't?"

"Because I wanted it to be, Max! I don't know!"

"Well, glad I wasted the application fees. If I get in, I won't go." He dusted his hands off. "That's that."

"I don't want you to turn down an Ivy League school."

"Well, then, what *do* you want, Paige?" he asked, exasperated. "I feel like I'm torturing you in some way, but I have no clue what I'm doing wrong."

"I don't want to be responsible for your future at all. I don't even know what I want for *myself*!"

"Okay . . . I mean, you're not responsible for my future, so problem solved?"

"How did this become a fight about that?" I whispered, more to myself than to him.

"It's late." He rubbed the bridge of his nose, his glasses shifted upward. "I have to get home."

I didn't want to leave it like this. I was still mad about feeling judged, but I also knew Max. Smart as he was, he short-circuited when he couldn't understand something. And I was ever changing, a dynamic human and not a fact, not a trig problem with a clear result.

"I still feel off balance after the car accident," I said, calm now. "And waiting to hear from colleges feels like being buttoned into a too tight coat at all times. Maybe I am off. Teetering a little. I'm not always going to be the exact same person, though. I don't expect you to be, either. So, can we just try for better tomorrow?"

Some people have visual cues to show they're deeply considering something: a thoughtful nod, a bitten lip. Max fiddled with his watch sometimes, twisted it on his wrist. But he also, I had noticed in the past year, went still—blank and unreadable—when he was truly taking something in. Like a retreat so far into his mind that he stopped moving. And I *knew* that, from watching his face in class and across the table at the coffee shop. But in this moment? Damn if I didn't second-guess myself, wondering if he was stonily furious.

"Yes," he said finally, coming back to me. Something about his eyes softened. "We can."

"Thank you." My hand went to the door. We'd landed in a good, safe place, and I had zero interest in continuing to argue. "And thanks again for coming to get us."

As he backed down the driveway, I held up one hand to wave as if things felt resolved, fine. If they were, why did I feel like we'd peeked into a stuffed-full storage room and, seeing the mess, slammed it shut? Hugging my arms to my chest, I turned back toward my friends.

CHAPTER NINETEEN

I submitted my college applications the first day of Decem-
ber. All that work down to a few clicks. I thought I'd panic,
wishing I could grab my portfolios back from the digital
ether. But I felt lighter, reams of paper sloughed off.

I answered Maeve's video call from my desk, where I was
watching pilot episodes of new TV shows instead of doing
homework.

"Did you do it?" she asked, instead of saying hello. Her
bedroom was filled with light, California sunshine pouring in.
Even through a computer screen, I felt warmer.

"Yep!" I held out both arms, a free woman.

"Good. So, the scene you sent me for our time-travel
teen drama." She ducked off-screen, reaching for something.
"Everything okay?"

"Yeah, why? Were my pages that bad?" Without the
restraint of our applications, we were free to blue-sky, free to
cowrite. We'd been playing around with some pretty out-there
ideas.

"No! They were good. I mean, heavy-handed at moments."
She leaned forward, circling creamy foundation onto her bare
skin. "I just assumed, based on the heatedness of the dialogue,
that you'd been arguing with someone."

I trained my face still, trying not to look caught. Everything was fine with Max now, so it didn't seem worth revisit-
ing. "Nah. Just reliving old feelings."

"Mm-kay. Just wanted to check. Everything else good?
The parents?"

"Yeah, actually." My dad's move into the house had been
uneventful, even for me. "So far, so good. Where are you
off to?"

"Just lunch with parentals. But, you know. Always gotta be
ready. Never know when I could meet a film agent or a lover."

She said it like *lov-ah*, in a throaty voice of an old Hollywood starlet.

"Can I ask you a weird question?" I asked, and Maeve nodded. She was on to mascara, pulling the wand quickly. "How
would you react if someone called you his 'dream girl'?"

"Ooh." She tapped her chin. "Is this for real life or a script?"

"In real life, say."

"Depends on who, obviously. The creepy freshman who
stares at me a lot? Gross. But River Lee?" Maeve's number one
celebrity crush lived in LA, enough to make their relationship
an eventuality in her mind. They'd bump into each other at a
coffee place, discuss acting methodology. "If it was River Lee,
then book your plane ticket out West, baby, because I am to
be *wed*."

She raised her hands in triumph, and I laughed, though my body refused to unclench.

"Wait," Maeve said, lowering her arms. "Why are you asking this? Did someone say this to you? Max?"

I angled my head, an exaggerated *duh* look. "Who else would say that to me?"

"Was this like . . ." She trailed off, raising her eyebrows. "During a private moment?"

"No!" I walloped the laptop screen with a nearby pillow, hoping she felt the effect. "God!"

"Well, just asking! Context is key!" We both settled down, letting the revelation of these words sink in. "Paige. That's, like, very sweet. You are *such* a dream girl."

"Shut *up*." The pillow was still in my hands, convenient for immediately covering my face.

"I'm serious!" Maeve said. "But why are you asking? You don't know how you feel?"

My hand went to my chest, pressing down like my rib cage was a dam, holding emotions in. "It's so sweet. But then, I start to wonder if that was a very serious thing to tell someone? I don't know."

"Did he say it in a super-serious tone? Like . . ." She leaned forward, gripping her screen, and dropped the pitch of her voice. "Paige Hancock, you are my dream girl."

"No," I said firmly. "No, it was way sillier than that."

"Paige?"

"Yeah."

"I don't want to downplay this if it's anxiety related," she said, "but you're a known overthinker. Which I love about you! Parsing out feelings is a great skill."

"But?" I guessed.

"But . . ." Her cheeks pulled up, just barely. "I think it's okay to simply enjoy the fact that the guy you love is in love with you back."

"Yeah," I said. It was so obvious, when she said it like that. "You're right."

Maeve made a knowing face—lips pursed in a way that accentuated her cheekbones. "He freaked you out with the college stuff. I knew it. He totally freaked you out."

"No," I scoffed, staring at the pillow. "Why would you think that?"

"First of all, it is really good that you're not pursuing an acting career," Maeve said. "Secondly, there's a vein of hopeful cynicism in everything you write. You're trying to believe, but helplessly waiting for the anvil."

I pulled the collar of my shirt up, covering my chin and mouth. Truly, this pronouncement felt like being completely naked and having someone explain my body parts to me. Only my inner self, exposed.

"It seems rude," I said, from beneath the cotton of my shirt, "to verbally character-sketch someone to their face."

Maeve opened her mouth to respond, but her dad's voice cut in from the background—something about five minutes and attending brunch, not the Oscars. "*Okay*, Baba."

"Thanks for checking in," I said. "Tell River I said hey."

CHAPTER TWENTY

It was a drippy December, halfhearted rain falling from marbled skies. In my room, I skittered like a caged mouse without a wheel—decluttering, list making, list crumpling. I picked up extra hours at Cin 12 and rallied my friends toward activities, into the outside world. We checked ice-skating off the List, and, next to Max, I thought of Rockefeller Center next year, the tall tree and the lights. The cinematic magic of winter in the city. Max and I likewise skated around the college topic—we simply clasped hands, holding steady in our precarious balance.

On the last day of school before Christmas break, I practically sprinted to the exit by the parking lot. Tessa was waiting at our usual spot, wrapped in a tweedy gray coat that I'd never seen before this week. It was somehow both well tailored and stylishly oversized. And it also, simply by existing, made me self-conscious about the toggle-buttoned red peacoat I'd worn since I got it for Christmas freshman year.

"Freedom!" I said when I was close enough to be heard. "Two solid weeks."

She was smiling, close-lipped like she had a secret, and she held up her phone. The screen displayed an online confirmation from Tate College, the place that had enamored her in Chicago. "I got in."

"Ah, Tessa!" I said, squeezing her. "Congratulations! I can't believe you found out so soon!"

When she stepped back, her eyes were alight; she was as happy as I'd seen her in a while. "I know! God bless early admission. And right before break! A Christmas gift from the universe."

"Wait." My head snapped back. "You did early admission? Doesn't that mean you're, like, definitely going?"

"Yeah! It was my first choice." She was still smiling, but hesitantly now—confused by my reaction. "You knew that."

Did I, though? My expression drooped; I could feel it, and my mouth was refusing to spring back up. Tessa decided on Chicago, on being near Laurel. And she was . . . delighted. No second thoughts; no hesitation.

"What's wrong?" she asked.

"Nothing!" I said. "Nothing. I just didn't realize that it was, like, settled."

"Oh. Yeah!"

We'd lived side-by-side lives all these years, and this, right now, was the moment we knew it was over? That didn't warrant even a tang of bittersweetness? I imagined Tessa bustling through the Chicago winters, past the lit-up department store windows. Tucked into cafes with exposed brick, dancing at underground venues on the weekends with Laurel. I wanted that for her, but my protective instinct reared like a wild horse.

"But," I said, trying to puzzle out the plan here, "what will you do if you and Laurel break up?"

She settled back on her heels—only a centimeter farther from me, but I could feel a divide opening between us. "Uh, I dunno. Be sad? What are you talking about?"

"Just, like . . . could you transfer?"

"I wouldn't want to," she said, crossing her arms. "I didn't choose Tate based on Laurel. Did you not hear anything I said when I came home from my visit? And if it's not a good fit, I'm not stuck. Of course I could transfer."

Of course she could. Tessa had space to mess up—big and expensively. College wasn't a single shot on the pool table, one she had to line up and sink with precision. "Yeah. I guess *you* could."

"What's that supposed to mean?" She squinted, trying to figure out if I was conceding or further criticizing her. And, God help me, I chose the latter.

I raised my chin and said evenly, "It means you can afford to change your mind. So, that's great. Good for you."

Tessa recoiled, eyes springing wide. "You're making this about money? Why are you turning this all around?"

Her eyes went watery, and I floundered. Why *was* I doing this? Before I could stammer an apology, she touched her pointer finger to the corner of her eye, clearing the tear pooling there. "Excuse *me* for being capable of committing to something when it feels right. And not because I've wrung a pro and con list dry."

Tessa, normally a slouchy house cat, had flicked out her

claws and swiped. I blinked at her, processing the sharp heat of scratches.

"Oh yeah," I spat. "I'm *such* a loser for having to consider my options. So uncool for not having rich parents who can pay for any college scenario."

"How is that my fault?" Tessa demanded. Two guys walked past, craning their necks at the sound of raised voices. Tessa gave them a vicious glare, then turned it on me. "What am I supposed to do? Not go to the one college I like because . . . why? Some judgmental friend might act like I'm codependent with my girlfriend?"

"I'm just saying you could postpone the decision a little, so you don't wind up hurt!" God. This was honestly the least controversial feedback imaginable.

"Oh, please. This isn't about me at all. This is about you and Max," she said, and I blanched. Then anger poured back in quickly, a red lens filter dropping behind my eyes. Tessa waved her hand. "This is about you sabotaging a good thing with hesitation and hypotheticals. But that's not my problem, Paige. It's yours."

The thick skin I'd developed in summer workshops gave way, my cheeks blooming with heat. Why would she throw that in my face? "Yeah. I wonder why I'd play it safe. I wonder why I'd be scared of impermanence or losing someone."

I regretted it immediately, using Aaron to make a point. Using my parents' divorce, my grandmother's death.

"You're seventeen years old, Paige," Tessa said, unmoved. "At a certain point, that's not a reason; it's an excuse."

My mouth fell open. Tessa had had a front-row seat to my life these past years, closer than my own mother. She'd witnessed every low moment, and all that time, she'd made me believe I was strong, that I was a good person trying my best. But here she'd been saving my faults like stones in her pocket, waiting to pelt me.

I turned away, and bolted so fast I almost tripped. I couldn't stand the sight of Tessa's face for another second—let alone get a ride from her. Max or Kayleigh would take me or, hell, I'd walk home.

"Paige!" she yelled. Then quieter, "Jesus."

I'd heard the phrase "burst into tears" plenty of times but rarely had my tears truly burst. I was just worried, like any good best friend. Which path was more loving, in the end: To be blandly supportive no matter what? Or to help anticipate problems and save her from pain? I'd reacted with caution, like I usually did, and was that really so wrong?

I found Max walking away from his locker, and he stopped at the sight of me.

"Whoa, girl." Like I was an agitated filly. "Hey, hey, hey. Come here."

"Can you take me home?" I asked, pressing my face into his chest. "I know you have tutoring, but—"

"I'll reschedule," he said. "What happened?"

"Tessa and I . . ." I shook my head because how could I recap what just happened? *Imagine us flinging balls of flame at each other, only words instead of fire. Imagine the cruelest thing I could hear about myself, then imagine Tessa saying it without a single whiff of remorse.*

Max kissed the top of my head. "C'mon. Let's get hot chocolate on the way home."

I clutched his hand on the way out of the building. At the beginning of the year, I'd walked out of school musing about the last first, the start of the end. But this, really, was the moment. Tessa had a plan far away from me, and my friend group would never be the same. We'd scatter, meet new people, our texts and visits thinning so gradually that we'd hardly notice. It was enough to make me wipe a tear with mittened hands, and Tessa, on her way home without me, was—as always—too cool to even care.

CHAPTER TWENTY-ONE

My mom served Christmas brunch in her two-tone kitchen, bottom cabinets now white as brushed teeth. Last week, she'd struggled back tears, drill in hand, as she reattached the hinges. The project was taking longer than she expected, work deadlines jutting into her free time. My dad had shuttled Cameron and me out the door to pick up Thai food, giving her a moment. She'd turned a corner, though, over halfway done.

"The white paint makes the countertops look nicer, no?" She handed me the pie server to cut a slice of quiche. "We'll replace them someday, but until then!"

Was it the royal we—our family? Or did she mean herself and my dad, planning into someday with him? I found myself glancing under the tree for any small, square packages.

For the first time in years, all four of us sat around the tree Christmas morning. Christmas Eve used to be at my dad's, with stockings and matching pajamas. He'd drop us off here late, so we could wake up at home to cinnamon rolls. My mom and grandma, sipping morning tea as they watched us open gifts.

Having my dad here helped. Not because he replaced my Grammy—I was still playing her memory like an all-time favorite song. But because she'd like that we were all here together. She'd like watching my mom open the gift from him, an oval chalkboard with a sage-green frame.

"I thought you could use it for a business name, if you decide to sell your furniture at the flea market this spring," my dad said. "Or you could just put it up in the kitchen. No pressure."

"Have you been thinking about getting a booth, Mom?" I asked.

"I have, yes," my mom admitted, smiling down at her sign. "I'd need to apply soon. And come up with a name."

"Something simple and classy," Cameron said. "Hancock Design."

"But you should play up the upcycling aspect." I swiped through my vocabulary. "Renovate? Refurbish?"

"Kate Renovates," Cameron said.

"Kate's Kreations," my dad suggested, spanning his hands out like the name was up in lights. "With a *K*."

Cameron gestured to the back door. "Get out."

She held a serious face for a moment and then we all laughed. Even my dad, as he exclaimed, "What? It's good!"

"You know, I could do a booth, too . . . ," Cameron said. "Sell cookies. Beats working for someone else at a summer job . . ."

I gave her a pointed look, sure she was referencing my cinema tuxedo.

"Oh!" my mom said, clasping her hands. "Would you? Let's do it together!"

The refurbishing theme continued as Cameron and I took my mom to the garage to unveil our present. We'd bartered down the price for a beat-up old credenza at the antique mall. It took both of us, my dad, our neighbor, and his truck to get it here. A behemoth of a thing, scuffed to hell—the roughest shape of any piece so far. A near black varnish, and outdated and chipped. But with delicate bamboo edging, hinting at a previous life. A stately foyer, a hotel mezzanine?

I glanced at my mom, wondering if we'd missed the mark, buying a disheveled Christmas present. But she was starry-eyed, running her fingers over the detailing. "Oh, this is going to be *beautiful.*"

After that, I opened a sweatshirt from my dad, "NYU" across the front in clean white letters.

"Before you start with 'But what if I don't get in,'" he said, "you got into the summer program, so you *are* an NYU student. And also, you *will* get in, even if you wind up deciding on a California school."

I hugged the sweatshirt's purple sleeves. I'd coveted NYU apparel at the on-campus gift store this summer. But could I really wear it? Wouldn't that be mortifying if I did and then they rejected my application? Beside me, my mom smiled a bit stiffly. When I caught her, she quickly murmured, "Looks great, sweetie."

After presents had been opened and wrapping paper cleaned up, my dad trooped upstairs for his traditional holiday nap.

Cameron, putting away her new baking supplies, sighed. "I really thought Dad might propose."

"*Cameron.*" I said it in my most serious, line-drawing voice.

My mom opened and closed her mouth several times, an aquarium fish watched by two unblinking spectators.

"It . . . won't happen like that," she said finally. "Don't expect a big proposal, okay? Your dad has made it clear that he's invested in a long-term future. Anything else will be mutual decision making as we go."

"Wait." Cameron was agog, eyes flickering. "Did he already ask?"

"Cameron," she said firmly. "I respect that this affects you—both of you. But I need to go at my own speed here, okay? I promise I'll tell you when there's something to tell."

Regardless, Cameron pranced around the kitchen like Cinderella, tidying up beside invisible birds.

Once we were alone, my mom sighed. "She got her hopes up, didn't she?"

"He did ask you, didn't he?" I countered.

We looked at each other, silently agreeing that this topic would not be delved into any further. In the Mother-Daughter Olympics, we'd medal in repression, worrying, and aimlessly online shopping without ever buying anything.

"I'm trying to do the right thing for everybody," she said.

I thought of her face last year, solemn across a checked restaurant tablecloth. She'd seen my hesitation—in swimming, in opening my heart up to anyone new. Tessa hadn't been wrong: I couldn't stop tabulating risk, weighing negative consequences until they bogged me down. But my mom understood that in me then, the way I understood her now.

———————

Max stopped over in the early evening to exchange presents, though it took almost an hour for my family to let us be. Once alone in the living room, I handed him a tellingly rectangular gift, wrapped in red-and-white-striped paper.

"Whatever could it be?" he joked.

Max had always been more of a comic and graphic novel reader, but he loved *The Phantom Tollbooth* in that specific way of childhood books: the ones that are yours completely, signposts that marked the person you were becoming. Over the summer, I'd found a used copy in a rummage-y city bookshop. It wasn't a first edition, not a signed copy. But someone had added marginalia: *Ha!* and *magic* and assorted questions filled the otherwise blank spaces. Those ballpoint pen scratches gave this copy a story within a story—a past life, a singularity that I thought Max would appreciate.

He turned it over in his hands.

"I love *The Phantom Tollbooth*," he said, sounding surprised. Like I wouldn't have remembered this small factoid from an early conversation.

"Look." I pressed my fingertip to the first word on the first page, which had been underlined. *There.* I turned to the last page and pointed to the last word of the book, likewise marked. *Here.* "I never noticed that when I read it in school."

"Me neither." He ran his thumb over the words, over a tale

about going from there to here. He grasped the book to his chest for a moment. "Officially my favorite book I own. Okay, open your gift."

Reaching my hand into the gift bag, I felt a momentary flash of panic—what if he'd gotten me something fancy? And I got him an old book?

Beneath sparkly tissue paper, I unearthed two white candles in pretty glass jam jars. I never splurged on candles, and when I received them as gifts, I burned them slowly, trying to make them last.

"Here, guess." Max unscrewed the silver lid and held the first candle out to me.

"It's . . . ," I said, inhaling. Subtle, oaken. Wood shavings.

My eyes welled up. Not because the scent was particularly strong, but because it smelled like mid-August, like fresh starts, like jitters.

"Number Two Pencils," Max said, too excited to wait.

"Yes." To be known this way—I felt socked in the gut. The other candle was called A Formal Library, hints of old leather and pulp.

I kissed Max in the glow of tiny white lights, reflected doubly in the windows. Pulling away, I glanced toward the kitchen, where my parents and sister were doing a Christmas puzzle and working on yet another batch of cookies, respectively. They couldn't see us, but I wondered about eavesdropping, even over the sounds of The Carpenters. "Kind of wishing for a *Home Alone* family disappearance right about now."

Max laughed. "Kind of wishing you were coming upstate with me. Maybe next year."

The annual Watson-Chase ski holiday usually took place in upstate New York. It was easy to daydream: Max and me reading by a fireplace in a lodge. Snow drifting down outside. But a whole year from now?

"Maybe," I said.

"Have you talked to Tessa?" Max asked, and I flicked up eyes heavenward, an eye roll and a prayer for patience. As much as I'd wanted to vent to him, Tessa's words rang in my ears— blaming my hesitation, saying I was creating problems with Max. How could I repeat that to him and explain?

"No. She's clearly having a blast in Tulum." I said it as snottily as I could muster. *Tu-loooom.* I didn't even have a passport.

Tessa had posted a picture of the ocean water like blue agate, captioned: *View | Tulum | 12.24.* The luxurious beauty of it and her nonchalance made my point for me. It felt like an intentional slap in the face. Before it, I'd been expecting an apology text. Now I didn't even want one.

"Janie," Max said. "You really can't tell me what happened?"

If I told him that Tessa and I'd fought about college next year, about her mixed-up priorities and her obliviousness about money, he'd take it personally. Max was about to leave for a nice vacation himself. I had almost cried spending twenty-five bucks to replace my black work shoes, rubber soles worn down from the past six months at Cin 12. "It's best friend stuff."

"I know, but . . ." He sat back.

"It's fine. We'll talk when she gets home. If she's not too busy with Laurel."

"Paige," he said, surprised at me. "She's just doing what she thinks is best for her."

"And I'm happy for her. I know distance is hard," I said, voice cracking. "That doesn't mean you alter your life's whole path."

"It doesn't mean that for *you*." He said it gently, but I knew what he meant: I wouldn't change my plans for him. Not college and not even an internship that I'd chosen over QuizBowl. But I couldn't do this—not here, not now. Not under gauzy Christmas tree lights, with my perfect present.

"C'mon," I said, climbing up. "She'd never admit it, but Cameron totally has her heart set on you decorating cookies with her."

I held out my hand to him, and he took it.

CHAPTER TWENTY-TWO

The day after Christmas was a Cinema 12 nightmare. Every showing of every movie, packed. We sold out of Reese's Pieces, which is how I learned what a grown man's hissy fit looks like. My back ached, and I longed for my pajamas in a way that felt like hunger, like thirst.

Somewhere after the halfway point of my shift, in the sea of grumpy, scrunched-up faces, I spotted Max. He mimed drinking and thumbed behind him, toward Alcott's across the street. I wanted to cry from the relief of his familiar face and the possibility of getting away from the madness. I held up a finger and grimaced toward the clock, and he nodded.

"Your ticket machine out front isn't working," the next man in line began. "It's just ridiculous. I bought tickets online, and—"

Max got to the front eventually, and I nearly whimpered. "Gosh, you're a sight for sore eyes. I didn't think I'd get to see you before your flight."

"Figured it might be a rough day here. You get a break, right?"

"Yeah. Eventually."

"I'll hang to the side," he said.

Hunter appeared a few minutes later, looking fresh. Untainted by the past four hours of mayhem. He had, of course, persuaded Donna to schedule him for a shorter shift. I gave him a helpless, harried look.

"Go," he said, slipping behind the counter. He'd brought my winter coat from the break room. "Get out of here. I've got it."

"I have never been happier to see you," I muttered.

"Now, that's saying something! Considering my face." He held my coat open like this was a between-scenes quick-change in the wings of a theater, and I slid my arms into the sleeves.

"Back in thirty," I said, fastening buttons, hurrying on my way.

"Merry Christmas, The Boyfriend!" Hunter called to Max. Then, to the restless crowd, "Sorry, folks! Quick change of elves. Let's keep things merry for you, shall we? Next!"

I followed Max, who was walking a step too fast for me. Snow had started to fall over the parking lot, tiny white feathers against black sky. When we reached his car, I looked up, dots of cold pecking my cheeks. Max had his hands shoved in his pockets, looking perplexed.

"You okay?" I asked.

"Yeah."

"Max."

"Sorry. That guy is just . . ." He gestured back to the theater. "Very obviously into you."

THE MAP FROM HERE TO THERE   211

It took a second to register, and I almost laughed. "Wait, *Hunter*? He is definitely not."

"Okay," Max said, sarcastic. I'd heard Max's sarcasm plenty, but never *at* me—never to dismiss something I said.

Suddenly, I couldn't feel the cold anymore. Heat scanned down my body, a warning flash. "Are you being serious?"

It was partially a rhetorical question, directed at his behavior. But *was* he serious? He thought Hunter was into me? Hunter Chen, who once called me "indoor recess in human form."

"You know he is, Paige." He sounded genuinely frustrated. Hurt, even.

"That's his personality with everyone. He'd try to charm a *mannequin*. It's, like, a hobby for him. Ask him! He'll tell you."

It was hard to form a coherent defense when I was so baffled. Why would he start this fight when I was at work? When he was leaving for almost a week? When I'm caught so off guard that I don't know what to say?

"I don't think of myself as a jealous person," Max said. "But I'm not sure at what point I'm just being dumb."

My exhale puffed out, the breath a cloud in the cold air. I closed my eyes, trying to visualize all the parts of this argument, charting how we'd arrived here. "It feels like you're accusing me of something. Like you don't trust me."

He shook his head, alarmed that I'd think that. But how could I not? "I do. I just . . ."

"Okay." I took both his hands, trying to channel my feelings to him like warmth. The Cinema 12 marquee reflected in his glasses, obscuring my view of him. "Then trust me. It's maximum Max over here. No one else."

"Okay." He shook his head, snowflakes bright on his dark hair. "Yeah. Sorry."

"It's fine," I said, though I still felt puzzled.

He kissed my cold nose. "Let's get you some food."

"Could you take the side exit?" I asked as I buckled myself in. And simply because I didn't want to delve into the remnants of my car accident, I added, "It's usually faster with the timing of the light."

"Really?" Max said. "Huh."

On the outside, we had a brief, nice coffee date before he returned me to work.

Internally, I retreated. I spent a lot of time with Hunter out of necessity—we were together with time to kill at work, and that meant I sometimes wound up telling him things. He was an unbiased third party. And then, right as Max and I were walking out the front doors, my phone buzzed. Hunter, clearly texting from a phone hidden in his pocket.

Donna got herr don bee late

I glanced at the message, mouthing the words as I deciphered. "Ah. Hunter warning me that Donna's back from break."

Max laughed—a sound with sharp corners. "I mean, you do see where I'm coming from, right?"

"Not really," I said, honest. "You and Tessa text all the time."

"She's your best friend."

"Make friends with Hunter, then!" I said. Max glanced around, fearing bystanders. It wasn't like me to cause a scene, but more and more, I couldn't find it in me to care.

"I don't get the impression he wants to know me, Paige, considering that I don't merit a first name."

We climbed into his car, the too contained space like a pressure cooker. I crossed my arms so defiantly that it seemed like they should make a sound—a clank as I closed myself off. Max went through the main intersection, and I squinted my eyes shut, pretending I was somewhere else—anywhere else. Part of me waiting to be rocketed sideways, Max's car T-boned. Part of me praying he wouldn't notice my fear, lest I have to reveal every undreamy fixation that my brain compiled.

By the time he pulled in to park, Max's side of the car had eased. He turned all the way to me, twisting in his seat. "So, um, apparently I've been bottling this up, and it all came out at once. You started hanging out with him, and then all of a sudden you seemed more excited about IU, and Ryan's brought up the idea of rooming with him? And . . ."

"I've always liked IU," I pointed out. "You do, too!"

"I know. But have you seen that dude, though?" Max said, trying for levity. "He's like . . . one of those guys in teenager magazines at the grocery store."

"Teenager magazines?" I stifled a smile. Oh, Max, talking about heartthrobs like someone's grandpa. And maybe he had a point. If he spent a lot of one-on-one time with a beautiful girl I didn't know—one who was really great to him—I might not *love* that.

"And I kept thinking, I'm going to leave for a week, and you're here with him, and—"

"Excuse me," I said, the anger rumbling back up. "You think the only thing keeping me from being a cheater is your relative proximity to Cin 12?"

"Well, no, but—"

"Okay," I said, one hand up and final. "I'm about to be late. I hope you have a good trip."

"Paige," he said. "I'm sorry."

"I'm not mad," I said, surprised to find that it was true. I felt . . . sad and defeated, a little hurt. "Text me when you land."

"I will," he said, and I pulled my coat around me, to head back into the bedlam.

We were sweeping up one of the last theaters, finally in a lower gear, when Hunter said, "You're quiet."

"Mmm." I reached down for a discarded candy box, M&M's still rattling inside. Honestly, who didn't finish their movie theater candy? Who didn't take it with them? "Not a great day. Week."

"Aw. Shitty Christmas?" He glanced up, excited. "Hey, there's your holiday movie title. Trademark Hunter Chen."

In other circumstances, I would have remarked that "shitty Christmas" was basically an entire subgenre of film. But I just smiled wanly, unable to muster the energy for casual conversation.

He was still looking at me—I could feel it. "You wanna talk it out?"

I tried to say *No, thank you.* I really did. But when I opened my mouth, instead of answering like a calm and rational person at her workplace, I began gushing out words like a three-tiered fountain of emotional repression. "It's just that I'm upset about stuff with Max, and I'm upset about stuff with Tessa, and I'm starting to think I must be doing something wrong because I'm the common denominator there, right? Everything is falling apart, and also senior year is somehow already halfway over, and—"

"Whoa, Hancock. Hey." He sat in a nearby seat and tugged me down beside him.

"Sorry." I wiped my face frantically, clearing evidence of my outburst. "God, this day completely wrecked me."

"It sucked." Hunter leaned in, elbows on his knees as if he were sitting in the dugout. "Okay. One at a time here. What's going on with Max?"

Obviously, I couldn't tell him about today's bickering match. Besides, I'd spent the past few hours wondering if some bigger issue lurked beneath Max's gripes about Hunter. Hunter's presence was an easy problem to latch onto, more immediate.

"I don't know." I threw my hands up, embarrassed to sound like such a dramatic person. "We're *off*, and I can't figure out what I'm doing wrong."

"You want my advice?" When I nodded, he frowned thoughtfully. It warmed my mood a bit, that Hunter Chen would take my problems seriously. "Keep fighting. It means you're trying to get your side out there, that you care."

"Keep fighting?" I scoffed. Clearly he didn't know that part of that fight was about him.

"Look, I don't really know Max. But I know you, and I know the way you talked about him all summer."

It felt like a long time ago, when our idea of the future extended only to being back in the same city. Everything revved toward that, the anticipation. Now we were angled toward next fall, parting ways. Or at least, I was.

Hunter turned, a sad smile. "You don't want to wonder whether you left it all on the field."

It seemed simple when he said it that way.

"Yeah," he said, more sure this time. "Trust me on that."

"Is Julia home for the holidays?" I hadn't wondered about her until this moment because apparently this was Paige Is a Jerk to Her Friends Week.

"She is," he said, unreadable.

"Are you going to see her?"

"Probably on New Year's. Friend-group overlap. You know." Defeat looked out of place on Hunter Chen's handsome face, and I hated dragging his mood down with me. "I think she's going out with someone at school. He's shown up in a few pics."

I knew how to get a smile out of him, and I only hesitated because I could hear Max's voice, accusatory. And it was partially out of lingering annoyance that I said, "Well, I bet you're better looking."

He pointed a finger at me, like he knew exactly what I was doing. After a moment, he smiled. "It's true; I am."

———————

For the next few days, a dusting of snow made the world seem quiet, and I went quiet inside myself, too. I texted with Max, but only surface updates, and I chatted with Maeve at length.

I knew Tessa was home by now, but I hadn't heard a word from her. Her Christmas gift sat wrapped on my dresser, a painful reminder festooned in gold paper.

After I finished with Maeve, I wandered downstairs. My dad had taken Cameron to spend a gift card somewhere, and my mom was on a step stool, straightening a drop cloth on the countertops. The paint cans were popped open and waiting.

"Hey, sweetie," she said. "How was your chat with Miss Maeve?"

"Good. Can I paint with you?"

"Sure. You want to prime that section?" She pointed near the sink.

Lately, she'd taken to wearing silk scarves that belonged to my grandmother, tied neatly around her neck or, like now, pushing her hair back like a headband. We worked in silence, under the sounds of NPR on an old radio my dad dredged up for her. After I rolled the first few stripes of primer evenly, my mom nodded approvingly, and I took my moment.

"Did you have a boyfriend when you left for college?" I knew she had a boyfriend or two in high school, one longer relationship in college. But she never shared details, and I'd never wondered before.

"I did. Pete Warner."

She said the name as if it contained all necessary information.

"When did you break up?"

The pause she took—I knew it well. She'd paused like this many times in my life: when I asked why swear words were bad if they were only words, when I asked if getting your period hurt. When I asked anything that didn't have a straightforward answer.

"About two months into college," she said finally.

My mom, by all observation, enjoyed telling me what to do. Curfew. Rules. Various and sundry nagging. And Lord knew, she was always asking about Max and me. So why, when I actually wanted her suggestion, was she making me work for it?

"Gotcha." I tried to mask my disappointment, but my voice sagged down.

"He and I . . . we had a fun time together," she said. "But it wasn't a very deep connection. It didn't hold up when we were apart. Not meant to be, that's all."

Did Max and I have a deep connection—is that what she was saying? If someday I had a teenage daughter of my own and she asked about my high school boyfriend . . . would Max be an old memory, a name I hadn't said aloud in years? That seemed unfathomable, Max Watson as a footnote in my life story. Besides, our relationship *did* hold up apart—three summer months that felt steady and good.

I sighed again, closing my eyes for a moment. "Tessa's officially going to that school in Chicago."

She nodded, like it all made sense, but she didn't look away from her painting. "Ah. Near Laurel?"

"Yeah."

"She was considering LA and New York before, right?"

"And Nashville." I mean, this wasn't just about me. "It's not like her, right? To base a decision around someone else."

"Hmm." My mom kept her lips together, mulling. "She's excited about the program?"

I idly swiped more primer, stretching up as far as I could reach. "Yeah. I guess it's kind of an alternative school. Which is great. But, like, if you were Tessa's mom, wouldn't you be worried?"

She raised her eyebrows, and I hoped that meant she was stumped. Like, as a mother, she had to admit this was a bad idea. "Well, to be fair, I'm always worried."

The comment was meant to put me at ease, but I couldn't be deterred.

"Don't you think it's going to end badly?" I prodded. God, I was being so transparent, trying to pry my mom's opinion into my own. Desperate for the win. "What kind of friend would I be if I glossed over that?"

"You know what I think?" She smiled, a bit sadly. "I think this isn't the last time you'll approach a major life decision differently than Tessa. Or any of your friends."

I wanted to mumble about this cop-out answer, but even I had reached the limit of my bratty streak. I felt my shoulders droop.

My mom continued. "You wouldn't base your college decision around Max—I know that. Partially because of who you innately are and partially because, well . . . half your childhood, you had a single mom."

"True." And I absorbed a few important things: that my mom had a happy life without partnership, and that she had independence through work she cared about. I wanted those things. I prioritized those things.

"Tessa's grown up with her parents' relationship as a bedrock for what happiness looks like in adulthood. Does that make sense?"

So had Morgan, with her so-in-love-it's-gross parents. Kayleigh and me, not so much. I nodded, considering this. "I'm not a total cynic—maybe she and Laurel will be together forever! I just don't want her to lose her whole self in it."

"I know," my mom said. "But maybe trust Tessa to know herself and her priorities, eh? It sounds like she'd love this school regardless of Laurel."

I sulked a little, loathing to be wrong. After a moment, I sighed and looked up at the cabinets, blocks of streaky white soaking in. I'd have to go grovel.

"I'll finish it," my mom said. "It's okay. Go."

"Thanks," I said.

Instead of giving me a directive to return before dinner or wear a coat, my mom—was I imagining it?—looked a little proud of me.

"We don't have ice-cream sandwiches," she said. "But I'm willing to donate two of my Klondike bars to the cause."

When we were little, Tessa saw a movie on vacation that we'd promised we'd see together when she got home. She wanted to see it again anyway, but my tender fourth-grade feelings were still hurt. She came over to apologize with two melty ice-cream sandwiches in hand, and it had been a tradition ever since. We just didn't often have occasion to apologize to each other these days.

I walked the line of trees between our neighborhoods, wet leaves glomming onto my boots. The cold kept the ice cream from melting, though I longed to put my hands in my pockets.

Tessa's parents had video security, and I held up the Klondike bars to the camera. She must have checked the screen because, opening the door, Tessa looked unsurprised. Her skin was tan and freckled against an oversize cream sweater, and she'd wrangled her curls into a loose braid. Truly, I aspired to this level of weekend loungewear instead of flannel jammie pants and faded T-shirts from random middle school events.

"I was a jerk," I said.

She leaned her head against the doorframe, appraising me. "Maybe a little. But I bit back way too hard."

I lifted one shoulder. Sure, her words punctured like darts, but mostly because they hit the bull's-eye.

"And I do know . . . ," she began, trailing off with a sigh. "I do know that my life is cushy. I'm really trying to own that and, like, figure out how to put it to use."

I nodded, hearing Laurel in between her words, the rests between the notes. The conversations, slow and steady, that become the ways love changes you. "Mine is too, honestly. But I got jealous. I got jealous that you have a set plan."

"You got jealous." She laughed, blowing a curl out of her face. "*I* got jealous of you in New York."

I furrowed my brows. She did? "But when you visited in June, we had such a good weekend."

I'd wanted to laugh-cry in relief to have the person I knew best in a city I'd only just met. I'd introduced Tessa to my new friends like an overeager kid at show-and-tell. After that, Tessa and I camped out in her hotel room, switching intensity between elation about her new girlfriend and the pressing issue of coming out to her parents.

"I know," Tessa said. "But you were so clearly clicking with Maeve and everyone. And I don't know any of that film stuff."

She stared down at her bare feet, toes painted burgundy. Had I ever seen Tessa McMahon look embarrassed? She was . . . jealous. Or at least, taken aback to see me fit in somewhere other than with her. Before I could explain how no one—including Maeve—would ever supersede our lifetime of friendship, Tessa held up a hand and repeated, like she could hear my thoughts, "No, I know."

If she'd gone off to New York and made a new close friend—found a future that excited her—I would have been sucked into jealousy like quicksand. But I always thought Tessa was impervious to envy like that. "I should have thought about that."

"Nah," she said. "I should have gotten over myself. I'm happy for you."

"I'm happy for *you*," I said. "About Tate. I really am."

She held out her hand, waiting for the ice cream offering, which I placed in her palm. Then she stepped back and opened the door for me.

CHAPTER TWENTY-THREE

New Year's Eve, we'd always lounged at Tessa's house. But the List dictated a New Year's Eve party, so I shimmied into a silver dress drudged up in the messy Target clearance aisle. Tessa got us tickets to a local band showcase at the Carmichael, and I got a rare, one-night curfew extension. But Max was still skiing, so it's not like I had someone to kiss. And it's not like he would have danced with me anyway.

But I liked the music so far, and I liked Laurel's friends from home, who were mingling with us, laughing. My mind tugged toward Max again, the unsettledness I still felt between us. Fanning my face, I stepped toward the bar.

Laurel sidled up to me. She'd swept her box braids into a bun, showing off a low-backed velvet dress. "Having fun?"

"Yeah! I know cover bands are supposed to be cheesy or something, but I'm into them!"

"Me too!" Her smile was bright, but I could feel her hesitating—waiting for something. "So, uh, I heard you and Tess went a couple of rounds about Tate."

She mimed fisticuffs, punching the air gently, and I wanted to sink into the sticky cement floors. I pressed my hands against my face. "Oh God. I'm so sorry. I hope you don't think that had anything to do with—"

"Sorry?" Laurel leaned her elbows on the bar. "I was going to thank you."

"Thank me?"

"Yeah! I was freaking out about Tess going to school in Chicago." I recoiled in surprise, and she laughed happily at my shock. "I was thrilled, too. But I didn't know if she was going because of me. What if I want to transfer schools in the future? What if she hates the school or the city and resents me for it? What if the choices put so much pressure on our relationship that it breaks?"

That sounded familiar. "Oh my God. *Yes.* Exactly."

"Plus, Northwestern is something I worked really hard for! Chicago feels like *my* thing, even though I want Tess there with me every second."

"No, I *totally* get that. Completely."

"But since you brought it up with her, we talked it out. I mean, maybe you didn't approach it perfectly . . ."

"I did not," I confirmed, and she laughed again.

"But we had a great talk, and I feel solid about it now."

"I'm glad. Not my finest hour." The bartender plopped two waters in front of us, and I left two bucks on the bar—something I'd learned from watching Tessa. "Is it hard being long distance?"

"Sometimes. I'm trying not to grip too tightly, you know?"

Laurel opened her hand, as if setting a lightning bug free. "Because that'd be desperation at work. I'm trying to give her room. Give myself room. And hope that this keeps being what we both want."

"That's good advice," I said.

Seconds before midnight, the countdown mounted higher and higher, voices rowdy. I stood in the center of it all, still. Why did this feel like a seismic shift, from 11:59 p.m. to midnight? One year was always becoming the next anyway, and this was only one calendar, one way of counting. But suddenly, it was here: my graduation year, the year I'd leave home. I sent Max a kiss emoji, lost for any other shorthand to convey how I felt.

Incongruous. That's how I felt. Sulking in a glittery dress, worrying about the future while standing in a celebration of now.

Kayleigh slung an arm over my shoulder, smacking a kiss onto my cheek before racing to join Tessa and Laurel near the stage. The cover band shrieked into a Queen song.

Morgan stayed behind, close to me. "You missing Max?"

"Something like that." I clasped her hand. I wasn't sure if she even remembered talking to me about fertility in a stranger's bathroom, but I kept my promise not to bring it up. Still, I couldn't un-know the fact that my friend was hurting.

She squeezed my hand. "He'll be home soon."

We'd been in touch, of course. Ryan's sister brought her boyfriend, the first outsider to get an invite. (Max liked him.) Max's mom seemed relaxed, which made Max happy. (She beat him in Scrabble, which made him mad.) Max loved the slopes. (Ryan wiped out hard on a snowboard but sustained only ego and tailbone bruises.)

Ryan had posted a photo of Max in the hot tub yesterday, glasses off and glancing at the backdrop of snow-capped hills. Only his shoulders were visible, so it wasn't a scandalous pic. Ryan had, however, captioned it: *YOU'RE WELCOME, PAIGE!* By the time I saw it after work, Max had already commented *When did you even take this, creep?* and our friends had left a series of enthusiastic, teasing messages.

For a brief moment, everything felt normal. Like summertime, like we were a given. Before complications crawled in like vines overtaking a garden.

A text came in, the same kiss emoji returned to me. *Miss you, girl.* I imagined him in the ski lodges I'd seen in movies, crackling fires and hot toddy. Ryan singing "Auld Lang Syne," probably. Bing Crosby making late-night sandwiches.

Come back to me soon, I wrote. A text, a benediction, a New Year's wish. As I sent it off, I closed my eyes and saw flashes of the year I'd left behind, an Oscars reel in my mind. Losing my grandmother. Plummeting off the deep end, racing after Max. New York. Every long hour at the cinema, every hour hunched behind my computer writing. Staggering out of my battered car, Hunter's arm braced around me. Struggling to breathe, to calm my mind.

For being the same 365 days as any other Gregorian calendar year, my God—what an incredibly long year it had been. Four months until May 1, when college decisions would be final. I looked down at my silver dress, at the girl I was right now, the one who'd worked so hard on her portfolios and aimed high. I thought of the lost, grief-stricken Paige of sophomore year and the hesitant junior Paige, baby-stepping out of her comfort zone. What was I doing now, side-lining myself and watching the fun from afar? That wasn't me—not anymore.

I squeezed Morgan's hand again, and she looked over, eyes pulled from the crowd she'd been watching contentedly. For the briefest moment, I hesitated, thinking of Max's disinterest at Homecoming. "Wanna dance?"

Morgan gave me a look, eyes bright beneath the purple mascara she used on special occasions. "Um, only always."

CHAPTER TWENTY-FOUR

You think you understand reluctance. You think you have procrastinated before. But not until second semester of senior year do you truly understand the depths to which you, a supposedly good student, can sink.

I was less "reading" *Beowulf* than "dragging my eyes across the words of" *Beowulf*. I reminded myself that this was foundational literature. That Seamus Heaney translated it, and I liked his poetry. That once I managed to craft a coherent paper, I could move on to Kate Chopin and Toni Morrison.

Alcott's was Kayleigh's idea, since she still had a house full of wedding prep and brothers, who weren't due back to Bloomington till Monday.

"I'm done," Kayleigh announced from behind her laptop.

I glanced up. "With the whole paper? Already?"

"Oh my God." She gave me a look of genuine disgust. "*No.* With homework, as a concept. With high school."

Tessa removed her headphones. "Did Morgan ever text?"

"She said she's working on research. I assume with Gabby."

Morgan and her Empower cofounder had been doing a deep-dive into curricular change, into precedents set by other states and what their options were.

"Okay, I'm going to say it." Kayleigh had fire in her eyes, or at least, the look of a girl about to set something aflame. "I think Morgan's hiding a boyfriend. Or a crush, anyway."

Tessa blinked at her, considering whether to indulge the accusation.

"Nope," she decided, looking back down at her laptop.

Kayleigh pointed her stare at me, and I sighed. "Fine, I'll bite."

"Consider the facts: last weekend, we're at that New Year's concert with a smorgasbord of hot guys, right?"

Smorgasbord? "Gross. But I guess so."

"And did Morgan bring her flirt A-game?"

I remembered Morgan looking . . . content. Relaxed. "No?"

"What's with the question mark at the end of that statement? No! She did not. Not even *close*."

"She was a little mellow, maybe."

"That was Morgan's prime hunting ground. I'm telling you, something is up. Secret. Boyfriend."

"That's quite a leap you took there," I said. "The track team could use you."

"I'm not kidding," she insisted. "Something's up. I can feel it."

We all went back to work.

Ryan stopped by, still in his workout clothes, and slid into our booth. He'd barely said hello before I felt him looking at me. "Are you and Max still in a fight?"

I didn't look up from my computer. "We were never in a fight."

God, the irony of Ryan getting on my nerves at Alcott's, the site of my first real interaction with him last year.

"You and Max got into a fight?" Kayleigh asked, and I acted as if I hadn't heard her. "About what?"

"No idea," Ryan said, hands splayed. "But I shared a room with the guy over Christmas break. A real treat, let me tell you. Very merry."

I could feel Tessa looking at me, surprised that I hadn't told her.

Kayleigh's gaze drifted off, as if she was solving a riddle. "I didn't see you guys together all week."

"Yeah. We're both busy." It wasn't a lie. Max had QuizBowl, robotics, tutoring, college visits with his mom, babysitting the Kelly kids. I had work, more work, and now the play. "We're fine. Promise."

And we were. He came by the cinema on Wednesday night to drive me home and was perfectly nice to Hunter, even. He was babysitting tonight, and I'd see him tomorrow.

Tessa left early, citing a photography assignment in the morning, so Kayleigh drove me home. I didn't notice the diversion in route until we were already in Morgan's neighborhood.

"What are you doing?" I asked. She'd slowed the car, the driving equivalent of a tiptoe. We were almost to Morgan's house.

"Seeing if someone's here. A boy."

"You dragged me on a *stakeout?*" I demanded, piecing this together. "I'm an accomplice?"

I held a hand out at the empty driveway. Morgan's bedroom light was on upstairs. "This is *bananas*, Kayleigh. What is going *on* with you?"

She leaned against the headrest, groaning. "I thought maybe Morgan was . . . It sounds stupid to say it."

I turned as much as I could in the passenger seat, intrigued. In the yellow light of the streetlamp overhead, she winced, hesitating. "Last time you saw Morgan and Reid together, were they weird?"

I'd seen them at Kayleigh's house in late summer. I did remember Reid making a crack about a CNN correspondent that I didn't get, and sure—Morgan laughed in a sort of starstruck way. "Weird how?"

"Come on. Flirty."

"With each other? No. They were . . . I don't know, like they always are. You think . . ." I stared at my friend, flabbergasted. "Oh my God, you thought Morgan was secretly dating your brother?"

"I don't know! They've been all buddy-buddy since summertime."

"They have common interests—advocacy and all that. Morgan looks up to him."

"Mmm, I dunno," Kayleigh said, tapping a finger to her temple. "I can *sense* something there. It is gross and it is wrong, but it is there."

I would have laughed except that her tumult sounded so genuine. For some anxious people, worst-case-scenario thinking was a disaster. But it helped me to assume the worst and come up with a plan based on that. "Okay, say you're a hundred percent right. They're together and hiding it from you."

"Jesus Lord," Kayleigh muttered, puffing her cheeks out like barf was imminent.

"Would it really be so bad? I mean, they're both old souls. Cheesy. Into politics . . ."

"Yes, Paige! It would be so bad. What would I *do* if they broke up? I can't avoid my own brother. And I'd *never* cut ties with Morgan. So what would I do?"

"Keep your relationships with them separate? I don't know. What would you do if Max and I broke up?"

She gasped. "Don't joke about that!"

"I'm not." But nice to know how us parting ways would go over. "It's a thought exercise."

"Well, then . . . easy—pick you. I love that guy, but if he wronged you, I'd feed his comic collection to a pack of wolves."

"No, you wouldn't."

She pursed her lips. "You're right. I'd keep the *Ms. Marvel*s."

"You know what I'd want you to do?"

"What?" she grumbled.

"Be glad that two people you care about made each other happy for a while. A little of that is better than none. Trust me."

I had played that dark game sometimes, when my grief for Aaron was still a wound, barely stitched closed: Would I walk away from him, that first day we met, if I knew the shattering that would follow? No. I really wouldn't. I was glad to know him, to witness him for even that short amount of time.

"But you and Max are okay, right?" she asked. God, her hopeful voice, like Cameron's years ago, after hearing our parents fight.

"Yeah," I said, and I sounded sure.

"Okay," she said. "You're right. Morgan would tell me if there's something to tell."

True to her word, she steered us away from Morgan's house. But she was gnawing into her lower lip, her gaze out the windshield more like a trance.

"Kayleigh. What?"

"It's not them," she said, waving one hand back down the street. "It's not *just* them, anyway. It's, um—it's that I miwanago a you see."

"What?"

She pulled up to a stop sign, braking, and said meekly, "I might want to go to UC. University of Chicago. I applied."

"Oh." That, I had not seen coming. "Not IU?"

"I mean, I *love* Bloomington. Obviously. But my mom went to UC. When I visited, I felt . . . connected, I guess." She glanced over quick, afraid to see my reaction. "I haven't told Morgan."

The pieces interlocked in my mind. Maybe on some

level, she'd hoped Morgan was keeping something from her. Because she was keeping something from Morgan.

"Kayleigh. C'mon. It's Morgan." I said. "She'll understand."

"I know," Kayleigh said. "But we've planned on IU together for years. And I'm going to topple that whole plan?"

I reached a hand out, stilling her. "How long have you been holding on to this one?"

"Months." She sighed. "Maybe years? In the back of my mind. I talked about it with Laurel some this summer. About wanting to be in a bigger city. And there's this historically Black sorority that I'm interested in, and I'd be close to Sawyer . . ."

"But then Morgan got her diagnosis . . . ," I guessed.

Kayleigh nodded. "And I know she's putting all her energy into the school board stuff, and I love her for it. But I see her hurting, you know?"

"I do know. But you can be there for her from afar, too." I reached over to touch Kayleigh's arm. "She will want this for you. I *swear*. I swear on my bookshelves."

Kayleigh faced me, pitiful. "On your shelf of favorites?"

"On my original copy of *The Goose Girl*," I said, eyebrows raised at the severity of this offer. "But maybe tell her via text, yeah? Give her a moment to react alone."

"Yeah," Kayleigh said. "Okay. I can do that."

I smiled at my friend, who was staring down at her lap. "Did you know that sometimes, when I'm unsure about a situation, I ask myself what you would do?"

"Really?" This seemed to perk her up.

"Really. Usually when I'm trying to be brave."

"I'm not always brave," she said.

"I know. But you usually try to go through with it anyway."

One side of her mouth lifted, a half smile. "Yeah. I do."

The next week, Ryan made his own addition to the Senior Year List with reservations at a little teppanyaki place he'd always wanted us to try.

"So," he said, raising his glass of water. "To our graduation year. And to never, ever applying to colleges again."

Kayleigh lifted her glass but said, "I mean, I'm probably going to get my MBA eventually."

"Yeah," Malcolm said. "As a philosophy major, I kind of have to get a PhD if I want to teach. And Max might go to med school, so . . ."

"Stop ruining it!" Ryan demanded, and he laughed as we clinked our glasses. "So, top-choice schools: let's hear 'em."

Max groaned, a sound that matched the sinking feeling in my stomach.

"Tate," Tessa said, though she didn't look my way.

Morgan named IU, and then smiled encouragingly at Kayleigh, next in line. After Kayleigh told her the truth, Morgan came over to my house, cried on my bed, and made me swear never, ever to tell her.

"UC." Kayleigh nodded, confident.

"Penn State?" Malcolm said. "I guess?"

Josiah said Corry Tech, where he'd study supply chain

management while working at his family's dry-cleaning business. Then it was down to only Max and me.

"NYU." I said it to get it over with. It seemed obvious, didn't invite any questions.

"Max?" Ryan prompted.

I could feel him tense up beside me. "Columbia, I guess."

"Ah, you guys are cute," Malcolm said. "Moving to New York, living the dream. Send us a postcard."

I took a sip of water, both to hydrate and to cover my expression. Max had probably named Columbia for the same reason I'd said NYU: to be done with the interrogation. But as the conversation moved on—speculation about dorms and roommates—I could feel myself sweating. And not because of the sizzling griddle in front of us.

I placed my napkin on my chair, excusing myself to the bathroom. There was no one in the stalls, so I paced by the sink, huffy breaths loud against a roomful of tile. Reeling in the panic that wanted to zap out of me like electricity. I looked wild-eyed, a spooked creature in the woods. Cold water—the ache in my hands tethering me to my body. There. Okay. I managed to breathe through my nose, slowing down. I'd just about handled it—quickly, I thought—when Tessa stepped in, brows furrowed.

"You okay? Is it your tummy?"

"Oh, I'm fine," I said. "Sorry."

She looked flummoxed. "Why would you apologize?"

"I don't know." I patted my cheeks, trying to cool them down, and then admitted, "I don't feel well."

"Physically?" she asked. "Or emotionally?"

That's what you get for cultivating a near decade of best friendship: the inability to hide, even when you want to.

"Both." I wiped my hands. "I should get back out there."

I could feel Tessa watching me in the mirror, searching for her move. "You have to tell him, Paige. Whatever it is you're thinking."

My eyes shot up and returned to my own reflection, which looked more miserable than I imagined myself. "I would, Tess, if I had any idea."

I let the door swing closed behind me. It felt like that god-forsaken nightmare, my feet welded to the bottom of a pool. In this version, my friends were reaching out their hands, and I was too panicked to clasp them, my grip just missing.

On the way home, I could feel the discord swelling. As soon as Tessa shut the car door, calling thanks to Max for the ride, he looked over at me. "So, we probably need to talk, huh?"

"About?" Good Lord, but I was a bad actress.

"Okay," Max said, eyes on the road. "I said Columbia so no one would ask any follow-up questions. It was the path of least resistance. Like we talked about, even if I get in, I don't have to go."

"I know," I said, throat tight.

He sighed. "Do you? Because it feels like the idea of me in New York is a full-on dystopia for you."

I wiped my face preemptively. *You have to tell him, Paige.* "Well, it's a no-win situation, isn't it? If I get into a school in California or New York, and you're in Indiana or Chicago or wherever, we don't stand much of a chance, right? But if you choose a college where I am . . ."

"See, this is the problem, Paige." He rubbed his forehead. "You're being so fatalistic about this."

"Well, I'm sorry," I said. "But when you grow up in a household where a relationship is painfully falling apart, you're sort of programmed to avoid idealism."

He looked around the car as if he'd been dropped into an alternate reality. "And what great love story do you think I grew up around? Why can't we just see what happens?"

"Because if I rely on you too much, I'll get blindsided!" Once I started, I couldn't stop. "It'll be great until I'm swamped with classwork and all of a sudden some pretty girl from your dorm sits by you in bio lecture, and she's glancing over when she thinks you aren't looking. And you'll notice her, and I'm not around enough, and it will *crush* me, Max. Or maybe! Maybe we'll end in a whimper, two people who can't reach out far enough, fast enough. And I'd rather keep our friendship forever than try to grip onto love for now. I don't know, Max! I don't know."

My heart hammered so loud that my hearing went fuzzy; that telltale pulsing spread down my arms, threatening to whoosh me into a full-blown panic attack. I wanted to keep going, to qualify the things I'd blurted out, but my brain could only chant the word: *Stop, stop, stop*, a command that my adrenaline ignored.

"Okay," Max said, worried. "Paige?"

"Sorry," I managed. *Tell him it's bad. Tell him your brain has*

places like the intersection outside Cin 12, where you can't go with-
out dissolving. Tell him that panic rears up when you think about
getting rejected from every college, about the car wreck and it-
could-happen-anytime death, about your parents breaking up
again when it's only Cameron living at home and you're not there
to support her, that falling in love with him has apparently made
other people think we're settled for life, and should you be with some-
one who won't dance, who won't balance you, are we too similar,
are we too different? "I'm sorry."

"It's okay," he said. "That's a lot to have going on. But there's no girl in my dorm, okay? There's not going to be."

"You don't know that," I said, genuinely surprised by his naïveté. "And I hate the idea of her. But I also hate the idea of holding you back."

We were in my driveway now, and Max put the car in park, then crossed his arms. "Or do you hate the idea of me holding *you* back?"

For all my imaginings—new friends in my film program, hopefully ones I'd like enough to introduce to Tessa, to Kayleigh and Morgan—I'd truly never thought of anyone but Max. "That has honestly not been a consideration."

"Really? Because it feels like you're searching for something. And I don't know what it is, but it's not me."

"I'm searching for something?"

"Going to parties, panicking about me applying to colleges near you, all the Hunter stuff."

"There *is* no Hunter stuff," I said, frustrated that he'd reduce it to that. "He's on your side of this, if anything."

The gap in conversation stretched too long, and his face darkened. "My side of what? My side of being into you? Because yes, I agree."

"If that were true, why would he tell me to stay in the game with you?" I gestured between us. "And I'm *trying* here."

Max's jaw locked and for an instant, I thought it was a moment of stunned revelation. Like, *Oh yes, my girlfriend is correct.* But now, now he was gritting his teeth, barely able to speak. "You talked to him about us? And, I'm sorry . . . you were considering exiting the—what was it?—the *game*? With me?"

"No. Just . . . after everything around Christmas." Okay, I could see how that sounded a little bad. "I couldn't exactly talk to Tessa about something like that. So, what were my options?"

"Why wouldn't you talk to *me* about it, Paige?"

"I'm talking about it with you now!" I flung my hands out wide. "And it's going *great*."

That's right, I could be sarcastic, too. I stuck the landing with an indignant look, expecting Max to lob another comment in return.

He shook his head at me, huffing out an exasperated sigh. "If you're going to break up with me, could you just get it over with?"

My chest deflated, empty of air. I sat stunned, both at his words and at the resignation in his delivery. "Is that . . . what you want?"

"No. God, no, Paige. But I can't keep doing this."

And I really, truly couldn't keep doing this either. Not after half a childhood full of tense silence, living in the wreckage of two people who held on for too long. The way they both resented themselves, each other.

"Okay," I said evenly. My jaw wavered, my entire body about to shake from holding back sobs. "I think we just need to cool down and sleep on it."

"Yeah," he said. "Sure. Let me know what you come up with."

My lips parted, ready to tell him that he could stop being jealous about Hunter. He could stop getting frustrated with me when I acted differently than he expected me to. He could fight with me and not shut down every time it got hard.

For the first time, I couldn't look away from the truth: this might be a broken thing. Damaged by, as Tessa so delicately put it, my hypotheticals and hesitation.

"I'll text you tomorrow?" I hadn't meant to whisper it. But I didn't have enough air left for much more.

He nodded, unable to look at me.

After I walked inside, I waited by the door. Hoping that he'd charge out of the car, past the jumble of the words and feelings we'd tried to exchange, and straight to me. But when I got the nerve to look out the window, I saw only taillights.

We stood like two distant hearts on a too big map. The dotted line between us grew ever farther, a distance no longer easy to walk. My hands ached to grab us both, to push us together where we belonged. But it didn't work like that.

I stood there for minutes or hours, crying noiselessly. Absorbing the sound into my chest as I leaned against the door.

"Paige?" I barely heard my sister's voice.

When I turned, she was frozen on the stairs, watching me like she'd spotted a ghost. And maybe I was, stuck in purgatory between love and whatever comes next.

"What happened?" she asked, hurrying down.

"I don't know." I hung my head, pressing both hands to my eyes. God, hearing myself say the words made it hurt even worse. "Max and me—I don't know."

The hug surprised me, the jolt of touch as my sister squeezed me tight. I recovered fast, relaxing into a full-on snivel against her shoulder.

"Okay," Cameron said after a minute. "C'mon. I have cookies."

CHAPTER TWENTY-FIVE

When I arrived at Alcott's the next afternoon, Max was sitting in the back, fingers laced together. I felt ridiculous showing up here, my personal haven, to conduct a relationship forum. But it was neutral territory, away from eavesdropping parents.

I'd rehearsed my opening statement on the drive here in my dad's car. Cameron had stayed up late with me, asking probing questions and repeating *Mm-hmm, mm-hmm* until I wanted to flick her. But finally, she amassed all my responses to inform me I struggled with vulnerability. That bridling emotions was a form of control for me. Additionally, last night, I learned that my sister listened to quite the array of self-help podcasts.

So I'd tell Max, mortifying as it was, that people joking about us getting married had derailed me. That hearing "dream girl" became this pressure, this commitment I hadn't meant to make. But first, I'd say sorry for bumbling along the way.

Max looked up, noticing me. His hair was rumpled from—I knew—his hand passing through it, fidgeting. He looked exhausted, lilac beneath his eyes. "Hey."

"Hi." I sat down with nice posture, like I was on a job interview. "Max, I'm really sorry about last night."

"Me too. I've gone over it and over it in my mind. I barely slept." He spun one finger, signaling an endless circle. It was easy to imagine him awake and at his desk, scribbling equations into a notebook. If Paige = x and Max = y . . .

"Same here."

"Paige." He wet his lips, like his mouth was too dry to speak. "I think I've gotta let you go for a little bit."

He said it fast, like he had to get it out, and I couldn't quite register what he'd said. The world tilted on its axis. I braced my hands on the edge of the table, like I'd go flying from my chair. "What?"

"Hear me out." He had his hands raised, and I stared at his palms, at his love lines like shallow topography, etched rivers. "Paige?"

"Yeah," I said, to acknowledge I could still hear him. My body had gone clammy and cold, the café around us suspended in a blur.

"You don't want me to factor you into my college decision," he said. "And I'm trying not to. But if I'm being totally honest, it's hard to tell if I am."

"I know," I said, eyes filling. And I did know, because it was hard for me, too. I'd been thinking of IU so fondly since I visited with Morgan. But subconsciously, was that simply a desire to stay near my friends? And if so, was that even a bad thing? "So, you're ending our relationship over that?"

"No. Well, sort of. I think we should step things back until one or both of us make a decision about school. That way,

I can't factor you in because I won't know where you'll be anyway. And you won't feel any kind of pressure. It'll be like a gap year."

"A gap year," I repeated.

"Not a year, obviously. A month or two?" he said. I felt like I'd dunked my head beneath water, words gone garbled. I stared at the nearby coffee display, bags of beans in rows like squat soldiers. "Because I can feel myself making it worse for you. I'm not sure how, and I'm not sure what else to do about it."

My eyes filled with tears again. Hadn't my body rocketed into panic, tears, heaving when the college discussion came up? I'd wanted, so badly, to stop it. But here we were.

"We could just agree not to talk about college, right?" I said pitifully. But our friends were always in our business, with their little jokes. The heat of it, the pressure.

"We could, but . . ." He studied me. Under the table, his hand covered mine, resting on my knee. "What you said, that you'd rather have our friendship for life. That's how I feel, too, Janie. This needs a step back. Doesn't it?"

He said it so sincerely that a tear slipped over the rim of my eye. I'd tried to make him see me as Summer Paige, the girlfriend—fun, witty, someone he thought about happily. Not his friend Paige, who made basic interactions into emotional disaster zones and worried herself sick.

"So, do you think the gap year idea would help? Honest reaction." Max's voice was almost begging. "You can tell me no."

Wasn't this what I'd been asking for? To make separate decisions so I could breathe, focus on my own murky path forward? I dabbed the corner of my eye.

"You know, it's funny," I said, voice oddly calm. "Just last night, Cameron got me thinking about how I go straight to binary outcomes. This or that. Extremes."

Life or death. Together forever or painful divorce.

"Okay . . . ," Max said. He'd pulled his hand back. Now, one finger circled the face of his watch.

"And this gap year idea, it's an in-between," I said, nodding. Deciding at the moment I spoke the words. "It's not us ending things entirely or spinning our wheels trying to stay together. It's good. It's a good idea."

I had absolutely no idea if I meant it or if my brain was trying to save face on my behalf.

"It is," Max said, hesitant—nearly a question. Like he hadn't thought so until now.

"I think so." Finally, I could meet his eyes, pale green as hydrangea. "What would the rules be?"

"The rules?"

"Do we see each other? Talk at all?" He looked utterly mired, like he hadn't gotten this far into the thought process.

"Maybe not one-on-one. With friends."

"Do you . . ." I bit the inside of my lip hard enough to leave tooth marks. I clasped my hands, damp as they pressed into each other. "Do you want to go out with other people?"

"No." He leaned away, taken aback. "Do you?"

"No!" I swiped my hands out, an umpire's signal for

safe. Hunter had taught me that, and I dropped my arms guiltily. "No."

"But . . ." His eyes slid to the ceiling as he thought. "Oh God, I'm about to puke saying this. But if we don't put the 'go out with whoever' option on the table, I think I'm always going to wonder."

About other girls? Who?! I went wide-eyed, surely nearer to puking than he was. But no. He meant wondering if I was secretly harboring feelings for Hunter.

"Max, I would tell you," I said, and I meant it. I'd cry as I spoke, but I wouldn't lie.

He held the eye contact across the table, and I wanted to think he believed me. Or maybe he believed I was in denial, as I had been about him for much of last year.

"So, um . . . ," he said, "let me know, I guess, when you're closer to a college decision. I'll do the same. Then we'll reconvene and see where we are?"

Reconvene. Max. My arms ached to push the table between us aside. The idea of not texting him before bed, of not catching his hand in mine between classes.

"Okay. But." I swallowed, hard, fighting the wobbly pressure against my tear ducts. "What do we tell everyone? That we're cooling things off for a bit? And we'll leave it at that?"

"Yeah. We tell them we're fine, but not together. That we can both hang out with them."

"Okay," I said once more.

"Okay." He sat back, hands out like he was steadying himself. "So, um, I'm gonna go, then."

That couldn't just be it. Max and me and this love that felt written, as destined as anything I'd ever found. But he stood to walk away and, on his way past, paused. He took my hand, kissing it quick, as he said, "Hey. It'll be okay."

"I know," I lied.

It might have been the mildest, most loving way to part in the history of temporary breakups. So why did the divide between us feel like a canyon that could swallow up every good thing on earth?

We'd pulled the emergency brake, I told myself. That had to be better than flying off the edge, crashing something so precious in the rift below. But, if that was true, why did my heart feel totaled, smashed inside my chest?

I put my head down on the table and, not for the first time, cried into my arms on the back table at Alcott's, feeling completely tossed at sea.

CHAPTER TWENTY-SIX

The news hit our friend group like a stone hits water. Max and I suffered the impact most, but it rippled out wide. In some ways, their sadness and surprise comforted me. *You guys just need a breather,* Morgan said. *It's not a* breakup *breakup, right?* Kayleigh asked. Tessa stayed quiet mostly. She'd known the discord was building, felt the change like a drop in barometric pressure.

At work, I found relief in drudgery. In busyness and especially in the no-phone rule, which kept me from waiting for texts or obsessing over Max's social media. But I flinched at the sight of every teenage guy, tall with dark hair. I wished I could reprogram my entire nervous system, which felt automatic excitement at the possible sight of Max.

He'd been out of school at the end of the week, visiting colleges with his mom. He posted a picture of himself with a friend from his private school days, now a freshman at Notre Dame. He looked happy.

I looked like hell. Sleepless, defeated. I had no idea what Max was doing tonight, tomorrow night, or ever, and I hated it.

Hunter tried his best to cheer me up, which I noticed, appreciated, and also had no patience for.

"So, between the three actors on that poster," he said, pointing, "who would you screw, marry, and kill?"

I gave him a look. "That's crass."

"Oh, come on."

"Screw . . . ," I said, pretending to think, "this question."

"Okay, Sad Face, that's it," Hunter said, in a tone that suggested an announcement would follow. "My parents are out of town this weekend. I'm having a few people over tomorrow, and you're coming."

I stared at him, waiting for the stupidity of this idea to become apparent to him. When his expression remained confidently decisive, I gestured at myself. "Yes. Because what a great energy I'd bring to a party right now."

"That's the point!" He laughed. "Look, you need to ride it out—I get it. I know you'll be back to sad on Sunday morning. But take *one* night off this."

He waved his hand at my face, at my entire essence as a person. That's how it felt, anyway. I worried strangers could see sadness like a gray-blue aura all around me, like gloaming. Really, I should get extra credit on the *Wuthering Heights* unit for personifying both the moors and the angst.

But Hunter's friends hardly knew me, and they didn't know Max. I could pretend to be fine, and no one would remind me. No one would look at me with pity.

"I have no way of getting there."

"Bring your friends. Or I'll pick you up and drop you off myself." Before I could ask, he added, "Yes. I will stay fully sober at my own party to drive you home if it means you'll come."

I smiled at the offer, tempted.

"Come on," he said. "You can see my embarrassing childhood stuff. I had huge glasses in third grade. Huge. There are pictures."

"Okay."

"Okay?" he repeated, jubilant.

"Yeah, sure." I squinted one eye. "Why not?"

———————

Hunter's condo reminded me of my own house—not big and not fancy, but care in every folded throw, in every framed photo. As he gave me a quick tour, I felt like I'd been there before. Like we'd known each other as kids but drifted apart.

I felt the same way about his friends, who let me slide into their dynamic without a moment of awkwardness. They poured cheap vodka, razzed each other, demanded details about Lane's recent second date with a girl she'd met at the theater. They were completely cool when I declined a drink. After an hour or two of slow sipping and hanging out, Lane said, "Oh, hey! Let's show Paige our Twister!"

Their Twister, it turned out, was homemade—primary color circles drawn on a white vinyl shower curtain. Each spot meant a drink or a challenge. They let me observe the first round, and I tried to sit out the second, but the peer pressure became heckling.

"Paige!" Lane, last round's winner and therefore presiding Gamemaster, spun the dial. "Left foot blue."

I stretched to reach, my legs now bridged uncomfortably. I hadn't put my arms down yet. Lane read from the blue circle stack. "'Player must wear underwear on the outside of clothes for duration of the game.'"

Fortunately, I'd been prepared for this one, as a guy named Riley had been required to do this last round. He'd emerged with boxer briefs stretched over his jeans. I had a cute bra on anyway, so I chose to include that in the definition of underwear. In the bathroom, I fastened it over my T-shirt and tugged the straps back up my shoulders. I returned to the board with totally feigned confidence.

"Hunter," Lane said. "Right hand red."

Hunter looked down at the board. "Shit. How?"

There was only one way, and it involved Hunter being in a crab pose between my legs.

"Just do it," I said, hoping the command would cover up my embarrassment.

"He's gonna fall," one of their friends—Gabe—said, gleeful.

"I'm sober, dummy. I'm untouchable."

Sure enough, Hunter managed to twist himself between me and the dot he needed.

"Oh my God," Lane said, laughing. "Have we ever had this many hands and feet on the board without a fall? This is a record."

"Spin again!" Gabe yelled. "What's taking so long?"

"No yelling at the Gamemaster! Booty shake penalty!"

There was some movement near me as Riley groaned, "Oh, God, no. So close to my face."

The game broke up after Gabe dropped hard, taking half of us with him. They opted to play quarters, and I went to the kitchen for some water. On my way back, I poked my head into Hunter's room—he'd taken me in during the tour, so I figured it was okay. Unsurprisingly, Hunter's walls were papered in photos—friends squeezed close together, his brother and sister as middle-schoolers holding baby Hunter and recreating that photo at a recent wedding, a photo of a beautiful older woman in a cheongsam. Hunter and Lane, grinning and goofy in suits at a recent formal. I wondered if any of the pretty, smiling girls were Julia, the one who got away. I'd only been looking at the shelves for a minute when a gasp came from the doorway. "Trespasser!"

"I was promised the goods," I said, gaze sliding to Hunter. "And I've found them."

"Did you now?"

"Never, in all of our shifts together," I began, reaching for the trophy, "in all those hours, through every teasing comment . . ."

He covered his face with one hand.

I presented the trophy to him as if he didn't know its inscription. "Linwood Elementary Spelling Bee Champion."

"My first and only nerd achievement."

Dramatics, I knew. He did fine in school. "What word did you win on?"

"Elegy."

"I love that word," I said.

Hunter smiled. "Yeah? What other words do you love?"

Was he collecting intel—things he could tease me about later? Or did he really want to know? I didn't care. "Whimsy. It sounds like what it is. Smithereens. Sonnet. I love a lot of words."

He sat down on the edge of his bed as I put the trophy back on its shelf. "You feel any better?"

"I do." I sat beside him, the mattress dipping.

"No, you don't." He said it pleasantly, like he enjoyed my effort to fib.

I tipped my head back, and I realized, with some surprise, that my hair nearly reached my shoulder blades. "I keep trying to pinpoint where Max and I started going in different directions, and I just can't find the spot where our path forked."

I separated two fingers into a peace sign, trying to demonstrate a path forking, but it was too late. Hunter looked delighted. "*Oh.* This is about forking?"

"Shut up." I shoved his shoulder with mine. "God. No. It's everything else. I probably shouldn't even be here, for starters."

"Here?"

Normally, my thoughts made ten pit stops in my brain before exiting my mouth. Tonight, they bypassed all of the usual checkpoints and flew into the air. "Kinda drove Max nuts, us hanging out. Isn't that ridiculous?"

Hunter leaned back, elbows on the bed, casual as could be. "I dunno. Is it?"

My eyes shot to him—he wasn't confessing feelings for me, was he? His eyes went wide, hands splayed out. "Oh no. I don't mean—"

"No, I know!" I insisted, mirroring his gesture.

"But if I weren't hung up on Julia. And if you weren't still completely in love with Max . . ."

He paused, giving me space to correct him. I didn't. My feelings pointed at Max like a laser beam, direct and bright. But if I'd never met Max Watson. If our history didn't bind us, if my heart had space. Wouldn't I be smitten with Hunter? Wouldn't anyone be?

"We have fun," Hunter continued. "I think you're interesting and pretty. And, as you know, I'm extremely good-looking and talented."

I lagged my head toward him. "It's your modesty, really, that gets me."

"I'm just saying. That's not where I'm at. But it's not *ridiculous*. Is it?"

Well, when he said it like that . . . Hunter Chen and his big grin and his big heart, scooping me right up into his world. "No. I guess not."

Not ridiculous at all. So un-ridiculous, in fact, that I felt embarrassed to meet his gaze. There was a part of me that could see the whole montage: Hunter fast to pull me onto the dance floor at prom, his fun-loving side a counterweight to my hesitation.

Suspended in that strange, candid moment, I felt the choice so clearly. I could have kissed Hunter in that moment, and he might have kissed me back. Maybe it would have become more, our connection eclipsing older loves in the end. Hunter Chen was really something. But I wouldn't try to soothe my

THE MAP FROM HERE TO THERE   257

heartbreak with him, not at the expense of our good, easy friendship. And as I finally managed a small smile at him, I suspected he thought the same of me.

"Maybe give the guy a break, yeah?" Hunter clapped my back, nodding toward the living room. "C'mon. Let's have fun."

I didn't see the picture till after I'd climbed into bed. Lane had posted it hours before, their Twister board with a record-setting number of people still in the game. My head was thrown back in embarrassed laughter. At least from this angle, you couldn't tell my bra was outside my clothes. You could, however, see my legs spread over Hunter's precariously balanced pose.

I rocketed up, horrified. There was enough overlap between my friend group and Hunter's—someone would have seen it, maybe even Max. I dove into who followed Lane, deciphering my options. I could just text her to take it down, right?

But when I clicked to Max's account, trying to figure out if it was too late, I found a photo he'd posted. The QuizBowl varsity team, mid-celebration. It was a great shot—Malcolm and Sofia high-fiving, surprise on both their faces. And then there was Max, his open-mouthed grin an exact mirror of Aditi's—their profiles aligned as they locked eyes. They looked . . . close. Not only in proximity, but in connection.

It felt like taking a punch. Maybe because the photo was from a QuizBowl match, with Aditi in my former chair. But hadn't I chosen to walk away from it? Hadn't I chosen to walk away from Max?

I wasn't even sure when it was from. Did they have a match

after Max got home from Notre Dame? Was this before? I hated not knowing the whens of Max's life almost as much as I hated this picture, and I couldn't resist any longer.

Hey, how was Notre Dame?

Good. Really good.

Good.

This is what we were reduced to—Max and Paige and our bond that used to feel inevitable. "Good" had never felt so terrible.

Maybe texting isn't the best idea.

My jaw dropped open as I reread the words. Of all the cold-blooded power moves. To act like he didn't even want a quick check-in, a checking of our friendship's pulse. But fine. All connective tissue severed. A clean cut.

Yeah, you're right.

See you at school.

I stared down at the exchange. Why—*why?*—did I feel the tiniest bit of relief beneath my sadness? I'd been so fixated on the idea of losing Max eventually—eyes locked on when it would end, how much it would hurt. I finally knew: here and now, with words dissolving between us.

CHAPTER TWENTY-SEVEN

I didn't feel like talking—not in class, not to my friends, not to my mom. So the start of thrice-weekly *2BD, 1BA* rehearsals served me perfectly. Monday, Wednesday, and Friday afternoons, Tessa dropped me off at the nearest city bus stop and I rode downtown to Mythos. My dad picked me up after his evening class. Inside the rehearsal room, my role was essentially silence: listening closely, taking notes. Cris told me exactly what she needed, and I reveled in the straightforwardness. I was a runner, a task-doer, a list-keeper.

I knocked on the green room door, where one of the leads paced, memorizing lines.

"Hey, sorry to interrupt. They're almost ready for you."

"Oh, thanks!" Marisol hurried to the hallway with me. "You're Paige, right?"

"Right," I said. "Your audition was phenomenal."

"Oh. Thanks. The script really spoke to me, so . . ." Her dark eyes widened. "Ugh. That was such an actress-y thing to say. But it did."

I liked her for deflecting the compliment to the writer.
"Oh, I understand. For me, too."

We chatted on our way to Cris, who stood gesturing at the
taped-off floor where a couch would be.

"Hancock, can you duck in the prop room? Find a pizza
box? Or something similar in size and weight."

"Sure thing," I said, and I disappeared.

On Sunday afternoon, I arranged a hierarchy of work I had to
do: finish calc homework, study for a history exam, make a
dent in my English paper. I'd only gotten as far as cursing
Gottfried Leibniz and Sir Isaac Newton when I heard Morgan
arrive downstairs. She'd asked my mom to be a professional
mentor, as required by her Women's Studies final project. True
to form, Morgan was co-writing an op-ed for the school paper
about sex education reform.

The two of them settled into the kitchen table, and I sat
at the other end, laptop open to my English paper. As Morgan
explained her many resources and binder tabs to my mom,
I busied myself making popcorn. I'd seen her fired up before,
obviously, but this had the focused power of the sun through
a magnifying glass: a precise burning.

"Why had I never heard of PCOS or endometriosis?"
Morgan was saying. "I took an entire semester of health. Plus,
there's more from Gabby. Like, does our curriculum even
acknowledge queerness? Seriously."

"This sounds very close to you," my mom said. "That's

good. A human angle—a personal lens—can make a strong point."

Morgan glanced over at me, and I nodded, encouraging her.

"Yes." She pulled her shoulders back. "If you think it's helpful and appropriate for the article, I'm willing to talk about my personal diagnosis and all the frustration. Reid says it made a big difference when he was writing articles for the *Warrior Weekly*."

Sitting there, I couldn't resist opening a recent screenplay outline, one I was still dabbling with. A girl whose brother died in a drunk driving accident crusades for local reform. She joins forces with her brother's best friend and battles her own grief and anxiety along the way. It was a little bit me and a little bit each of my friends, the parts of our stories that might make other people feel less alone.

I wasn't trying to think about college. But there, at that table, my mind skipped off to that coffee shop in Bloomington and a seat there next year, across from Morgan. Rallying each other as we tried to turn the things that hurt us into something bigger than ourselves.

CHAPTER TWENTY-EIGHT

I always imagined being in my bedroom, on my laptop, when I received my first answer about college admission. Instead, I got the USC e-mail on my phone—notifying me that my status had been posted—while I was at Mythos. I sat down in a back row, shielded by the balcony's shadow. It felt full circle here, a place that reminded me of my grandmother. A username, a password, a breath held in so tightly that it ached.

An answer.

I scanned the first lines—*committee has reviewed applications carefully, most impressive pool of candidates to date*—until my eyes snagged on the word.

Unfortunately . . .

Of course. I knew that was coming, right? I was 99.99 percent sure.

Still. When people called it "the sting of rejection," they weren't kidding. It actually stung, like a slapped sunburn. I blinked back tears.

I am one hundred percent not going to USC. Another feeling swept through me, like a quick breeze on a stifling day. Finally, I knew one detail of my future with total certainty. And once that relief wriggled in, it expanded. I knew all the reasons I should have wanted this school; I knew the opportunities it held. Getting in would have been an incredible affirmation, and maybe I would have thrived.

But it was off the table.

God help me, I wanted to tell Max. It had been almost three weeks of our gap year, of wan smiles in the hallway and limited eye contact in group conversations.

No from USC, I texted Maeve, lump in my throat. I sent a frowny face, and immediately wished I hadn't. I didn't want her to feel guilty if she was accepted.

I'm rejected, too, Maeve said. *LOL-oh-well. We're meant for other greatness.*

I exhaled in relief, if guiltily. I'd wish Maeve well at any school; I'd keep working with her as long as she'd have me. But I did hope we landed somewhere together.

"You okay, Hancock?" Cris Fuentes was glancing down at me. I hadn't heard her enter, even with the clunky boots.

"Yeah," I said, sitting up from my sloppy posture. "Fine. Just a college rejection that I'm being a baby about."

"Ah," she said. "Been there. You're not a real theater kid until you have your own personal hiding spot for crying. C'mon. Let's go talk to the crew and find you something to hammer."

———————

USC was the jab. On Saturday afternoon, I took a hook to the jaw—a rejection from UCLA. I was on my laptop in my room for that one, the place where I'd written and rewritten my portfolio. This time, I didn't cry. I stared. I would not be living in LA.

Maeve got in, and I felt genuinely happy for her. But the reality of back-to-back rejections spread through me like darkness. The anxiety began to swirl, a galaxy churning. What if I didn't get into any colleges at all?

I cut the thought off, guillotined it in my mind. No. Tonight was Lane's eighteenth birthday, a giant bash with her entire Venn diagram of Oakhurst, Linwood, and college friends. I packed my overnight bag for Tessa's house, stuffing in a pair of ripped jeans and a black top I found secondhand in New York.

My parents were on the couch, deeply invested in their favorite murder-mystery show. They looked happy and innocent, unaware that their daughter was 0 for 2 on college applications. "Hey. I'm walking to Tessa's."

My dad glanced up, face bathed pale in the TV light. "Tell the girls we said hi!"

"Do you work tomorrow?" my mom asked.

"Yeah. Evening shift."

"Well, home from Tessa's before noon, okay? We'd like to see your face at some point this weekend."

"Aye-aye." I saluted, and I stepped out into the night.

THE MAP FROM HERE TO THERE 265

Lane took us up to her bedroom for her private stash—a shoe-box full of half-empty bottles. My aversion to drinking had always been powered, like so much of my life, by the fear of doing something wrong. Tonight, I welcomed misbehavior. Why not? Everything was already screwed up.

We raised a glass to the birthday girl and drank down our shots—all except Tessa, tonight's driver.

"Not bad," I said. The burning felt good—cleansing. Or maybe that was just the lemon aftertaste, vaguely like kitchen soap.

"Help yourself." Lane handed me the bottle. "I drank lemon vodka after a breakup last year, and now I can't stand it."

Meant to be. "Thanks."

A sip for USC, a swallow for UCLA, and a glug for the NYU rejection likely coming my way. Cheers. I drove the rest of my life into the ground for screen writing, and for what?

"Okay," Tessa said, on our way downstairs. "You're going to need to tell me what's happening with you. Is this Max stuff?"

I adjusted my top, lower cut than my usual oeuvre. Ha-ha, "oeuvre." What a snobby-ass little word. I didn't really know how to do makeup, but I'd swiped on eyeliner, dark and glittery as granite. I felt beautiful and terrible.

"Just trying to have fun," I said breezily. Or the way I imagined a breezy person saying it, anyway. And really, this was just a *yes, and* attitude. Accept what someone is giving you and give something in return. Life had given me some flat-out rejection, *yes. And* I was going to do whatever I wanted now.

The weird thing about lots of alcohol is that I figured it would go: *fine, giggly, a lot less fine, drunk, whoa really drunk.* But that night, it went: *fine, fine, fine, my face feels weird, you know what's funny is platypuses, hahaha woooo, oh God what have I done.* I would have considered this progression a mistake, except that I couldn't feel anything but sloppy-armed blurriness.

"Is, like, half the school at this party?" I asked Morgan, in a voice that might have been too loud. We'd moved to the kitchen, where I responsibly, in my opinion, sought out water. Kayleigh was nearby with an extremely cute guy leaning in to talk with her. Tessa, last I knew, was consulting on a party playlist. I'd seen Hunter briefly, holding court in the living room. He'd held up both hands, gesturing in a way that I interpreted as *I'll find you later.*

"Seems like it. And lots of people who graduated last year." She was looking down at her phone, texting rapidly, and I kept looking around at vaguely familiar faces.

Once, when I was in fourth grade, I lost my footing at recess and fell backward off the playground equipment. It wasn't a long fall, and I landed on a patch of grass. But something about the way my back met the ground—I couldn't breathe. I tried to gasp, but my diaphragm had seized up.

That is what it felt like to see Max walk into the kitchen with Aditi. What was he even doing here? Oh God, of *course* Aditi would know Lane—tristate popularity.

Max was a half step behind her, like he might guide her by the small of her back at any moment. She looked beautiful, black hair tousled to one side like she'd casually raked it. She glanced up to say something to Max, smiling, and he laughed.

Oxygen disappeared from the kitchen, the house, the planet.

I'd watched the changing expressions on Max Watson's face in class, in the driver's seat, in birthday-candle light. I had never seen him look at another girl like that. I hated their height difference. Short as she was, Aditi had to tilt her chin up high to speak to him.

I hurried out of the kitchen, leaving Morgan there. I wanted to wreck my whole life. Swipe my arms across the game table, making the tiny pieces clatter on the ground. Start over.

The world looked like it does from a carousel—only the nearest things seemed stationary or even real. And my watery eyes made even those things appear through a fishbowl. Color swimming past. A carousel inside a fishbowl. Or something. And spinning! How was I spinning while standing still, eyes squinted shut?

On my way into the dining room, my shoulder knocked something with a hard edge. A shattering sound near my feet, a too fast cause and effect. I scooped up the picture frame and set it back on top of the piano. The glass had fallen out, smashed.

"*Shit*," I muttered, dropping to my knees. I tried to gather the shards into my palm as fast as I could. With as crowded as the party had become, tracking glass around would be a disaster.

"Paige!" Tessa's voice floated somewhere above me. "Up. Get up."

"I have to fix this! I broke it!"

"Okay, but get away from the glass. Let me find a broom or something."

I saw blood before I felt pain. I glanced at my right palm, confused, and unstuck a small shard from the fleshy part of my thumb. When Tessa hauled me up, it became fairly apparent that another had dug into my knee. I brushed it off, and it annoyingly bled onto my jeans.

"Jesus," Tessa muttered, pointing me toward the stairs. "Lane's bathroom. Go."

I cradled my hand, suddenly feeling totally vulnerable. Quietly, I said, "Can you get Max?"

She hesitated. To be fair, it didn't sound great: drunk, bleeding, and asking for a boy I was not supposed to be talking to.

"He keeps a first aid kit in his car," I said.

"Fine," she said. "Go. We'll come up."

I went, gripping the stair rail with my nonbleeding hand. It really didn't hurt! Mystery! Lane had her own bathroom, attached to her room like in a fancy master suite. In there, I folded up some toilet paper and pressed it to my knee. The blood seeped, warm. I ran my hand under the faucet, watched the watery pink. I opened the cabinets but found only a box of tampons and a basket of nail polish.

But wait! TV shows had taught me rudimentary medical care for dire situations! I unearthed Lane's booze shoebox. A few drops of plain vodka onto a wad of toilet paper and held to my bleeding knee. I sat on the bedroom floor, gritting my teeth.

"Paige! What on earth?" Tessa gasped.

I looked up. Max was blocking the light from the doorway, a red first aid kit tucked under his arm. His mom had put it in his trunk when he got his license. I knew that because I knew *him*.

He sighed, crouching down. "Disinfecting it with booze, eh?"

"I am," I agreed.

Tessa sighed, too. "I'm gonna round up Morgan and Kayleigh."

"Go. I've got her," Max told Tessa, and I did feel gotten. Getted. Had?

He hoisted me up so that I was sitting on Lane's bed. Near us, a picture of her and Hunter from childhood looked on, smiles with missing teeth.

"I'm sorry," I said. How embarrassing, for Max to see me nose-dive like this. Wasn't I proving his point about not acting like myself, about searching for something?

He was unzipping the bag, rooting around for supplies. "For what?"

"Being a disaster," I said. "Breaking things."

Picture frames, my heart, yours, my future.

"I didn't get into UCLA." The words tumbled out of my mouth, unbidden. "Or USC. I haven't told anyone else."

"Oh." He looked at me for a moment, registering my drunkenness in a new way, maybe. "Oh. I'm sorry. And surprised."

"I'm not!" I said, laughing darkly. "Surprised *or* sorry. Well, I am. But you know what? Part of me feels *relieved*. I don't want to be in California, thousands of miles from everyone I know. Even for prestigious schools. Isn't that so cowardly?"

"No," he said. "Hand, please."

I offered it to him. Maybe I should have anticipated it, but the touch shocked me—the warmth, the familiarity of his hand on mine. He studied the damage; I stopped breathing, hesitant of his nearness and my current lack of inhibitions. He came here with another girl. A better girl, whom I liked so much.

"This'll probably sting."

"Oh, I can't feel anything right now," I said, chipper. "Oh, ow. Ow!"

"Sorry." He blew on my skin, cooling the iodine faster. "Okay. Worst is over."

Was it?

"Can I make the hole in the jeans a little bigger?" he asked, his fingers poised to do just that, and I nodded. He ripped the fabric just enough to fix a bandage on the cut. I wanted to push my fingers into his hair and tell him he'd be a good doctor someday. I wanted to ask him if he was any closer to a college decision, but instead I sat quietly, still as I could be.

After a moment, he stood, satisfied. "You're fixed up."

No, I'm not. I smiled weakly, afraid I'd start crying if I tried to speak again. These few moments of amnesty—when I was too vulnerable to be held accountable, too pitiful to be mad at—sliced sharper than glass.

"You came here with Aditi." I said precisely as the thought entered my mind, where it absolutely should have stayed.

Max narrowed his eyes at me. "Yeah. We had QuizBowl in Anderson before this, and she asked to stop by on the way home."

"Oh. You carpooled. Right." I had no business asking any more questions. I was preposterously drunk—barely capable of walking straight, let alone lying, and so I wanted to tell him that there really, truly wasn't anything going on with Hunter. There never had been.

"Thanks for this," I said, but he had crouched down and was zipping the first aid kit shut. It sounded loud. Did it sound especially loud? Had he zipped it angrily?

"Max. Did I—? Whoa, hey." I touched his arm. "Are you mad at me?"

He turned back. Something about his expression—his jaw?—made him look stony. "I don't want to do this whole thing, Paige."

"What whole thing?"

God, I was so confused. I looked up at Max with a kaleidoscope view, and tried to blink away my triple vision. What did I miss? He studied me, tugging his forearm from my touch. "Why did you have Tessa get me?"

"Because you have a first aid kit in your car?"

"You knew I'd come." His voice was scornful, like he hated himself for it. And also me. "You knew I'd take care of you. I showed up to a party with another girl, and you wanted to make sure you still had me on the line. But you can't have it both ways. You can't reel me back in."

"Reel you back in? I didn't mean to—"

"I don't care what you meant."

"Okay!" I sat back, unable to keep pace. He'd pivoted too fast, the words exchanged too quickly for my sluggish, sloppy brain. "I'm sorry."

"Yeah, me too," he said, already on his way out. My friends were walking in the door, coming to collect me, and Max said something to Tessa—about water and throwing up. Or I imagined it, my head filled with disjointed images of my drowning nightmares, my lifelong bad stomach, all the sleepless nights. When my friends surrounded me, all I could manage was: please get me out of here.

I woke up feeling like hell. I showered in Tessa's bathroom, feeling the sting of bandaged cuts and self-loathing. Tessa made pancakes and a pot of coffee, and she sat me down for a kitchen-stool confessional. I spilled it all—the rejections, the myriad ways I had messed up my personal and would-be professional life. She grabbed the paper towels as I started to cry. And when I had emptied everything out, she sent me home to tell the truth.

My mom sat at the kitchen table, pulling out pages from home décor catalogs for inspiration. Our mornings, even weekends, used to feel frenzied. She'd narrate a to-do list, which seemingly had no end. These days, she looked content in the morning time—coffee and her robe, hair pulled back. She read the news, perused design websites. Maybe an effect of Cameron and me getting older. But maybe an effect of my dad, who slowed us down in a good way.

"Hey, sweetie," she said. "Have fun?"

She asked it so genuinely, like I was returning from an innocent middle school sleepover, sugar rushes and all-night movies. When really, her crappy daughter had lied, gone out, and gotten stupidly drunk.

I shrugged, sliding into my seat at the kitchen table. I'd borrowed an oversize sweatshirt from Tessa, the sleeves long enough to cover the Band-Aid across my palm. "Where is everyone?"

"Cameron got it into her head that she wants to make donuts from scratch, so Dad took her to the store."

Good. I could only handle one reaction at a time. "I didn't get into UCLA. Or USC."

There had to be a softer way to introduce my failure, but I was too tired, too ill.

"Oh." Her face fell. "Honey. You got both e-mails?"

"Yesterday. USC on Wednesday."

"Sweetie. Oh no. You shouldn't have been alone with that."

"I needed a minute to sort through how I felt." I peered at her, curious. "Are you glad?"

"What? Of course not!" She tilted her head, upset. "I didn't love the idea of you being that far away, but I would have supported your choice! How do *you* feel?"

"Like a failure. And also relieved," I said. "I think I wanted to want it. If that makes sense."

She removed her glasses, trying to get a better look at me. "It does."

"Could you tell Dad and Cam?"

"Sure." She reached across the table and gripped my forearm. "I'm proud of you, you know."

"You don't have to say that."

"I know I don't." Leaning back in her chair, she considered me, slouched across from her. "You pushed yourself. I'm very glad to know you, honey."

"Thanks." She'd feel less glad, I imagined, if she knew the choices I'd made not twelve hours before. And then I said, because I was already on a roll, "I haven't been feeling great. Like, emotionally."

"Okay." My mom stayed in her leaned-back position, afraid to make any movement and shut me down.

"Not because of the rejections. Before. Way before."

"When?" she asked, trying to say it easily. But I could tell—she wanted to know what, exactly, she'd missed as a parent. "In New York?"

"No, not really. After. But it's hard to pinpoint. I know it escalated by, um, November, I guess?"

She startled—the facade of calm, receptive mother falling. "When Dad moved back in?"

"No. I mean, yes, that was also happening, but—"

"Your car accident."

"Yeah. But not just those things. It's everything. It's like my brain can turn anything, even good things, into panic." I imagined a bizarre conveyor belt where thoughts entered my mind—a good grade, Max's smiling face, a tiny comment from a friend—and came out as an electrical storm on the other side.

My mom nodded, accepting this. Accepting that the problem wasn't the outside factors. Or at least, it wasn't only them.

"I'd like to see Dr. Hernandez again," I said.

After Aaron died, my mom read online that a full year of

therapy would be good for a grieving teenager, and that's what I did with Dr. Hernandez. I liked her, after I got used to the oddly one-way conversation. I made progress, and I wanted that so much now, that room and her attentiveness and the way she never startled, no matter what dark thing I said.

"I'll call first thing Monday," my mom said simply. "That sound okay?"

"Yeah. Sounds good."

"Thank you for telling me. But, Paige?"

"Yeah?"

"None of this is an excuse for bad decision making," she said, dangerously calm. Maybe she sensed the foolhardiness on me; maybe vodka came off my skin like cheap perfume. Maybe she was, as I'd long suspected, capable of low-level mind reading. "I'm going to assume that whatever happened won't happen again."

Well, crap. "And I'm going to assume I'm grounded for at least a week?"

"Smart girl." She smiled thinly as I trudged upstairs.

CHAPTER TWENTY-NINE

Monday morning, I hated walking through the school hall-ways. I remembered everything from Saturday night, but I wondered which classmates had seen me talking too loudly, breaking a frame. Loss of control: not for me.

I saw Max briefly between a class change, but he didn't see me. Or pretended he didn't, anyway. Just as well—Tessa had advised me to give him the space he'd asked for. She'd said it so reluctantly, hating to make herself the go-between, but I heard her.

Instead of going to my lunch period, I stopped by Ms. Pepper's room, hoping to find her free. She was finishing up with someone from her previous class but waved me in.

I waited until the other student was fully out the door and still hung back. It spoke to how severely I'd gone awry, that I'd lose face in front of Pepper on the off chance she could help even a little.

"Hey there," she said pleasantly.

"Hey," I said. "Um, if I have a total breakdown to you about colleges, you can't, like, rescind the recommendation you wrote, right?"

She smiled, acknowledging my little joke, and pointed to the seat nearest her desk. "Tell me."

"I wanted to update you, as my senior adviser." This was a guise, actually. I mean, I did want to update her. But really, I wanted her to magically surmise my problems without me articulating them, and then offer succinct and sage advice. "I didn't get into USC or UCLA. Not shocking, but . . ."

Ms. Pepper winced a little, bobbing her head. "Which is not to say anything about you as a student—but the numbers alone. Those programs accept so few people compared to large applicant populations. Still waiting for IU and NYU?"

"Yeah," I said, hoping that my single syllable would portray my desperate desire for affirmation from Pepper that I would, in fact, get into one of those schools.

"If you get into NYU," she said, "is that your first choice?"

"Not necessarily? I went back to IU with Morgan last fall, and when I think about campus, it's like . . . I don't know. A perfect cake. A classic. Yellow with chocolate frosting, maybe." I looked up, hot with embarrassment. I wandered into her classroom and was now rambling about cake? "Sorry. My sister got really into baking this year."

"No, I follow you," Pepper says. "I love yellow cake."

Pepper wasn't one to share personal information. She shared anecdotes about her dog, Grendel, but that, over time, seemed calculated to me—her way of sharing something about her life, just not something about her. This once, though,

I hoped she'd waver under direct questioning from an emotional student. "Um, I was wondering. Did you stay in-state for school?"

She smiled, like the answer might disappoint me. "For undergrad. Did my master's out of state. But you know, for what it's worth . . . you spent a month in New York. So you have evidence that you connect with students at NYU, and you felt challenged and excited to be there. But I bet the same would be true at IU—at a lot of schools."

I huffed, a half laugh at myself. In a strange way, was NYU the safer choice? I already had proof that I could fit in, that I liked it. "You're right."

"Also, I hate to break it to you," Pepper said, "but which university is just one choice. A huge choice, yes. But once you get to campus . . ."

". . . I have to make even more choices," I guessed.

"Bingo. Your experience will be made of a thousand little choices as much as the one big one." She straightened, pressing her hands together. "Now! Tell me about Mythos! I've been hoping you'd stop by with an update."

A gray cloud trailed over me all week, heavy with water. I wanted it to open up already, douse me completely. I was still waiting on Friday, when Morgan ran up to me. Her fingers gripped my arm like a claw machine. "Have you checked your e-mail?"

I got into IU, with a really solid academic scholarship. So did Morgan and Kayleigh, though she'd already decided on

UC. A great and affordable in-state school that I liked. I got into college. I covered my face with one hand, overcome. The hallway suddenly felt like the first day of fall; I could finally breathe more easily.

"So, you think you'll send a deposit?" I asked Morgan.

"Yep." She made a checkmark in the air, the decision as simple as a pen slash.

On the map in my mind, I pushed another red pin into Bloomington. Ryan and Morgan at IU; Tessa and Kayleigh in Chicago. At least I could visualize those for sure. My pin was still stuck in Oakhurst, waiting. Two months maximum. Like a gymnasium scoreboard, bright red hours counting down.

"Did Max tell you?" Morgan asked.

Depends. He certainly told me off, that's for sure. "Nope."

"He got into IU, too. And Purdue."

"That's great." And it was—really. But I should have heard that from him.

"Paige," Morgan said, pained. "What are you guys doing?"

"Can we not?" I put my smile back on and nodded. "C'mon. Let's go tell Tess about IU."

———————

I told my dad when he picked me up from Mythos, and he did the Dan Hancock specialty of joyous and tearful. Instead of driving right home for dinner, he stopped at Kemper's to buy me a sundae with sprinkles, like he used to after final report cards. My mom jumped up and down, clasping me tight. They were the picture of proud parents, and I glowed in it.

Which is exactly why I didn't see the fight coming. I'd

gotten up to brush my teeth, awake later than I was supposed to be, when I heard the hushed voices downstairs.

I sat on the top step, toothbrush still jutting from my mouth, trying to make out the low tones of my dad's voice, the higher pitch of my mom's. *Leaving for school. NYU. Doctor. Anxiety.* My dad was worried I'd decide against out-of-state schools solely due to anxiety, that I'd internalize my mom's worries about New York. My mom countered that IU was a great school, with so many options that I wouldn't feel locked into one. I crept down a few more steps, in time to hear them accuse each other of pressuring me.

Neither one was wrong, exactly. My dad's no-holds-barred enthusiasm for NYU made me feel like IU would disappoint him. My mom's trepidation about NYU gave me secondhand doubts. In a way, their perspectives balanced out, and I considered barging downstairs to tell them so.

Cameron padded out of her room and sat by my side. She wrapped her arms around her knees.

"What's it about?" she whispered.

I pulled the toothbrush from my mouth, swallowing the minty foam. "Me."

We strained to listen, and God—the flashbacks. To being five and eight, me sending Cam back to her bedroom, reassuring her.

"They don't have any space to calm down and regroup," I said, quiet. "Now that they live together. This is exactly what I was worried about."

And when they couldn't escape each other—when they imploded again—it would be partially my fault.

"I'm going to bed," Cameron said, annoyed with me.

In the morning, I lingered at the kitchen doorframe, taking the temperature of the room before entering. I expected a chill on par with Narnia. I always knew when they'd disagreed the night before—the skillfully averted eye contact, no words exchanged unnecessarily. Sure enough, my mom sat at the table with her laptop and a legal pad.

"Little more?" my dad asked her, coffeepot in hand.

"Sure." She said it pleasantly enough. "Thank you."

"How's the interview list?"

"Robust," my mom said, tapping her notes. "The more perspectives I jot down, the more people I think of. It'll take me months."

"Feature potential?"

"I hope so," my mom admitted. "A series, maybe."

I stepped into the kitchen, confused. They seemed . . . calm. Happy, even.

"Hey, kid," my dad said. "I made you some decaf. How'd you sleep?"

"Okay," I hedged.

"So," he said, hand cupping the back of my head to get me to look at him. "Mom and I talked last night. Wherever you decide to go to school, we're gonna find a doc there—okay? Not just here at home."

Huh. A therapist, I assumed, in case my anxiety kicked into an unmanageable gear.

"It costs a lot," I said, my voice breaking. "Probably in New York especially. And wouldn't it be out-of-network? Or something?"

"There will probably be some hurdles to clear," my mom agreed. "But there are new options—online, even. We'll look into it."

My dad ruffled my hair. "And I'm all for IU, too. You know that, right?"

"Yeah, I know."

"I've just always wanted to live in New York myself," he said. "And what, really, is parenthood if not living your unfulfilled dreams through your children?"

I smiled begrudgingly. "I haven't even gotten in. And I'm trending toward rejection here."

He threw his hands up in playful exasperation. "You two and your negativity!"

"Actually," my mom said, smiling from behind her coffee cup, "I have a good feeling about it."

CHAPTER THIRTY

Kayleigh claimed she was using her birthday as an excuse to check off karaoke from the Senior Year List. It became clear during the second verse of "Always Be My Baby" that she was using her birthday as an excuse to belt Mariah Carey jams to an audience. And sing she did, in the private karaoke room her dad rented for us. The screen cycled through stock images that had nothing to do with the lyrics; the lights flashed magenta and unicorn purple.

It would have been purely fun except that I was trapped in a small, dark room with my ex-boyfriend and all of our mutual friends. Max and I were operating under the tacit agreement that the other person did not exist. We smiled freely at everyone else but avoided eye contact with each other. We sat on opposite sides of the curved bench facing the TV, me sandwiched between Morgan and Josiah so I couldn't even see Max in my peripheral vision.

All things considered, we were handling it. Or so I thought.

When Tessa dragged me up for an old Lilah Montgomery

song, I realized that I must be giving off bad energy. Tessa hated being in the spotlight, so this was clearly a concerted effort on her part. I got into it, serenading a delighted Kayleigh.

I did not look at Max Oliver Watson for even one flicked-glance second.

After that, we went down a Disney rabbit hole that began with Morgan's rendition of "Part of Your World." Josiah and Malcolm did an adorable and off-key duet from *Frozen*. Ryan hopped up to the machine and picked up two mics.

"Come on," Ryan said, motioning at Max.

Max made no movement whatsoever, like maybe we wouldn't see him. "Yeah, I think I'm good."

"Come *on*," Ryan insisted. To the rest of us, he said, "He was obsessed with *Toy Story* in kindergarten. He made me sing this a thousand times. You *owe* me, dude."

The song was beginning, so Ryan started in with the opening lines, angrily singing about persistent friendship.

"You can't leave him up there!" Tessa cried, thumping Max with one of the couch pillows. He trudged up to the microphone, laughing.

Max spoke more than sang, looking at Ryan with rueful head shakes. Ryan, meanwhile, hammed it up like he was born to.

"This is . . . maybe the cutest thing I've ever seen," Kayleigh marveled. The lights caught on her plastic, party store tiara.

Morgan held up her phone. "I'm legitimately going to cry. And send this to their mothers."

I patted Morgan's leg, motioning for her to slide out so I could go to the restroom. Under the fluorescent bathroom lights, I washed my hands with painfully cold water. I hated the tangy smell of cheap pink soap, and it didn't make me feel cleaner anyway. I stared at my face in the mirror, willing myself to get it together.

Kayleigh was waiting outside our karaoke room, leaning against the wall and texting.

"Hey," she said, straightening. "Stay here a sec."

She ducked back into the room, and I froze, more out of surprise than obedience. In seconds, she popped back out, and I frowned. "What's up?"

Max appeared behind her, and I opened my mouth to rage about this apparent conspiracy between the two of them. He got Kayleigh to act as the go-between? But when he glanced up, he looked just as surprised to see me. And just as unwilling.

"What is this?" I asked Kayleigh.

"How long until spring break?" she asked, unfazed by my hostility.

"I don't know. A few weeks?"

"Right," Kayleigh said. "And I worked very hard on planning our trip, wouldn't you agree?"

"You did," Max said, tentative. We both felt something coming, Kayleigh working up to her point.

"Okay. So are you two going to pollute my birthday party *and* my trip with furtive glares and sulking?"

"We weren't—" I began, at the same time Max said, "I'm not *sulking.*"

"Bah, bah, bah." Kayleigh waved her arms, silencing us. She stepped a few feet to the left and opened the door to the room beside ours. We'd heard people in there earlier, during lulls in our own performances, but it was empty now. "I know you have some no-talking thing, but we're all over it. Go hash it out. Find a way to coexist. Consider it my birthday present."

Max understood first. "You're sending us into a room to fight? Like an emotional cage match?"

"Fight wherever you want. But you're killing my party vibe." She circled with her arm like a baseball coach waving us home. "Go on. The music is loud. Scream at each other; screw each other. Don't care—just work it out."

"Charming," Max said.

Kayleigh pushed him lightly, enough to move his feet a few steps forward, into the room. Heat burned my cheeks, but I followed. A novelty light spun yellow stars across Max's annoyed expression.

"Thanks, love you, bye!" Kayleigh called, slamming the door.

We stood there, bass from the other room thumping against the floor, and crossed our arms. On the table, a tray of abandoned appetizers and a few mostly empty beer glasses from the last group in here. God, of all the awkward things. The audio system cycled through example karaoke tracks, on to a peppy Whitney Houston song.

I wanted to go back to this time last year, when I'd first realized that Max Watson could make my heart beat so hard that it almost hurt. Before we'd tangled every line that drew us together. Back then, I had no idea how good it could be. How complicated, how hard.

Now I did know. I knew that this boy who brought out the best in me could also spur the worst of me.

Woo, Whitney sang. *Hey, yeah.*

Max sighed. "I'll be the one who leaves, okay? I don't mind."

Like he was so magnanimous, deigning to leave the party first. I opened my mouth to say *Great*, snottily. But here we were, right? Relative privacy. And honestly, I wanted it over with even more than Kayleigh did. Wouldn't it feel like such a relief, to empty our heavy pockets of the grudges and slights? "Or we could get it over with."

"Get what over with?"

Seriously? "The tense silence, the glares. The whole thing, Max. God, just yell at me! It can't be as bad as this."

"I don't want to yell at you."

Fine. Maybe he needed me to start him off. Jiggle the handle of a locked door. I drew in my breath and my nerve. "Oh no? You want to be shitty and passive-aggressive instead?"

That'd do it. His jaw unhinged a little.

"*I'm* being shitty to *you*?" he said, pointing to himself and then to me as if I didn't understand pronouns.

"You're the one who ended it, so why am I getting treated like the antagonist?"

"Are you kidding me?" His anger felt real, at least—the molten core of a problem, buried deep beneath an icy surface. "I ended it *for* you."

Oh, that's the story he was telling himself? Because in my version, Max Watson couldn't handle my friendship with another guy. "Why would you suggest something you didn't want?"

"Because I thought it would last a week!" he yelled back. "Two, tops. I thought I was giving you space."

Oh. I settled back on my heels. His calmness as we broke things off at Alcott's—it wasn't resignation. It was . . . confidence. What had he said at Alcott's that day? *You can tell me no.* He meant it. He thought I'd be able to see the big picture, see him. And hadn't I?

"But instead," he continued, "you're with Hunter the next *second*. Which, whatever! Fair enough, I guess! But I don't have to pretend to like it."

My fingers bent, like I could claw at all the ways he was wrong. "Argh, Max! I wasn't *with* Hunter."

He narrowed his eyes, leaning in—like he'd already thought of this side of the argument, already bested me. "So, if you saw photos of me at a party with Aditi, having a blast days after we ended things, that would be fine with you?"

I averted my eyes, wishing I could deny it. If I imagined Aditi—this girl I liked so much—becoming closer and closer with Max? It would draw up every insecurity I damped down, every negative voice that whispered inside my mind. "There's no pressure with Hunter. He's a friend, so I can't screw it up."

"Why is there pressure with me, though, Paige?" Max asked, seeming equally exasperated.

"I—I don't know." What was I supposed to say? *I'm*

worried you think we're committed for life? It sounded absurd. It *was* absurd. I closed my eyes, teeth clenched, trying to find the right words. I could say that I never expected goodness, this much and this soon. It would be so easy to fan our relationship to fire, letting it overtake my future. But I feared snuffing it out, too. "A lot of reasons, Max. But I am sorry, okay? And I wish I could take it back."

When I opened my eyes, he'd eased away from frustration. "Take which part back?"

The part where I agreed to the gap year. But . . . *did* I regret that? Because now I saw, so clearly, that I shouldn't have been hiding my panic from Max. Telling my mom had felt like working up the nerve to peer under the bed, to check for monsters. If I could look right at the fear, confront it, at least I had some power. But I regretted the place we were in now, that's for sure.

The song faded out, replaced by the driving beat of a pop-rock song from middle school. Somehow, with a brain cluttered by trivia about Napoleon and geodes and Area 51, I still knew every lyric.

I stared up at Max, lips parted with unformed thoughts, and he nodded, jaw set. Like my silence decided something. "Okay. Well, I think we're done here."

He moved forward to leave, expecting me to step aside.

"No, we're not." I backed up against the door, fully blocking it. Blinking up at him, I said, huffy, "Don't do that—don't make unilateral decisions just because it's taking me longer to figure something out."

He was too close—already leaning down, arm out and his hand on the doorknob by my waist.

"Okay," he said, mostly out of surprise, I thought. That I'd said, clearly, exactly, what I meant to. We were both breathing fast, flustered from arguing. So often when emotions spiked, my instincts screamed *flight*: retreat to a quiet place where I can collect myself. Not this time.

"I'm not done," I said, and I lifted my eyes to Max's, ready to hold my ground. But his gaze glanced off my mouth, giving himself away. Or maybe I looked first, judging the distance I'd have to close. Maybe we were both halfway there before we realized we'd left.

Of all the ways our mouths had met before that moment— gently, intently, finally—Max had never kissed me with frustration revving beneath. I'd never kissed him back like I wanted to push him, even while pulling him closer. The pulse in my wrists, in my neck: *Uh-oh, uh-oh*, and *oh well, oh well*.

What was different? Everything else had been giddy and breathless. New. That version of us was a photograph framed in good light. Or frantic, in his basement and me trying to prove something to myself. Now he'd seen me hold back from him, retreat when I couldn't deal with the consequences. I'd seen his sarcastic edges become sharp and directed right at me; I'd seen jealousy ding his hard-won confidence. We'd wielded our worst qualities and shone our best qualities on each other, and I still wanted to kiss him. I still really, really wanted to kiss him.

The door lurched, someone trying to enter, and Max's arm shot out, holding it shut.

"Oh my God." I tugged my shirt down, wiped my mouth off on the back of my hand.

"Uh, hello? We reserved this room," a voice called from the other side of the door.

My many hours at Cin 12 took over. I grabbed two empty beer glasses and shoved the appetizer tray into Max's hand. The door opened to a group of frowning college-aged kids.

"Sorry 'bout that!" I pasted on a smile. "We were just dealing with our mess."

I mean, trying anyway.

"No sweat," the speaker—a guy in a blue hat—said, relaxing his stance.

"Room's all yours!" I said, cheerful. "Have fun!"

After everyone had filed in, we set the tray and glasses outside the door. I turned to Max, ready to exhale and laugh it off. "Well! Good instincts at least, you holding the door shut."

But Max frowned in consternation, not inside the joke with me or even close. "That . . . should not have happened. What am I supposed to do with that, Paige?"

He said it like I was the sole perpetrator of our extremely mutual make-out. Like it was something I had done *to* him.

"I'm gonna go," he said, turning away from me. I opened my mouth to yell after him that he would *not* bail on Kayleigh's birthday without saying goodbye, no matter how much she had meddled. But he stopped on his own and glanced back. "I'll pretend to get a text from my mom."

"Great," I snapped.

"Great."

He shook his shoulders out and took a deep breath before

reentering Kayleigh's party. And I was so pissed at him—for shutting down, for acting like my confusion was a personal affront, for expecting me to know what I was doing. He was the one who always acted so sure of himself, so sure of me.

So why did I also love this infuriating person?

When he did react to a supposed text from his mom, he made a good show of seeming regretful. He bid the birthday girl farewell, waved to everyone, and I really thought he pulled it off.

It took Tessa less than five minutes to plunk down beside me and say, "Well, that text was pretty fake, huh?"

I almost denied it, almost put up the energy required to fib. Instead, I gave a defeated smile. "I hate that we can't even disguise our drama."

"Well. You're so alike, you and Max. That's why it's so good. It's also why it's hard sometimes."

"That is . . ." I glanced over, studying her profile in the rainbow dots that swirled above us now. *Whatever souls are made of*, Emily Brontë wrote, *his and mine are the same*. I'd read that in class and thought: huh. "True, isn't it?"

"Yep." Tessa shrugged, like it was a very simple assessment. "Same for me and Laur."

"Why'd we fall for them?" I asked grumpily.

"Pure narcissism," she said, deadpan. Then, elbowing me, "No, c'mon. Because they're also the people who really get us. Right?"

Until recently, being with Max gave me a familiar feeling— like changing into pajamas, like scrubbing makeup off my face.

That *ah* moment of stripping away my time in the outside world. He'd fallen for me like that—absent of my defenses. And what had I done? Tried to be some simpler, girlfriend version of myself he didn't ask for.

"Okay," Tessa said. "To cheer you up, I'm willing to duet one more time. And—one-time offer only, enjoy it while it lasts—you can pick the song."

My smile spread slowly. Finally, an easy choice.

CHAPTER THIRTY-ONE

The rest of the weekend, I seethed. I pined. I daydreamed about charging into Max's house unannounced and pointing my finger up at his face while I yelled. I imagined that scenario turning into another imprudent make-out session. And while I knew drafting a list of all the ways he could have acted better was not the solution, I typed one out for my personal satisfaction anyway.

I found myself pacing my room Sunday evening, hands itchy for something to do. I went downstairs to see if Cameron would accept help with baking, but she was deep in homework at the kitchen table. I wandered out to the garage, where I'd noticed a pine dresser my mom had sanded down already, the raw wood like pale skin waiting to be clothed. The drawers had a floral pattern etched into the wood, more intricate than the electric sander could reach. The last of the lacquer needed some sandpaper and elbow grease.

I scrubbed at the arches and petals till my arm ached. I blew away the sawdust and traced my finger on the now smooth curve, warm from friction. The progress gave me the same satisfaction as picking at nail polish, only angrier.

All my feelings about Max, channeled into the scouring of old furniture. I could sand every drawer into a pile of dust and I'd probably still feel heated.

I barely registered my mom entering the garage, but her shadow stretched into my patch of light.

"Hey." I sat back on my heels.

"Hey." She was wearing her work button-down, hair tied back. "I didn't know you were out here."

"Yep." Only in this moment did I realize she might not have wanted this particular part to be sanded. Maybe I had just ruined her project. "Did I—I thought it would be okay if I finished this part?"

I held a hand to my forehead like a visor, trying to make out her expression.

"Of course," she said. "I'm happy for the help."

She pried open a small canister and stirred the primer while I finished my task. The scratch of grit on wood sounded louder than when I had been out here alone, and I eased off, to cover the aggression behind it.

"Did you know that sandpaper isn't made of sand?" I asked. "It's aluminum oxide, usually."

"That's interesting," my mom said pleasantly.

It wasn't, really. Just useless QuizBowl knowledge stacked into the crawl spaces of my brain.

Maybe I opened my mouth with trivial commentary because I didn't know how else to start. But my mom took the hint, only a beat passing before she said, "You wanna tell me what's going on?"

"Max," I said, like that explained everything. I wasn't going to tell my mother that Max and I had accidentally kissed mid-fight, further scrambling the entire dynamic. "We're a disaster."

"Well," she said. I appreciated that she wasn't looking at me, trying to study me. She kept priming the wood, watching each stroke of white. "You and Max care a lot about each other. Makes for big feelings when it's good. Big feelings when it's bad."

"Yeah." I sighed, sitting back again. "But it's like . . . how much work is too much work in a relationship?"

My mom exhaled, lips buzzing. "Well, my love. That's a very big question."

"I know." *Scritch, scritch.* My scrubbing was solely catharsis at this point. "On the one hand, I know all relationships take work. But I'm seventeen."

So often, my mom was quick to tell me what to do—or, more likely, not do. But she seemed to be really considering this one. "Didn't you have an argument with Tessa not too long ago?"

I furrowed my brows. Was now really the time to point out that I occasionally had problems with *all* relationships? "Yeah."

"How'd you fix it?"

"I don't know," I said, defensive. "I apologized?"

"Right. But before then?"

The conversation was beginning to feel like a game show

called *Screwing It Up*. Are *all* of Paige Hancock's choices wrong? Let's find out! With your host, Kate Hancock.

"I realized I probably should have reacted differently. So I told her that?"

"But Tessa didn't react perfectly either, right?" It wasn't really a question. She'd heard all of my grievances against Tessa's response. "Do you think if the situation happened again, you would behave differently?"

"I hope so," I said. I did wish for a do-over with Tessa, that I could match her excitement about Tate instead of questioning it. "I think so."

"Right. That's a relationship you value, and you put the work in to learn and do better."

I thought of Tessa and the plants in her room, of her plucking off old leaves, reconsidering the water frequency. Willing to confront what she was doing wrong.

"So, you're saying I should keep working at it with Max?"

"Not necessarily. I am your mother, after all." Sometimes, she stamped this phrase like a wax seal, the end of her argument. But sometimes, like now, her motherhood functioned as a simple explanation. Her opinions would always skew toward my safety and, given that, my goodness. My happiness. "I don't ever want to see you force a relationship that drains your spirit."

I startled at the dramatics. Max didn't *drain my spirit*. He and I clashed like colors—not armies meeting mid-field in battle. We were green and blue, sometimes in tones too similar to complement. But sometimes as natural as summer sky and the green lawns below.

"But," my mom said gently, when I hadn't spoken after a minute, "I also never want to see you give up when something isn't easy."

This whole year, I couldn't seem to find the balance: When to work harder, when to let it go? What was meant to be a challenge, pushing me to get up and try again? What was meant to be a lesson learned, asking me to walk away with some semblance of grace? When to say no, and when to say yes? "It's a fine line, I guess."

"It always is." She gave me a sad smile, genuinely sorry to tell me so. "As much as I love a pro-and-con list—and you know I do—sometimes you have to ignore all of that. Your gut instinct can say a lot."

When I relaxed my mind a little—past the complicated facets that made this year with Max so good and so difficult— the core feeling beneath the rubble was clear. I didn't even really need to soul-search. I didn't need to ask anyone else what to do about Max.

"Yeah. Thanks, Mom."

"Sure," she said.

I stood, brushing off my pants. "I'm gonna head in."

She stretched, readying her arms for a new section of un-primed wood. "Thanks for finishing the drawers for me."

We both knew my attack on the drawers was for me, but I appreciated her attempt at preserving my dignity.

Up in my room, I thought of last summer, when writing to Max felt like flooding. How the words rushed from my mind, past my shoulders and arms, straight out my fingertips. And talking to him felt like an extension. Sometime since then,

I'd tried to live up to his idea of me. So dazzled to be loved that I forgot Max really knew me—all last year, before I cared if he thought I was pretty enough, fun enough, easy to be around.

What was I so afraid of, anyway? *It's just you and Max.* But I'd stumbled onto something rare, and I collapsed under the fear of squandering it. How foolish, in the end.

The first e-mail took me over two hours and four drafts. I made myself go to bed without sending it, and I sank into my pillow. Just typing out the words felt like I'd taken a long walk or a particularly hot shower—like I'd been wrung out and cleansed. In the morning hours, I sipped my coffee and reread the words. It wasn't everything I wanted to say, but it was a start.

Dear Max,

I hope it's okay that I'm e-mailing you. It seems like the right option since we agreed not to text, and every time we talk, the conversation escalates faster than the time I need to think.

Tessa recently told me that you and I are a lot alike—it's why we connect. That's also why it's hard sometimes.

I keep thinking that getting frustrated with each other is a new development from this year. I've blamed our schedules, the mounting pressure of senior year, the fact that we started our relationship after three months apart. I've blamed myself. I've blamed you.

But the truth is . . . we butted heads last year, too.
We bickered one of the first times we ever spoke! I'm
not sure why I scrubbed that from my memory.
Classic romanticizer, I guess.

Every time we bicker, I wish it away. But the reasons
we clash are also the reasons we were drawn to each
other in the first place. Me & you, Watson—too alike
sometimes. So I can't wish we were different people.

I can wish I had handled those differences better.
And I do.

So, here's something I wish I had told you a long time
ago: It felt like a lot of sudden pressure, being together.
A few "old married couple" jokes here and there, and
I panicked that we were somehow in a more serious
relationship than I thought. I didn't tell you that the
"together forever" stuff made me nervous because
I thought you'd be like, "Whoa, those are jokes, why
would you think otherwise?" (Which would have been
fair.) But I think a little part of me also worried you were
fine with those assumptions. (This is . . . very
embarrassing to type out.)

It felt like our relationship had to be all or nothing.
Planning college around each other or calling it
off. Planning for the thing mostly likely to happen,
instead of what I most want to happen, you might say.

This is a long way of saying I'm sorry. The road in front
of us stole all my attention. I was squinting through the
windshield, trying to spot the point on the horizon when
our paths would diverge. You asked what I would take
back, and that's my answer. I should have enjoyed
being next to you, like I always have.

Love,
Paige

CHAPTER THIRTY-TWO

With *2BD, 1BA* rehearsals ramping up, I had blessedly little time to think about Max and the state of our non-relationship. He didn't reply to my e-mail the next day, or the one after. I accepted it, with some mortification, as a clear signal. When I saw him from a distance at school, I ducked down the fresh-man hallway, out of view.

At Mythos, I held my raincoat closed as I hurried out for espresso runs, jotted down notes as Cris debated blocking changes, ran to the campus store for more safety pins. During breaks, I chipped away at a paper for English class. And obses-sively refreshed my e-mail in case there was something from NYU or Max.

I'd seen each scene rehearsed at some point, but never all the way through. The first time they attempted it, Cris kept calling, *Cut.* I'd assumed that Marisol was hot under the stage lights, but no—she was flushed with nerves and frustration. Even Ella, normally so cool, flubbed a few lines. Other cast members missed cues, didn't shut the front door of the set apartment hard enough, forgot to walk in with a pizza box necessary to the scene. At one point, Cris craned around to look at the director's box, her arms wide like *What the hell?* The spotlight was supposed to follow the second lead, but it hadn't budged.

"It's always like this," Marisol assured me. "Like cleaning out your closet. The mess means progress."

Despite her confidence, she looked near-tears frustrated later in the week, when she botched her pivotal monologue. Cris called for everyone to take ten.

But Friday night. Friday night, no one forgot props in the first act. Doors were closed properly. I held my breath as Cris yelled for them to run it through, no break. We were on a roll. I mangled the end of my pen cap completely, tooth marks and frayed plastic.

Ella was winding up to her big scene, stepping out to center stage.

"Come on," Cris whispered under her breath. If I had to guess, I'd bet she hadn't meant to say it out loud. Ella glided through the transition, finishing the speech with an emotional tremble in her voice.

I was close enough to the stage that I could see Marisol resisting the urge to scoop Ella up and spin her around.

With a few pauses for adjustment, the play gelled before my eyes. It needed work still. We weren't in costumes; mics weren't placed for sound checks. But I saw it—the difference between paint on a canvas and art.

Cris smiled over at me. "You hooked?"

I could almost feel my own bright-eyed newness, the soundboard panels glittering in my eyes.

She laughed a little, looking back at the rest of the team. "She's hooked."

———————————

In my only block of free time, I met Ryan at the Linwood vs. Oakhurst baseball "friendly" after my second therapy appointment. My dad let me borrow the car, which I still couldn't drive through that stretch of road outside the cinema. Dr. Hernandez, upon hearing this, seemed completely unfazed. We'd talked about medication, and she'd sent me home with brochures.

The teams were still in pregame stretches, Hunter warming up his arm with the catcher. Ryan and I found a spot low on the bleachers, and I set my book beside me.

"So, you and Hunter becoming buds?" I asked. Hunter had texted me after hanging out with Ryan and, if I understood correctly, also Max. I'd stared down at my phone, perplexed by the situation. But it sounded, at least, like Hunter enjoyed himself.

"Yeah, he came over last weekend to play video games. Really fun dude."

"He is." I said it mildly—I really did. But the whole interaction still felt dense with unspoken meaning.

"It was Max's idea," Ryan said. "To invite him over."

I narrowed my eyes at him, disbelieving.

"And they were totally cool. We had a good time." Ryan fixed me with a look, unable to resist the meddling. "I'm not gonna defend Max, okay? He goes into full porcupine mode when he feels threatened—prickly as hell. You can bet I've been on the receiving end of it, too."

"Mmph," I said, grudging. But I did know that.

"You have to remember," Ryan said, "underneath the nerd swagger, he's still a guy who got pretty seriously squashed as a kid."

"That sounds like defending him to me," I noted curtly.

"No, just understanding him."

"He's the one who ended it, Ry." I thought, with no small amount of embarrassment, about the e-mail in Max's inbox—my heart swung open like a gate. "And I've tried to reach out. Honestly."

Before he could respond, Hunter waved, jogging our way. I studied him in the striped baseball whites, hat and eye black obscuring part of his face. In his element, comfortable. He and Ryan did a hands-clasped, back-pat hug, and he smiled down at me. "You came."

"I even wore half Linwood colors, thank you very much." In the form of a navy cardigan over a striped, Oakhurst-red T-shirt, but still.

"Hancock."

"What?"

He pointed to the bleacher space beside me. "Did you bring a book to my baseball game?"

"Yeah. Only for when you're not on the field."

"Don't take it personally," Ryan said. "She'd bring a book to her own birthday party."

They went down a sports tangent that I tuned out. After Hunter headed back to take the field, a pep in his step from knowing he had a cheering squad, Ryan looked down at his hands. "Sorry I got in the middle before. I always tell myself I won't. But I'm not always on his side, you know. Sometimes he's wrong. And he hates being wrong."

Ryan said this with a bit of relish. I knew Max confided in him—of course I did. But I hadn't considered how much of my behavior had probably been recounted to Ryan, in exasperation.

"He told you about karaoke, didn't he?" I asked. The heat rose from my chin to my forehead.

"No idea what you're talking about," Ryan said. He looked away, scanning the field so I couldn't see his face.

Even after Ryan's insight, I began to doubt Max would ever respond. But before bed, I checked my e-mail once more, and there it was. I rolled over, pulse banging against my throat.

Dear Paige,

Here's something I wish I had told you this year: I felt that pressure, too. And worse, I felt it freaking you out. I should have said, "Wow, how annoying are these little comments?" so we could laugh about it. But I worried that would sound mean? Ridiculous, right?

I agree with the assessment that we are alike. But I'd also like to posit another theory: I am an asshead sometimes. (I've been sitting here trying to think of a more poetic way to put this. Long-form correspondence! Shouldn't I be fancier? I am obtuse sometimes? Bumbling? But sometimes an asshead is just an asshead. Some things can't be English Romanticized.)

I was an asshead to you after what happened at karaoke, and I'm sorry for that. When I told Ryan that you and I fought, he kind of laughed. According to him, I'm too used to being good at anything I want to be good at. I hope I don't sound like a braggart when I say I think he's right. I spin out in frustration when I can't make sense of things, can't fix them like a malfunctioning circuit.

I'm sorry it took me a few days to respond. I could blame it on my schedule, but the truth is that I wrote and edited and rewrote and deleted and started again. I wanted the whole thing to sound concise but thoughtful, sincere but clever. Took me a while to decide on "braggart," which seemed more elegant than "jerk." And then I just went and showed my hand anyway. That always seems to happen, sooner or later, with you.

Man, I missed talking to you. Typing to you. Hearing from you.

Hi. How are you?

Love,
Max

It was a door, cracked open, and both of us were peering through. When I couldn't sleep that night, it was because I was already planning what to say next.

CHAPTER THIRTY-THREE

Dear Max,

The letters of famous literary minds do notably lack the word "asshead." And frankly, I think they're worse for it.

As long as we're being honest, here is something else I wish I had told you this year: I haven't driven through the intersection where my car accident happened since . . . my car accident happened. If you are thinking, "But that is a major, almost unavoidable, area of town," . . . yes, correct.

Have you ever seen a military-training sequence in a movie? There's always that big wooden wall the cadets are expected to scale. At a distance, the challenge seems straightforward. Viewers watching the movie from home are like, "Just scamper up, easy!" But I can't get more than a few feet without falling to the ground.

I'm not sure why the things that scare me overtake me. I think about this a lot.

It's hard for me to decipher between legitimate fear— good instincts trying to protect me—and panic based on no threat whatsoever. Sometimes I think it's a mix? I don't know. That uncertainty is making college decisions really hard. It makes everything hard, in some way or another.

Relatedly, I'm nervous it's going to be weird between us at school tomorrow. But I missed talking to you, too.

Love,
Paige

Dear Paige,

Tomorrow won't be weird. I'll tell you exactly how it will go: I'm going to say hello. I'm going to ask how your weekend was.

Well, maybe you'll say something weird from there or maybe I will. Never know. But that's how I'm going to start.

Love,
Max

At school on Monday, I saw Max after third period. He showed up at my locker as he had for much of the year, with Tessa and Ryan.

"Hello," he said quietly. "How was your weekend?"

I laughed under my breath instead of actually responding.

Ryan looked briefly curious but held up one hand. "You know what? Don't even want to know. I stopped trying to understand the subtext between you two ages ago."

So it went: A few brief, comfortable interactions at school. And then, at home, during breaks at the cinema and at Mythos, at night before bed—reading and rereading e-mails from Max. Composing them. Falling asleep hoping for a morning response, bold in my inbox.

Dear Paige,

Well, it's that time of year again—my birthday nears, and my dad comes a-knockin'. Like clockwork. Curiosity or guilt, who knows?

But it's been weird this year. He got in touch earlier than usual and seemed more . . . desperate, I guess? I'm ready to see him, but even if I wasn't—my mom has been oddly insistent.

The last time I saw him, I was 13. My mom took me to Chicago for a trip to Adler Planetarium and arranged for me to have dinner with my dad and his fiancée at their

place. I'd never met Margot before then, and I liked her
so much. She's a few years younger than my mom and
an illustrator—knows a lot about comic books, digital
animation. I had fun with her, and with my dad. But when
my mom picked me up, her hopeful face at the door of
their nice apartment made me feel so guilty I honestly
thought I'd vomit. My mom, who did everything herself
and, in her barely existent free time, took me to the
planetarium. I cried in the car back to the hotel, and I
wouldn't tell her why. When she asked if I wanted to visit
again, I always said no.

That was that. Afterward, I felt furious at my dad in a
way I hadn't as a little kid. He had this nice life with
Margot. Why couldn't he have had that with my mom?
Of course, the older I got, the more I understood it
doesn't work like that.

Long story short, it sounds like he'll drive in from Chicago
for a dinner in the next few weeks. I have . . . absolutely
no idea how I feel about it. My brain skirts around the
thought, reroutes me to schoolwork, applications,
anything.

Sorry. Kind of an overshare. I haven't told anyone all of
this. When it comes to my dad, Ryan gets really
defensive of me. I love him for it, but I don't need any
help painting my dad as the bad guy. And I never want

my family to feel like they're not enough for me, especially my mom. I'm starting to realize that I told myself I was protecting her, but I think maybe I was protecting myself.

I hope you had a good week. How's Mythos? Any word from colleges?

Love,
Max

Dear Max,

Mythos is . . . magical? I love being behind the scenes. The playwright visited today to watch dress rehearsal, and I got to chat with her a little bit. Her professional title is dramaturge. DRAMATURGE.

The play is great on page, but watching it evolve with the actors and direction is amazing.

Thanks for telling me about your dad. I've wondered before, but I never wanted to pry. It's probably not my place, but I feel so protective of you seeing him. I want to sit beside you with my arms crossed, ready to tell him off. That's silly, I know. I really, really hope it goes well. Will Margot be there? Did they wind up getting married?

No word from NYU. But it's really okay. When I imagine
myself at IU, it feels warm and good. Solid, like I could
really build something.

Love,
Paige

Dear Paige,

Margot's not coming this time, but yes, they're still
married. And really happy, it sounds like from his
e-mails. So, that's good. Sometimes, when I consider
Northwestern, I wonder if it might be nice to live near
them. Now that I'm old enough to choose when and
how I get to know them. Depends on how dinner goes,
I guess. Ha.

I got into University of Cincinnati this week, which is
great! And miserable! All year, everyone praised me for
casting a wide net, for doing lots of school visits,
whatever. Here's the thing, Janie:

IT'S BECAUSE I HAVE NO IDEA WHAT THE HELL
I'M DOING.

Engineering? Premed? Still don't know! I have to decide
in a little over a month, and I feel no closer than I was
at the beginning of the year. And for the life of me,

I couldn't tell you why I bottled this up all year. I guess I thought saying it out loud would force me to confront it. I'm pretty used to knowing what the right answer is.

And honestly, maybe the idea of factoring you into the decision at least gave me a little more direction? Which isn't fair to you, I realize.

I keep stumbling on more apologies that I owe you.

You must allow me to tell you how ardently sorry I am. (Sorry enough to quote your pal Darcy. Eh?)

Love,
Max

Dear Max,

I mean, you know I felt weirdly relieved to be rejected from every school in the greater Los Angeles area. (Okay, it was two schools, but still.) Congratulations on Cincinnati!

These decisions are hard because they're expensive, and they'll route us in a particular direction, and they feel permanent. But recently, Pepper told me that which college you choose is just one decision. I'll have to choose how I get involved on campus, how I put myself out there with new people, if I ask for help if classwork or homesickness gets too hard. So maybe it's about being nimble, too. Adjusting as situations change. (This is, uh . . . something I am exploring in therapy. Ha.)

Also, I had this idea for you: You know how people are always asking what we're majoring in? Why don't you try answering like you know for sure? One week, say "Premed." The next, "Engineering." See which one feels right. I mean, you'll be spreading misinformation around Oakhurst, but since when is gossip around here accurate anyway?

Love,
Paige

Dear Paige,

I understand what you mean. When Ryan begged me to transfer back to Oakhurst before junior year, I admired him for admitting I'm a security blanket for him . . . I'm less forthcoming about the fact that he's mine, too. He drives me nuts, of course. But he's also the best friend I've ever had. And he'll be my family my whole life! I know that, and I still don't want to live in different states.

So, I decided to try saying "Premed" this week, and already did once! It was one of my mom's work friends, so she made an apple-doesn't-fall-far-from-the-tree comment. A generic sentiment, maybe, but I like the idea of sharing a field with my mom. I like the idea of having that in common with her, someday. When it's frustrating, I can vent to her, and she'll really, really know.

I heard from Northwestern (yes) and Wash U (yes) this week. And Tessa let it slip that you got into NYU. (Don't be mad—she was just bursting with pride and blurted it out.) I'm so happy for you, Janie—really. I thought, when you inevitably got accepted, I'd feel torn to lose you to the big city. But I only feel glad and really bowled over by your hard work. Here's hoping Maeve got in, too. Go out and celebrate after play rehearsal, eh?

Love,
Max

Dear Max,

Congratulations on those acceptances. Geez, Watson—cleaning up with these universities. Has any of that news given you a gut feeling?

And thanks. I'm relieved and excited and intimidated and unsure. Maeve got in, too, but neither of us has decided. Mostly, I'm glad for the validation of my writing portfolio! But now I have to make a choice, and, well . . . me and choices.

Here's something else I wish I had told you this year:
My anxiety flared up really, really badly after the car
accident. My drowning nightmare returned in full force,
too. It hasn't been great.

After Aaron died, the panic attacks seemed situational.
The therapist I saw talked about traumatic grief, and
I thought I worked through it. I mean, you remember
last year.

I've been going to appointments with that same
therapist and recently started a low-dose medication.
I'm hoping it's like how my sister describes getting her
glasses—she didn't even realize how bad her vision was
until she got the right prescription.

I don't know why I didn't tell you any of this. I'm not
someone who thinks mental health stuff is embarrassing.
But . . . I guess I wanted you to see me as a brave girl
who could jump off the high dive, who could tell you
how she really felt.

Turns out one or two bold acts don't change a person's
core, huh? It's a longer road than that, and I'm still
trying to square the girl I want to be with the girl I am.

Love,
Paige

Dear Paige,

I'm also not someone who thinks mental health stuff is embarrassing. Kind of crushes me that all of this was going on with you and I didn't even know. But then, I guess you could say that about a few things in my life, too.

Can I tell you what I would have told you then? It sounds like the car accident brought up some really dark stuff and now you're confronting it. That sounds exactly like the brave girl I met last year.

Love,
Max

Dear Max,

Well, I'm officially cheating on film and TV with theater. I didn't mean to—it started with a flirtation, a curiosity. But I fell fast and hard.

2BD, 1BA opens tomorrow, and I'm so tired, and I'm so excited. The rush of everything happening moment to moment. Watching the actors adjust subtly, grow into their roles. The way every part interlocks and creates something the same and slightly different each time.

And now I'm rethinking college plans, too. Do I want to skew toward theater now? I don't know! I don't know.

All year, I've taken offense when my mom has tried to suggest I broaden my career plans, that I don't box myself into screen writing. But really, I think she wanted me to leave room for new loves to grow. I didn't see theater coming, but here we are.

Anyway, good luck with prep for QuizBowl quarterfinals. You know I wish I could be there.

Love,
Paige

Dear Paige,

I'm in at Notre Dame, but got noes from Caltech, Columbia, and U of M. *(Womp-wah.)* Busy week in rejection over here!

I'm leaning toward premed, I think—chemistry, maybe. But then again, maybe it'll be like at a restaurant, when you can't decide between two entrées. You just blurt out whatever feels right once the waiter shows up.

College is a bigger decision than fish or steak. I know that. With spring break coming up, I'm hoping getting away will give me some perspective. Like I'll move down that map to Florida and suddenly be able to see the whole picture. I don't know if that makes sense.

Thanks for the QuizBowl luck. I'm trying to focus on studying for that instead of focusing on seeing my dad the night after. At least with trivia, I can prepare.

I'm excited for you about the play. Break a leg!

Love,
Max

CHAPTER THIRTY-FOUR

On opening night, I felt the gradual tightening in my chest.
It's normal to be nervous. Deep breath. You are not solely respon-
sible for the success of the show. My emotions wobbled like a
bike, but I remained on both wheels.

The show flowed from scene to scene, with only one lighting cue dropped. The audience would never know, but it left
room for improvement. One of the actors bungled an important line, and I held my breath so hard that my sternum hurt.
But Marisol picked the line up without a trace of hesitation—no
cue that her mind had been silently working the information
into her own character's dialogue.

When the curtain dropped, I slumped over, breathing like
I'd run a marathon. Was it really over? An eternity, a moment.
The cast filed back out for their bows, and the widest, most
helpless smile spanned my whole face. I wanted to cry a little,
exhausted from tech week and also because, what a small
miracle—for so many moving parts, so many people, to make
this bit of make-believe become so much more.

My parents came to opening night with Cameron, then again on Monday. My friends trickled in at various shows, depending on what activities they had at night. Morgan and Tessa brought an embarrassing bouquet of flowers. Ryan and Kayleigh cheered so loudly, you would have thought I was actually onstage. Malcolm and Josiah brought their parents the same night Hunter and Lane surprised me.

The week flew, a show every night, and on Saturday, a matinee and evening performance, our second-to-last. We ate pizza in the green room in between shows, the actors in button-down shirts to protect their hair and makeup, and I longed for all of this even as it was happening, even with everyone still in one room. It was probably time to step away—recharge alone for a few minutes. Leave it to me to find the most nostalgic of art forms.

My phone vibrated in my back pocket, and I expected a call from one of my parents or an unknown number I'd ignore. But glancing at the screen, I found Max's smiling face, a photo I'd taken of him at Alcott's. He was supposed to be at dinner with his dad. I hurried away from the particular noise of theater people unwinding—vying for attention, stories told and bits performed. I held my phone to one ear, plugging the other. If Max's dad ghosted him, I would drive to Chicago, Illinois, shaking with rage.

"Hey," I said. My voice bounced against the tiles in the empty hallway. "You okay?"

"Yeah, I'm fine. Am I interrupting?" His voice, low and hesitant. "I was hoping you were between shows."

"I am," I said. "Are you—? Is dinner still . . . on?"

"Yeah. Do you have a few minutes? I don't want to keep you."

No, please do keep me, I thought. "You're not. Perfect timing."

"Okay. Because I'm sitting in my car outside the restaurant waiting to go in, and I . . ." He trailed off, like he thought I'd get it. Did he want a pep talk? "I wanted to hear your voice, I guess."

The unexpectedness of this—I stopped walking right there, beside a framed show poster . . . Oh. My grandmother used to say she was glad to hear my voice, something I understood only after she was gone. The comfort in that familiarity, the way you can close your eyes and imagine the person beside you.

"Do you want me to ramble?" I asked. "Or talk about something specific?"

"Maybe you could tell me about show week?"

I did a solid three-minute monologue as I paced at the end of the hallway near a window, looking out at Indianapolis. I told him everything, from my first-night jitters to now, how I already missed the buzz of live theater, that I planned to attend the cast party tonight even though I'd probably feel shy and out of place.

"Thank you," he said, once I wound down. "I'm really nervous, Paige. I didn't think I would be."

"Well, lucky for you," I said, "really nervous is my resting state. Which part are you fixating on?"

I could almost see him ruffling his hair. Maybe fidgeting with his watch. "All these years he's asked to see me. What if he wants to see how I turned out and that's it—curiosity satisfied, the end? I have to be prepared for that, right?"

I sat back on the windowsill, trying not to smile as I stared at my Keds, floral and worn-in. "I don't know anyone who's met you once and wanted to spend *less* time with you."

"Well, even you took a second to warm up to me! I can be intense."

"Max," I said evenly. I took his fear seriously, but he really had nothing to worry about. "You are a parental dream. My mom probably said 'such a nice young man' a dozen times after meeting you."

He made a grumpy sound, reluctant. ". . . I guess."

"But you don't have to be charming or even nice. This is your dad. You can be sullen or guarded or however you feel. You guys have a tricky history. If that's enough to shake him, then I don't like him one bit, and you can quote me on that."

Max laughed at last, a break in the coiled tension I could feel through the phone. "For the past—what, almost five years?—I've imagined so many different ways this could go. And now I'll know for sure. It's hard to give up the possibility. Does that make any sense?"

"It . . ." My mind flashed to idyllic Bloomington, then to busy, breathing New York. "Absolutely does, yes. But maybe it'll also be a relief to know for sure."

"Yeah," he said. "Yeah, I think it will. Okay. I'm gonna go in."

"Okay," I said, pleasant. Because I had no doubt that he could do it.

"Paige?"

"Yeah."

"Thank you." The earnestness of his voice, like he really needed me to hear him. I wanted to tell him how much it meant, that he'd let me into his uncertainty. *I haven't told anyone all of this*, he'd said in his e-mail. I wanted to be the person he told, the person he trusted to talk him through it.

"Any time." I wouldn't pour more emotion into an already overflowing night for Max. But I hoped he knew how much I meant it: any time, from now until any future I could imagine, I'd pick up the phone. If we broke each other's hearts tomorrow or five years from now, if we drifted, if we went our separate ways. I would always be saving his seat, that spot in my life meant for him.

I got his text at intermission of the final show: *It was really good. Thank you for earlier.* I held the phone to my chest, so relieved for him. And then, when I glanced back down, *Can we talk tomorrow?*

Yes please, I texted back.

During the Sunday matinee, the last moments of *2BD, 1BA* I watched with a calm deep in my bones. It was the feeling of a plane's descent, of the steering wheel nudged toward the last highway exit. The distinct feeling of being almost there.

After final curtain, the lobby overflowed with people, and I lingered at the base of the stairs, glad for my all-black outfit, inconspicuous. Groups scattered about like clusters of stars, different sizes and spacing, but all aglow. I craned around, hoping to spot my parents quickly.

"Paiger!" my dad called, waving as if he were lost at sea and I was a passing boat. He and my mom were talking to Ms. Pepper and a man with a neat beard and warm brown skin.

My dad bear-hugged me, and I tried not to disintegrate from embarrassment in front of my all-time favorite teacher. Fortunately, both Pepper and the man by her side smiled at my dad's enthusiasm.

"Paige!" Pepper said. "Congratulations! It was wonderful."

"Thank you," I said, hands clasped. "Congratulations on QuizBowl. Heard the team cleaned up Friday night."

"It was impressive," she said. Then, touching the man's arm, "This is my . . . friend, Professor Choudhary."

"Oh my God, Rach," he said with a laugh. He reached for my hand, a polite shake like he was meeting a real theater professional. "Ayush, her longtime boyfriend. Nice to meet you. The play was great—congratulations! And congrats on being accepted to the ol' alma mater."

Whose alma mater? My eyes shot to Pepper—did I not know where she went to school? I'd never asked, and she'd never said. "Wait. IU?"

"Undergrad," she said, smiling. "Ayush teaches history there now."

"So, no pressure," he added, "but you should definitely join our ranks."

"I bet Cris would love to have you keep working here, if

you stay local." My dad nudged my arm, pleased with himself for making this connection.

Stay with Mythos? I'd hardly let myself imagine more than this week. But the thought of becoming at home in this theater? Was it my imagination or did Ms. Pepper look almost proud? That darn poker face, her well-cultivated teacher persona that I only rarely saw through.

"I'd love that, too," I said.

"Well," my mom said, taking my dad's hand. She smiled like she knew something I didn't. "We won't keep you."

I thanked them all for coming and promised to text on my way home. As they walked away, I wavered, unduly sad to be alone. I'd had friends or family at almost every show—total support. But the cast party was last night, and now there was nothing to do but gather up my things and go. I glanced around the lobby one last time, hoping for . . . something. For Marisol to run over, for Cris to give me a task.

I knew the crowds didn't shift specifically on cue, the whole room didn't conspire to make a path ahead. But that's how it felt. I saw him the way I always did, my body tuned to his presence like a radio station default. Even in the busy, buzzy energy of the lobby, I found his frequency, low and steady. Max.

Smiling hesitantly, he raised one hand. I'd read once that waving wasn't always a casual greeting. It had origins in a salute, a gesture to show you came in peace. Right now, it seemed like both.

I walked to where he stood and lifted to my tiptoes, fitting both arms around his neck.

"Hi," I said into his shoulder. I'd missed this smell—laundry detergent and shampoo.

He held me tight. "Hi."

When we finally pulled away, I held the lapels of his jacket, an olive green that made his eyes look bright. He kept his hands on my waist and nodded to the mezzanine doors. "It was amazing, Janie. Really."

"Thank you. And thank you for coming."

"Of course." His gaze moved between my eyes, reading me from left to right and back again. "Do you have plans right now?"

"Nope," I said, shaking my head slowly. "I'm all yours."

We drove to the outskirts of Oakhurst, where the farthest-back neighborhoods stretched into forest and farmland. There was a patch of undeveloped land out here, framed by trees, where Max once took me to watch airplanes. I parked my mom's car beside Max's, and he hopped the fence first, flannel blanket thrown over his shoulder. He offered me a hand, which I held as we stamped through tall grass.

We stayed quiet as Max laid out the blanket, and I held the corner to keep it down in the breeze. And finally, we sat, facing each other with legs crossed, two kids settling in for a hand-clapping game at recess. Two kids looking only at each other.

"So," I said. "Tell me about seeing your dad. You said it went well?"

"It did, yeah. Not as awkward as I thought. But there's some . . . news, I guess."

"Okay." I braced for terrible news—a genetic illness, a cross-country move that would impede their relationship.

"Margot, my dad's wife? She's pregnant."

"Pregnant?" I said it like I didn't understand the meaning of the word. A half sibling. Max's parents were a near decade younger than my own, so having a baby seemed downright ordinary. Why had I never considered this? Max, someone's older brother. "*Oh*. Holy *shit*."

He laughed, as if my crudeness resonated with his feelings exactly.

"Have you . . ." I ventured, hesitating, ". . . decided what you'll do with that information?"

"Yeah," he said, and I startled a little. I hadn't expected certainty, simplicity; I'd expected the debate between missing an opportunity to know a sibling and having to reconcile with his dad. Max gave me a half smile. "Easy decision, it turns out."

I waited for him to elaborate, but I didn't need to. I knew because he'd confided in me, about his dad and Margot, about Chicago and time lost. We weren't breaking gap year rules at all—he'd made a decision, at last. "You'll go to Northwestern."

He nodded. "I will, yes."

"I think that's exactly right." Northwestern seemed so Max-ish—the Midwestern hominess of Evanston, with a lake and a skyline nearby. And Adler Planetarium waiting for him, just a little to the south.

"Me too. It's close enough to get to know my dad a little, but on my terms. And this way, I can get to know my brother. I don't think I'll ever regret that, you know?"

"Brother," I repeated. It came out a whisper.

"Yeah." He all-out grinned, a flash of teeth, and shook his head in disbelief. "Wild, right? I know it'll be like more of an uncle-nephew thing with the age difference. But. Yeah. I woke up this morning and still couldn't get my mind around it."

"And you'll be in Chicago with Kayleigh and Tess and Laurel!" The realization came with relief—my people together, in a little pocket of Illinois—and searing jealousy that they'd all have each other close, a train ride away. "And oh—Kayleigh's niece is there! Maybe playdates with your . . ."

"Brother," Max finished, with an incredulous chuckle.

"Max." I marveled at him, sure and peaceful. I was grasping his knee, my hand having reached for him without meaning to. "I'm *so* happy for you."

He bobbed his head. "Thanks. It's a lot, still, with my dad. I'm nervous to put myself out there. Like, I'm literally putting myself in Chicago. Mostly because I see myself at Northwestern, but . . . you know."

Putting himself out there in Chicago, putting himself out there emotionally, willing to test the water. But this was Max, after all. Willing to go after the thing he most wanted to happen.

"What?" Max asked, paranoid. "What's that look on your face?"

"Um, thinking that I admire you, actually."

"Oh." A small smile. "Thanks, Janie."

In the distance, I heard rumbling, the sound growing like the orchestra tune-up before a show, and we scrambled to lie down. I imagined us from above, the way the approaching airplane would see us, if it could: A boy who thought about the improbability of flight: the engine, the dynamic angles soldered just so. A girl who thought of the people inside: The same takeoff point in the same vessel, but how many destinations? How many passengers with suitcases of bathing suits? How many with a rumpled black dress for an unexpected funeral? A change of suit for tomorrow's meeting. Joy, pain, drudgery. All crammed inside a metal canister with wings.

Max saw engineering and history; I saw short stories.

After the plane had disappeared, the sound remained in my ears. Or the memory of the sound, anyway. Max asked amiably, "You ever think about evolution?"

It wasn't what I expected him to say, but it wasn't surprising either. The reliable tide that pulled me back to Max: he always felt familiar, but never enough to predict his next move. "Sometimes. What about it?"

"Pretty much the only way anything survives is by adapting. And I'm not great at it." He cleared his throat. "I haven't been great at it, this year."

"Mmm." I wanted to comfort him, to say I'd watched him grow. But I didn't want to deny him this revelation or minimize whatever he was working through. "Me neither. But still trying."

"You feel any closer to a college decision?"

"No," I said, laughing. I'd feel certain of NYU one day, then wake up the next feeling a pull toward IU. I couldn't parse my feelings, and I had an appointment with Ms. Pepper after spring break for exactly that reason.

"You wanna talk it out?"

"Not right now. But soon."

Now, I only wanted to kiss him as I'd daydreamed about last year, in this same spot. It was hard not to feel like I'd wasted time since then, gone about this all wrong, and could we ever do it right. But as another plane rumbled nearby, I put my palm to Max's cheek. Between raw potential and near magic, after all, there is a lot of trying again.

CHAPTER THIRTY-FIVE

The next Saturday, I stopped by the Oakhurst flea market around noon. The forecast had called for drizzle, ninety-percent certainty. I knew this from Kayleigh, whose family had converged on her house for the wedding tonight. *If Lisa's mother quotes her ominous weather app to Lisa one more time,* Kayleigh had texted last night, *I'm going to snap. Should be a fun weekend!*

My mom had prepared her supplies despite the forecast, packing up the truck borrowed from a neighbor. And here she was, under a blue sky, with mild temperatures. She'd purchased a few decorative items to outfit the booth, made little pennant banners with patterned triangles. Already, two pieces boasted Post-its with *SOLD* in my mom's block print. The chalkboard sign sat at the front of it all: SECOND TIME'S A CHARM.

"Look at you," I said. "How's it going?"

"Good! Good," she said, nodding and wiping her hands. She wore her painting apron at my dad's suggestion, to "highlight her as the craftsperson." The flecks were a record of her projects, a story told in confetti pattern. "The mini cookies are helping, as an icebreaker. Cameron and I keep sending people to each other's booths. It's not a bad business model!"

"Is Dad with Cam, then?"

"You just missed him, actually. He ran to the grocery store." She gestured back at the navy credenza. A white vase had been relocated from our living room to its tabletop. "I forgot to pick up some peonies. I thought pale pink would make the color really pop."

"I could have stopped on my way!"

"That's okay, honey." She smiled at two women passing by, nodding as a hello. "He wants to help, but he worries about hovering. It was a good errand for him."

"It's really your pièce de résistance." I'd watched her crouched over the detail work, sweat on her brow. I'd seen her throw her hands up when the primer dried unevenly; I'd seen her call it a night in the throes of frustration. She was always back to it the next weekend, undeterred.

"Oh, well. Thank you." My mom glanced over her shoulder, surveying her work. "It has good bones."

An older couple paused near us, eyeing a small coffee table.

"I should get out of your way," I said. "Good luck!"

I stepped away from my mom's little oasis, the space that she'd carved out for herself. Every hour, toiling, scrubbing, detailing—she'd been working on something but also working through something. Trying to process life without her mother. Maybe visualizing her life without her oldest daughter living at home. And figuring out a life with my dad.

"Hey, Mom?" I turned, and she looked up. "You know I'm for it, right? If you say yes to Dad."

"Oh yeah? Why's that?" she said, a little teasingly. She knew why, but I think my reasons mattered to her, too.

And there were many. Because the man had done an all-out moral inventory. Because he kept showing up, present but not pressing. "Because he ran to the store for peonies."

She smiled, the creases by her eyes like tiny paper fans. As I walked off, she called, ever the parent, "Go say hi to your sister! And be affirming, okay?"

I bought cookies from Cameron, who was already running low on business cards. The man in front of me had been asking about custom designs for his son's fifth birthday; Cameron responded about turnaround time and bulk pricing. Her cheeks were pink, either from the bustle of talking to so many people or excitement. She looked both like the little girl I'd always known and as grown-up as I'd ever seen her.

"What?" she asked, when she caught me staring.

Grammy would be so proud of you. I'm really going to miss you next year, more than I ever would have imagined when we were kids. I can't wait to meet the girl you become, next week and next year and when we are both old. There are a lot of ways I wish I were like you, even though I'm the older sister.

"Nothing," I said. "I think you're going to have a busy summer."

"Yeah!" She exhaled, but not with her usual huffiness. With ready energy, hands on her hips. Sometimes, I saw flashes of our mom in her, so clear that it was almost startling. Then she added, a sly smile creeping up, "I might even need an assistant. You busy?"

"Taste-tester only. On a volunteer basis," I said, and she waved me off.

Cameron had never really needed me in an obvious way, but I was starting to realize that she was always paying attention. I wanted to be the older sister who could go off on her own to the big city, set an example of dream-chasing. But I also wanted to be the big sister who stays close enough to show up at the occasional dance performance, to drive home the night her little sister gets dumped for the first time. Both were good choices.

"Max and his mom stopped by earlier," Cameron said. "Bought a bunch of cookies to take to Ryan's track meet."

"That's nice," I said mildly, though I already knew. He'd texted before and since, on his way across town to watch Ryan compete. They'd stop by the wedding later, after dinner and first dances.

Cameron raised an eyebrow over the wire frames of her glasses. "Are you going to tell me what's going on?"

I most certainly was not. Because what was going on, for the past week, was Max and me finding ways to see each other every day without our friends noticing. Sitting in his car in the Cin 12 parking lot until the last possible moment I had to get home. Meeting at a coffee shop in Carmel after borrowing my mom's car. I'd kissed Max Watson more in the past week than I had in the past year, making up for lost time.

I bit off nearly half the cookie I'd purchased and, through

the icing and crumbles of sugar, quoted Cameron to her face.
"I dunno. It's just me and Max."

That night, Kayleigh's dad said his vows to Lisa in their
backyard, under a billowy tent. Lisa carried a pink bouquet,
complete with a few roses from the garden Kayleigh's mom
planted many years ago. All four Hutchins kids stood by their
dad, Kayleigh in a blue dress to match her brothers' blue suits.
Lisa's son stood at her side.

I sat between Tessa and Morgan in a middle row. A
strange parallel to the folding wooden seats at Aaron's funeral,
where my friends had been behind me. In Pepper's Shakespeare unit, I'd learned that traditionally, tragedies end with
death; comedies end in marriage. Life was both tragedy and
comedy—that seemed clear enough. It just depended on which
point you called the beginning and which part you called
the end.

During the first dance, I thought of my parents. Wondered
if I'd witness this moment the way Kayleigh did now. She
looked serene, Brady's arm around her as they watched their
dad whisper something to Lisa.

"You think she's good?" I asked Morgan.

She looked like a modern-day Lucille Ball in a halter-cut
sundress, one side of her hair clipped back. "Yeah. I think she's
really good."

The dance floor opened up after that, and couples swayed
to a Sam Cooke standard. We angled our chairs so we could
be full spectators.

"I love this song," Tessa murmured. "If the DJ knows what
he's doing, it'll be an all-generation fan favorite next."

As if on cue, the opening bars of "I Want You Back" sang out. Kayleigh burst onto the dance floor with her aunts, and I tugged Tessa up with me. TJ spun with his wife and tiny baby girl, who'd slept through most of the celebration so far. Brady gave a committed lip-synch, while Reid gamely played an invisible bass.

After a few songs, Tess and I retired to our table, winded and happy. Ryan and Max showed up shortly after, handsome in their ties. I thought of them appearing at my grandmother's repast, this time last year. Staying late, making sure I wasn't alone.

The speakers switched over to simple guitar chords, an acoustic cover of a song I'd always loved.

Catching my eye, Max signaled toward the dance floor with his thumb.

I cocked my head like, *Really? Dance? You?* and he shrugged. For the first time in a long while, walking toward him felt simple. Not loaded with emotion or nerves, preparing to plead my case or to mediate for space between us. Being near him felt like it used to: irresistibly easy, my home base.

We met somewhere in the middle, between other pairs. A short way to go, in the end—across a few squares of wooden flooring.

"Hello." I put my arms around his neck before he could change his mind. But he was relaxed; I could feel it before his hands even touched my waist.

"Hello," he said.

"Well, well. Look at you. Dancing." I hesitated, worried that he'd trot off like a spooked horse.

"Am I?" Only Max could make two words sound that self-deprecating. "Or am I swaying awkwardly with my arms around your waist?"

I smiled, eyes flicking down. "I like the tie."

"Thanks. It's no Armani but . . ."

"Saving that for prom?" I teased. But when I realized what I'd said, my eyes went wide. I hadn't meant to imply prom with *me*, necessarily.

"Would you want to go together still?"

"Yes," I said, surprised by the blunt question, and just as surprised by my immediate answer. "I would."

"Cool. Good. Sorry. Was that not fancy enough? I figured a promposal would be a little . . ."

"Oh my *God*." Of course I knew he'd read all my e-mails. But faced with my confession that I'd hated those marriage jokes . . .

"Too soon?" He grinned.

I pressed my face into his chest, both hiding and getting closer. I felt his laugh more than I heard it.

"We'll dance at prom?" I pulled back to look at him, suddenly needing a firm answer on this.

"Sure," he said. "Even if I embarrass us both."

I peered at him. Was this really a worry? I thought of Ryan's words at the baseball field, reminding me that Max guarded himself with good reason.

"You couldn't," I said. Sure, there were boys who would spin me with panache and finish with a dip—I knew that. Boys whose ease would compensate for my hesitation. But I'd rather figure it out with Max.

I rested my cheek on his chest. We were still leaving Oakhurst in mere months, and I had no idea what the time between would hold. Certainly no idea about the after.

"I can practically hear that, you know."

I looked up. "Hear what?"

"You worrying."

I don't think my mouth smiled, but my eyes did. "Ah, that."

"We're gonna figure it out, you know." The way he looked at me, brushing my bangs aside, it was a wonder everyone didn't know exactly what we'd been up to the past week.

"Oh yeah?"

"Yeah." He leaned down and said quietly, the words right beside my ear. "We're really smart."

———————

Mr. Hutchins and Lisa left through two lines of sparklers down the driveway, off to a downtown hotel for the two nights before our Monday morning spring break exit. They got into their car with *Just Married* scrawled in Kayleigh's brightest pink lipstick. It was driving off into the sunset, roll credits on a rom-com. A happy ending. But only if you saw it as an ending.

Morgan, Tessa, and I stayed after with the Hutchins kids, folding tablecloths and boxing up pillar candles. Kayleigh's brothers got into the leftover booze toward the end, and tried to one-up each other on the dance floor. Brady's boyfriend held his phone out, laughing as he took video. The Hutchins boys harmonized loudly, showing off their a cappella pipes.

I glanced over at Kayleigh, wondering if she noticed Reid

occasionally glancing at Morgan, checking to see if she was watching, laughing, impressed. I'd seen them talking earlier by the dessert table, and honestly, they wouldn't have noticed if someone had popped out of the cake.

"Yeah, I know," Kayleigh said. She must have felt me looking at her, must have heard my unasked question. "I'm . . . weirdly fine with it. Kind of makes sense, doesn't it?"

"Kinda does," I admitted.

Eventually, TJ's wife came out in her pajamas, baby monitor in hand, and TJ swept her into a spin.

"That first wakeup isn't gonna feel good," she warned, smiling.

"We're done out here," he promised. "Last dance."

Upstairs, we climbed out Kayleigh's window onto the flat stretch of roof outside her room. Her dad had always strictly forbidden this, but I figured he knew deep-down that we'd been coming out here for years. Kayleigh passed us the drinks she mixed downstairs. "Cheers. To Dad and Lisa."

We touched the cups together before leaning back, watching the moon creep over a neighboring rooftop.

God, I'd hated living here sometimes—Oakhurst and its superstores, so few things distinguishing us from the next suburb. The way I could never really outrun what people knew of me. And yet, all year, I'd wondered at my heels-dug-in reluctance to leave. Tonight, the reason seemed obvious. The world was full of spectacular girls, but these? These ones were mine.

"This was a good night," Tessa said, arms resting on her knees.

"I'm gonna miss it up here," I said, wistful. Glancing at Morgan, I said, "Sitting right there, you told us you kissed Isaiah Jacobs."

"Oh my gosh." She covered her face with one hand. "He's still really cute. Maybe it's not too late for our love to blossom."

I looked to Kayleigh, who'd become conspicuously quiet. It was dark, but that almost made it easier to catch the glint of water in her eyes. "Hey! What is it?"

"Sorry!" Kayleigh said, drying her cheeks with one palm. "God. Sorry. I'm going to miss this so much next year. Like, I know it'll be fine and we'll make it work! But it won't be the same."

Tessa reached across to put a hand on Kayleigh's knee. "I'm right there with you."

In this alternate universe moment, where Kayleigh was the one faltering, I naturally shifted to balance her. "And there's so much more to come! Our trip on Monday! Prom, senior tag, graduation parties. Like, half the List. All summer. Maybe you'll hate us by the end."

"Maybe," Kayleigh said. "After ten years of friendship, this is probably it for us. Ugh, I'm a disaster. Who made this drink so strong?"

Tessa gave her a look. "*You* did."

"Why, I *never*," Kayleigh said. Then, cheerfully, to me, "So! Are we going to address that little moment with Max on the dance floor or . . . ?"

I shrugged, coy. Max and I had been in the emotional equivalent of an awkward slow dance for months. Stepping on each other's toes and boundaries. Frustrated with ourselves, with each other. Feeling watched. But now that we'd found a rhythm, I wasn't going to perform a damn thing. Not until we got our confidence up.

"You still love him?" Morgan asked eagerly.

"Oh, c'mon." I flicked an annoyed glance at her. My friends looked away, chastened and accepting this as my final word on the subject. So I got an even bigger reaction when I scoffed, "Of course I do."

Morgan gave a kind of triumphant laugh, and Tessa bit both her lips, like she could hide the smile.

"You two better not be disgusting on my spring break," Kayleigh said, pointing a finger.

"Disgusting? We just started talking in person again."

Morgan craned toward me, like she'd caught that strange detail. "What does that mean? Have you been texting a lot or something?"

I hadn't decided yet if I'd tell my friends that I wrote my way back to Max. "Let's save some of this for the drive on Monday."

"Okay," Kayleigh said, standing up carefully. "Off the roof before the buzz sets in. Chop-chop."

"Oh, wait," Tessa said. "Stay there."

She climbed into Kayleigh's room and returned with her camera. "Yearbook goes to print soon and I need a picture of us. Okay. Timer's set!"

"You don't want to take a cuter one on spring break?" Morgan asked. Tessa slid in beside me and put an arm around my waist.

"This is more true-to-life," Tessa insisted through her teeth as she smiled.

"You'll barely be able to see us!" Morgan said.

"Yeah," Kayleigh said, "but we'll know."

"It'll be fine," I said, and I smiled against the flash.

I may not have known much about my future—my college choice or degree, my someday job and city, boys I'd love and lose. But I knew who'd be beside me. Chalk it up to too many movies, too many TV finales that flashed forward, but I saw these girls as clearly as I saw the moon overhead. Beyond college, beyond even our twenties. I'd drive across state lines to get to them, to soothe small disappointments and big heartbreaks. I'd come crawling home to them when I got lost, to guide off their stars. I'd be their witness to diplomas received, vows spoken to partners, oaths taken for office. And when the rest of the decisions felt like a tightrope, precarious with no back-stepping allowed—well, I had a net.

CHAPTER THIRTY-SIX

We left Oakhurst in the dark-sky hours, that thin edge between night and morning. Beating Monday morning rush hour seemed like a good idea when I'd agreed to the departure time.

I did not remember what five a.m. felt like when I agreed to it.

My parents wanted to drop me off at Kayleigh's, which I agreed to warily. Part of me believed that my mom—once confronted with the visual of eight teenagers piling into cars for a cross-country trip—would decide to take me right home. During the short drive to Kayleigh's house, my mother rattled off every last-minute thought and worry. Car safety: blown tires, gridlock, the importance of keeping music and distraction at a minimum for the driver. She hadn't even reached house or beach safety admonitions by the time we pulled into the driveway.

The three caravan cars sat waiting, all doors and trunks open and already near full with suitcases, beach towels, coolers.

"And we need text updates," my mom was saying, finishing a thought I'd tuned out. "That's part of this agreement."

"Katie," my dad said softly, one hand reaching to her leg.

"You can text me anytime," I said, in my most even-toned, mature voice. "But sometimes I'll be in the ocean or pool, so don't get worried if I don't respond immediately. I promise I will."

That sounded very reasonable to me, but my mom sighed for longer than seemed physically possible, given the limited amount of air in human lungs. Still, she got out of the car and put on her friendly parent face.

"You're a *saint* to do this," I heard her tell Lisa.

"Everyone feeling awake enough?" Mr. Hutchins asked us. "Don't be a hero. Tap out when you need to. Plenty of drivers to go around."

Ryan patted his cheeks, psyching up. "I'm ready. Let's do it."

"Then you can drive first," Tessa said, dangling her keys out to him. Her eyes were puffy, her mouth a grumpy little line.

"No problem. It's on. I've got this."

Max leaned down to me and whispered, "He had espresso."

I smiled a little, clutching my own coffee like it was a life force. "Can I ride with you first?"

"Of course. My backseat's got luggage in it, though. So it'll just be us."

"That's why I asked," I said, and he smiled. This early, everyone else's energy sounded too loud, like particles humming through the air. For a little while, my own thoughts were the only ones I could handle.

We formed a circle as Ryan spoke to us like a sports movie coach at halftime. "People are going to have to pee after morning coffee—I get that. But we're gonna try to get to past Louisville. No weak links, all right? Minimum drive time means maximum beach time."

"Caravan like we agreed," Mr. Hutchins said. "Passenger stays awake to navigate and texts the group if anyone falls behind. No crazy speeding or—"

"I will turn this car around," Kayleigh said, voice low in an impersonation of her dad. Lisa pretended she was itching her nose to hide a laugh.

Mr. H pointed at Kayleigh, smiling. "You joke, little girl, but I mean it."

"I know, I know." Kayleigh gestured to all of us. "Follow the rules so we can just get there with no drama, okay?"

"No weak links!" Ryan repeated, clapping. "Now let's get out there and road-trip."

Malcolm looked at Max. "He's going to calm down, right?"

"Eventually, yeah."

I cozied into the passenger's seat and breathed deep: the steamy hazelnut coffee, the wet, dewy morning, the just-warm April air. Somehow, I knew the sense-memory would stick around. Next year, grabbing cafeteria coffee before an early class, I'd be transported to this moment, a new day and the empty highway. Not dancing-around happy, not lip-gnawing anxious. Content, the good things wrapped around me like a favorite blanket.

Max followed Tessa's SUV, maneuvering between other

cars. The scenery changed from billboards and low-rise office buildings to heartland grass, tilled fields waiting for seeds. Tiny towns along the road like knots on a rope. I watched it all through the windshield, inside our shared quiet. Max held out his hand, palm up, and I laced my fingers through.

"I can't believe I'm going to be looking at the ocean by tonight," I said. Even if we didn't hit traffic or dawdle at rest stops, the drive would take a good twelve hours. "I'm gonna go right down to the water, even if it's dark when we get there."

"Yeah, me too." Max smiled over at me.

With each stop for bathrooms or gas, we changed drivers and seating arrangements. Morgan drove Tessa's car through Tennessee, the four of us talking and laughing through field after field. I read a retrospective on a classic sitcom while Ryan and Malcolm talked over sports radio.

We stopped one last time in Montgomery, Alabama, for a fast-food dinner. As we trooped back out to the cars, Max nudged me. "Finish the drive together?"

He offered me the keys, dangling from one finger. I hadn't driven on the highway in a while now, but I certainly *could*. My hand closed around the keys.

The medication, a few weeks in now, took me down a few notches. I could keep my body calm for long enough to practice what I was learning in therapy. I speed-walked around the block outside my house, I poured a glass of water, I scrawled my stream-of-consciousness worries in longhand. The change wasn't quick or perfect, but it was a littlest bit better, and I would take it.

I adjusted the seat and mirrors, and we were on our way. I'd downloaded a few podcasts—one about déjà vu and another about Agent 355, a female Revolution-era spy whose identity still remained unknown. Throughout both, Max kept reaching for the pause button, wanting to ask me what I thought, if I agreed with the interviewee. And once just because he wanted to talk excitedly about Hedy Lamarr.

As I steered, I imagined the car from above, gliding down the map. That mental image came straight from my grandmother's old guest room, where a vintage map of the US used to hang. The states were pastel—lavender and pistachio and butter yellow—all framed by the pale blue Atlantic and Pacific, by the Gulf of Mexico. I'd spent a lot of time studying the state shapes. Wyoming and Colorado, as perfectly rectangular as birthday card envelopes. Minnesota looked like an anvil, squishing Iowa a bit. My own Indiana, curved like a stocking.

The sun was sinking in the rearview mirror as we pulled off the highway. We made a few turns onto a long lane of beach homes. We'd fallen behind our friends by a minute or two, thanks to a semitruck that nosed its way in front of me.

"Should be the next right," Max said. I slowed the car to a crawl, and peered until I spotted the house. Dark teal with white trim, a bright yellow door. Adirondack chairs on the porch, begging for a cup of coffee and a book. The other cars were already in the driveway, Tessa's back door left open in the hurry to get down to the water.

We probably had a half hour of light but still, we bailed out of the car fast. Max reached one hand back, almost absentmindedly. I took it, and let him tug me around the side of the house, down the dunes toward the beach. Our friends were just ahead, stripes of movement on the horizon.

As far as sunset skies went, they weren't the most impressive I'd ever seen. No swabs of lavender, no spun-sugar pink. Just soft blue becoming palest orange, clouds fluffed like pillows across the horizon.

Kayleigh was running toward the ocean with arms wide, her shriek of joy carrying over the distance and call of the waves. Ryan, right behind her, hit the water so hard that it kicked up all around him. Morgan and Josiah lingered near the tide line, while Malcolm and Tessa waded slowly.

I hung back, a little stunned, and Max stopped beside me.

I hadn't seen the beach in years, but it's not the kind of thing that leaves you. The shush of the waves, the particular smell of sand—salt and something marine, organic. Dried-up seaweed or rotting driftwood, nothing you'd expect to smell good. But I inhaled, again and again.

"I was worried that I'd built it up in my mind," I admitted.

"As good as expected?" Max asked.

"Better."

"You wanna sit?" Max asked, and I nodded. I slipped off my shoes and dug my toes into the sand.

We stared at the Gulf, this beast with a belly full of wild kingdoms, secrets, tragedies. The vastness made me feel small in a good way. I couldn't believe that this world, which felt so far away from my everyday life, was only ever a day on the road away.

"Last year, I couldn't have been even this close to the water," I told Max. "Now, I like it so much that I'm feeling sad about those LA college rejections!"

"Same," Max said, raising one fist. "Damn you, Caltech."

We both laughed a little, and I curled my arms around my knees, smiling over at my pal, my love, my whatever-he-was. It was nice to see him so relaxed, leaned back like he was letting something—the breeze or a feeling—wash over him.

"Hey," he said, eyes finding mine.

"Hey."

Just for a camera flash of a moment, I felt a small kind of mourning. Missing Max even though he was right next to me. He must have noticed my mood change because he slung one arm around my shoulders, in the easy way of an old friend. I wanted to memorize him: the exact quirk of his eyebrows, the May-morning green of his eyes.

"They're going to be annoying this week," I said, nodding at our friends. "About us."

"Yep," he said, cheerfully enough. "I give it less than an hour. What do you want to tell them?"

Maybe I'd tell them that the first time I fell for Max Watson, it was because of his obvious goodness. His smarts and self-assuredness, the way he showed up for the people he loved. The second time, it was with full knowledge of his faults: the sarcasm born of frustration, his propensity for shutting down. "Um, probably that we've been making out and hanging out and pointedly not talking about the future?"

"We're a mess," he said, then laughed. By now, our mess

was simply a fact we'd both accepted. But beneath the scuff marks and scars, I could still see us in bright, glossy color—as blue green as seawater.

"We are. But you know what?" I peered at him, pointing between our faces. "This has good bones."

I watched his expression, waiting for him to understand what I meant. I believed in this enough to do the detail work, to return after I'd thrown my hands up in frustration.

"Yeah, it does," Max said, and I tucked myself into him, smushing my cheek against his shoulder. The breeze pushed at us, like the Gulf's heaving sigh. Cooler than I'd expected. But I still craved the water on my bare feet, the push and pull of the low tide. Proof that I'd made it here. Maybe I'd wade all the way in, drenching my clothes heavy.

"You two getting in or what?" Kayleigh yelled from the water.

Max looked my way, a question. He was learning to wait—learning that I wouldn't always keep perfect pace with him and he couldn't assume. But I'd learned a few things, too.

I stood up, brushed the grit from my legs, and said, "Yes."

ACKNOWLEDGMENTS

Thank you to Bethany Robison, Taylor Martindale Kean, and Mary Kate Castellani for trekking half-built worlds with me. Your insights, belief, and good humor are lifelines every time.

Team Bloomsbury, you are unparalleled: Erica Barmash, Anna Bernard, Phoebe Dyer, Beth Eller, Courtney Griffin, Melissa Kavonic, Jeanette Levy, Cindy Loh, Donna Mark, Brittany Mitchell, Oona Patrick, Claire Stetzer, and Nick Sweeney. (Thank you also to Cristina Gilbert, Linette Kim, Lizzy Mason, and Emily Ritter, whose work helped find a readership for Paige & Co.) Sending my gratitude across the pond to the team at Bloomsbury UK as well!

Additionally, thank you to: Ali Mac for the gorgeous illustration work, Taryn Fagerness for her work in foreign rights, and the Full Circle team for being the best in the biz. Thank you to my early readers for your keen and thoughtful feedback.

Special thanks to Shymaa Salih and to the family and many

friends who help me navigate making art and motherhood—
a river that always flows both ways. Thank you to my partner
and daughter for being my sunny day.

And, as always, thank you to the book community. Thank
you for caring and being willing to connect with characters and
with me, for posting pictures and taking the time to write
reviews. Thank you to the librarians and library workers,
the educators, the publishing pros, the writers, and the book-
sellers who champion lifelong readership.